WHERE THE VEIL IS THIN

Edited by
Cerece Rennie Murphy
& Alana Joli Abbott

WHERE THE VEIL IS THIN
All stories within are copyright © 2020 their respective authors. All rights reserved.

Published by Outland Entertainment LLC
3119 Gillham Road
Kansas City, MO 64109

Founder/Creative Director: Jeremy D. Mohler
Editor-in-Chief: Alana Joli Abbott
Senior Editor: Gwendolyn Nix

ISBN: 978-1-947659-81-0
Worldwide Rights
Created in the United States of America

Editors: Cerece Rennie Murphy & Alana Joli Abbott
Cover Illustration: Anna Dittmann
Cover Design: Jeremy D. Mohler
Interior Layout: Mikael Brodu

Printed and bound in China.

Visit **outlandentertainment.com** to see more, or follow us on our Facebook Page **facebook.com/outlandentertainment/**

CONTENTS

— INTRODUCTION —
by Jim C. Hines

Like many children, I learned to save my lost teeth for the tooth fairy. My mother even made me a little tooth-shaped pillow with a tiny tooth pocket. At the time, the tooth fairy was a whimsical story told by parents and innocently accepted by us kids. We all looked forward to finding those shiny coins the following morning.

If I'd known then what I know now about fairy lore, I would have told my mother to burn that damned pillow and get those cursed teeth as far away from me as possible. Fairies and spirits aren't generally known for altruism and charity, and a fairy bargain—even one so simple as trading a coin for a tooth—is a dangerous thing.

Most cultures have stories of fairies and spirits and otherworldly creatures living in the mist and the shadows, gliding into and out of our world to interact with humans. Sometimes, if the human treats those fey creatures and their powers with respect, and if the human is fortunate, those interactions are to their advantage. If, on the other hand, you dare to disrespect a fairy's power? Your role in the story is likely to be brief, noted only as a lesson to others.

Specific powers and magics vary from one story to another, from illusions and transformations to an endlessly inventive inventory of curses, but their strongest power, the power that grips us to this day, is Story. These beings from beyond the veil enchant us through the stories we share and pass down from one generation to the next. But what is it about these stories that capture and hold us?

One answer is that they help us to make sense of the universe, to impose rules and order and explanation on cold chaos. Your child becomes sick and behaves strangely? Perhaps they're a fairy change-ling. The crops all died? Someone must have angered the guardian of the fields.

Even fairies themselves, often creatures of id and chaos, are bound by certain rules. Human laws are fragile, easily-broken things by comparison, but fairy rules are inviolate. They provide order, and even control. No matter how terrifying and powerful and chaotic that strange, beautiful/ugly being might be, it's bound by rules. Through those rules, a clever human can triumph. In that way, these stories not only help to explain chaos, they give us hope to overcome it.

Many of these tales teach us that the universe itself is a place of hope, and that ultimately, the universe favors justice. Fairies and spirits are known to reward the just and punish the wicked. In a world where wealth and power so often triumph over fairness, who wouldn't find comfort in the idea that other beings wait just beyond the shadows to ensure justice is done?

Hope goes hand in hand with warning. For every story where kindness and cleverness are rewarded, we also see cruelty and selfishness punished. A lecture on right and wrong is easy to shut out, but stories pierce us like slivers of glass. It's one thing to tell children to respect women, for example. It's another to tell a story of those who didn't, and how those women returned as animal spirits to devour their tormentors.

Or maybe the true power of these tales is less about lessons and understanding the universe, and more about the sense of wonder that comes from things beyond our understanding. The discovery that our world is so much more than our senses suggest, with magic waiting beneath every shadow, just out of reach. When you finish reading these stories, you return to our world with new eyes. Every new-budded flower, every firefly, every raven watching you from its perch, becomes *more*.

Perhaps most importantly, these stories hold a mirror to ourselves. J. M. Barrie of *Peter Pan* fame wrote that when the first human child laughed, that laugh shattered into countless pieces, and those pieces became fairies. He was far from the first to note the inseparable bond between human and fey.

Through these stories, we examine who we are. We see our joy and our rage, our kindness and our greed. We laugh at Rumpelstiltskin's tantrum at the end of his tale, even while (hopefully) recognizing that we've all had our moments of melodramatic tantrum. We empathize with the suffering and inner strength of characters like Cinderella. We discover facets of ourselves in spirits and fairies and clever beasts and even the lowliest goblin.

It's hard to find a story that's truly universal, but the best fairy stories come close. Like fairies themselves, they defy efforts to pin them to a specific time and place. Instead, they draw on archetypes and collective belief, shapeshifting from one telling to the next, all the while luring us closer with riddles and knowledge and magic and insight.

Or maybe there's an even simpler reason why these stories are so prolific, why we've continued to tell them for so many centuries. Maybe in their wisdom, our ancestors made a fairy bargain many lifetimes ago to protect us. That the fairies would leave us in peace—mostly—so long as we continue to share stories about them. Fairies are known for being quite vain, after all. I imagine our fascination, our compulsion to tell tales of those magical beings from the other side of the veil is quite flattering to their egos. Maybe the sharing of these stories, the magic of our own storytelling, is what keeps us safe at night.

Or maybe not. Maybe it's nothing more than daydreams and whimsy and wistful longing.

But if it were me, I'd keep reading this book, just to be safe. Because if there's one thing I've learned, it's that the last thing you want to do is risk insulting a fairy.

THE TOOTH FAIRIES:
— QUEST FOR TEAR HAVEN —
Glenn Parris

The little brown girl's six-year-old tongue licked at a tooth. It wiggled in her mouth but refused freedom. Slight in stature, Shanny Prentice slept curled up on the sofa in a long T-shirt. The room was cozy and warmed by the hearth's waning fire. She cuddled up with a lap blanket; her head nestled gently into a soft down pillow. That tooth wobbled tantalizingly loose.

Dusk languidly faded to shadows as twilight ushered cool evening into deep darkness. Night always invited wayward blood thirst in one form or another.

Thumb-sized figures flitted about Shanny's head, anxiously stalking that dentine prize. Raz thought all little girls breathed through their mouths at night. While the fairies pondered their challenge, Shanny hummed a sigh and rolled over on her other side. This complication was unexpected.

"I almost 'ad it!" Hilde griped, her cockney accent out of place in the central Louisiana home. "Look at 'er massage that precious tooth... back and forth, back and forth." Nearly hypnotized by the movement of the tongue through the girl's cheek, Hilde added, "She's tormenting us on purpose, I tell you! Why won't she open 'er mouth?"

"She did open 'er mouth," a jovial declaration welled from near the others, "very wide in fact!"

Dressed in torn, hand-me-down Confederate-era mismatched doll's attire, Fin stood at his post by the window and made an honest effort to stifle his laughter at Hilde's expense. Drenched, she wiped clear mucus first from her face, then from the old English-styled hat and tattered outfit, weather-beaten over two centuries since she'd first wore them new. She fluttered soggily.

"Bad vantage point, lass," Raz said. "Downwind from that itchy little nose."

"Let's pour ice water in 'er ear," cackled Old Molly. "Just a few drops! Heh, heh, heh."

"Careful, she's a real sneezer, that one!"

"Yes, Hilde, we can all see that," Fin chuckled.

Cross, Hilde silently stomped her foot on the girl's forehead without the least disturbance to Shanny's slumber. Humans might measure a fairy's weight in nanograms.

Raz grew impatient despite Fin's good humor. "In all my years, I've never seen a brat go so long breathing through her nose."

After more than an hour of scrutinizing the little girl, the fairies' tempers had grown short. Even Raz, the leader of the band, second in age only to Old Molly and usually up for a good Tooth Hunt, grew eager to put this business behind him. The whole team inhaled together then sighed in unison. The fairies could almost taste the blood in the tooth socket.

Hilde buzzed around the sofa, flailing arms and legs to dry herself. Her gyrations fostered the semblance of a twisted, angelic hobo.

Fin was farthest away from the sofa, perched on the windowsill, safe from the girl's nasal squall. As sentry, he kept watch for the spider, his fairy staff at the ready.

"She's not dreaming," Raz complained as he noted the absence of rapid eye movement.

Like Rodin's *The Thinker*, Raz modeled the picture of monumental study; he brooded, chin on his fist, elbow on his knee, and foot propped angrily on the girl's forehead now. A moonbeam weighed more.

The blood would taste so much sweeter infused with liquid *fear*, the mead of adrenaline and endorphins. Fairies wielded magics apt to stir pleasant dreams into night horrors. If they got to the socket while it was still freshly bleeding, each could fill his or her second belly full of blood for their kinfolk. All four fairies felt their own rotting, flimsy fangs aching with drool.

"Let's pour ice water in 'er ear," Old Molly chimed again. "Just a few drops! Heh, heh, heh. That'll give 'er a nice nightmare!" she laughed. Molly's rags, a collection of cast-offs faded grey centuries ago, rendered Hilde's appointments glamorous by comparison.

Old Molly sat on the edge of a teacup resting on the coffee table between the girl and the fireplace. The cup was full of strawberry Kool-Aid diluted by melting ice cubes. Old Molly kicked the small icebergs away when they floated near her gnarled, crusty toes bathing in the crimson beverage. Most thought the 300-year-old fairy was getting addled in her old age, and her feet had grown numb from so many harsh winters over centuries past.

Old Molly held the dime they'd use to prop Shanny's mouth open when they finally got to the loose tooth. Molars were always the hardest to harvest, but they bled the best. The coin gleamed from Molly's neurotic polishing.

"Let's pour ice water in 'er ear," urged Old Molly again. "Just a few drops!" It became more of a chant than a suggestion. She rubbed absently at the silvery disc with her sleeved elbow.

Ignoring Old Molly's exhortation, the posse continued to mull thoughtfully over their little challenge. The security and glow of the fireplace comforted the girl even in sleep. Only its crackle broke the room's silence as the gathering sank into their hunger.

Despite the magical rules that bound other paranormals, fairies were allowed to enter a victim's house uninvited, as well as handle crucifixes with impunity. But in conjunction with other iron-clad limitations, each species of blood-drinker was saddled with at least one compulsion. Tooth fairies were neat freaks. Except for the coin used to prop the mouth open, fairies left no trace of their presence.

The perfect opportunity for the drainage of blood from a loose tooth came as it followed its natural course during the night. If the tooth was never found, the parent attributed its absence to a child swallowing the tooth in her sleep. The kid, of course, always believed the traditional explanation and cherished the little silvery treasure.

Shanny's useless little brother—TommiLee, as they'd heard him called—lay curled up on the floor. His head full of healthy, firmly implanted teeth rested on Rusty, the old Labrador retriever. The two were so inseparable that when the boy was called home, the dog often ran inside, too.

The hound was of no interest to the fae visitors. The dog raised his head up momentarily, then laid it back down again. Fin knew the animal by name, an unnecessary detail in his reconnaissance report. Who cared about dogs? The real purpose of the scouting mission was to make sure there were no witches and no cats on the property. Dogs they could always handle. Canine eyes couldn't see fairies anyway, and the dumb critters always fell asleep on a whiff of fairy dust if necessary.

Cats, on the other hand, were wily creatures with an innate sense of the occult. No one in either world ever rested certain whether felines boasted supernatural powers or not. Magic worked on them occasionally, but one could never be sure of the outcome. Whatever bore out, every vampire knew cats as witches' servants.

A savvy cat could make short work of a bunch of fairies, but a witch? Practitioners-noir could enslave them all and track them back to their village. A fairy village made for powerful magic potions. Such a wily conjurer could endanger not only fairies, but all kinds of enchanted folk.

The Lycan would be none too happy about such a development. Wolf-folk were not to be trifled with for sure. But fairies' larger kin, the Vampyr, would be furious.

The true vampires had seethed when a fairy village allowed several scouts to be captured by a class of fourth graders on a nature walk fifty years ago. The thought of a fairy-enriched stew nourishing a coven of invincible witches would enrage a pride of Vampyr. It could be all out war! Every fairy settlement in the southeast would be collateral damage of their wrath—and witches or other supernaturals would claim the enchanted girl as a prize if the fae safari were found out.

No, a fairy could never be too careful around cats, especially in mid-autumn when their feline powers peaked. Yes, dogs were much safer to deal with. Still, Fin did not trust *this* dog: it smelled funny.

Fin also didn't trust spiders. He kept staring through the cracked window at their little team of mounts. Trained in pairs to carry plump fairies long distances, the eight fireflies tethered to a web were vulnerable. Even the mosquitoes guarding them didn't bestow any confidence. Fin had hoped it was a cobweb, an abandoned spider web for which there was no resident spider. Before entering Shanny's house, the fae troupe had jiggled the web hoping to waken the spider and lure him to the center of the web. They got nothing.

Perhaps this beast had died, moved on, been killed by a larger animal, or run afoul of a human. Whatever the case, the spider was not in his lair when they tied the flies. Fin's greatest fear was that the spider was on the prowl down on the ground or in a nearby tree. If he came back unseen, there would be no way to save the fireflies. The mosquitos guarding them would be little deterrent. It was a long walk back home.

Although all four of the fairies could fly, their abilities were best suited for quick, short-range sorties. Sustained, endurance flights could easily wipe them out. They'd barely make it with four bellies over-filled with blood-mead if they successfully completed their mission before dawn. On the ground, they were much, much slower. Short fairy legs were just not made for running. Even young Fin wouldn't fare well on such a trek. The eighty-year-old youth maintained his vigil at the window.

The remaining three fairies ignored the other two occupants of the room, their attention firmly on the little girl. Limited psychic abilities revealed much. Her daddy was the only human who called her Shanny. Everybody else insisted on calling her by her given name, Sharon.

The fairies knew that. They knew what she liked, and they knew what she feared.

"Let's pour ice water in 'er ear!" hissed the old fairy again. Molly's voice was barely a whisper, less than a breeze. "Just a few drops. Not much."

Raz floated effortlessly in place, his wings just tickling the air, holding his position. He held one hand to his chin and the elbow on his other hand, which lay crossed over his bloated belly.

"She hasn't opened her mouth in over an hour," he exclaimed and belched loudly. "How does she do it?"

"We'll starve at this rate!" rattled Hilde, her figure finally dry, but nearly as deformed as Old Molly.

"Ever since the Hurricane that the juicy, big people called Katrina, it's become hard to find poor children with loose teeth," Raz moaned. "Ripe for feeding,"

Modern dentists had learned their craft too well for fae liking. It was over a mile to the rotting oak they, along with six dozen other hungry fairies, called Tear Haven. The trophy would be licked and polished of all blood and pulp, then set in place to contribute to the fortification, becoming one of over eighty thousand teeth that made up the hovels, roads, stairs, and towers of the hidden village.

Just then Shanny's eyes began to move erratically beneath closed lids.

"Now's our chance!" Molly said. "Make 'er open 'er mouth! You know we all have to eat. And we have hungry mouths to feed back 'ome."

"She's having pleasant dreams, curse her," Hilde scowled. "Why won't she have a nice nightmare to season that precious tooth? What's she got to be so bleedin' happy 'bout anyway?"

Grabbing at the rune staff Raz held tightly in his fist, Hilde implored him. "Go on, poke 'er hard. Maybe you can stir some adrenalin in 'er little head."

"That's how you broke your staff in the first place." Raz knew they all recognized the importance of the loss, but he still felt obliged to emphasize the need for caution. "We only have two left."

"Let's pour ice water in 'er ear," the old crone implored once again. "Just a few drops?" By now the chant had a rhythm to it. Old Molly seemed to derive great pleasure from just the thought of the despicable deed. Molly caressed the rim of the cup sensuously as she recited her litany. She still sat on the teacup's edge. The few remaining ice cubes still melting in the sweet strawberry Kool-Aid, provocatively reminiscent of the blood they all craved. The old fairy's little feet seemed impervious to the cold.

"Hush Molly!" Hilde followed the sharp admonishment by mocking, echoes of Old Molly's chant: "'Let's pour ice water in 'er ear.' She says. We don't want 'er to wake up. We just want a little nightmare."

"She's right, Molly," Raz said. "If she wakes up, we'll all have to wait for her to go back to sleep. There are only a few hours before dawn. We don't have time for this. You know how slowly little girls drain."

Hilde urged Raz again, "Use the staff."

Reluctantly, Raz nodded in agreement. "But we can't just 'poke' her. We need to craft a nightmare." He smiled now for the first time all night. "A nice, nasty charade. We'll use an incantation, an old one. Molly, I need you for this. Fin, it takes two staffs. Hilde's is gone and old Molly just has a wand. Come close."

Fin had his back to the whole affair. He was still peering nervously out the window. The large web was sturdy.

Where is that spider? Fin knew if anything happened to those fireflies, Raz and company could be stranded. Fin hesitantly joined the group.

As fairy hands clasped around the two staffs and raised them, Fin's nose crinkled. He looked back at the window. The fireflies rested, glowing at leisurely intervals. He looked at the lazy dog snoring, again motionless. Somehow, something about that dog still bothered him.

Raz and Old Molly began the incantation. Hilde and Fin bowed their heads. They began to whirl faster and faster around the axis of the two magic staffs. Fairy dust spouted out above them from the misshapen heads of the rune staffs, showering down upon Shanny's sleeping face. The incantation complete, Raz lit gently by her left ear.

In her father's voice, the fairy leader whispered, "Shanny, the wind is coming. So is the water." He followed the lie with a cool, damp puff of his foul breath.

"It's another hurricane, Shanny. Remember, like before? We have to hunker down, ride it out. Hope we don't drown like the Devereuxes did."

Shanny frowned frightfully in her sleep, her eyes moving frantically now through closed eyelids. Her father was an engineer and knew better than anyone how to survive a gale like Katrina. Still, they'd barely made it to safety that time. Shanny had lost her friend, Tessy Devereux, who'd perished along with her whole family.

The little girl began to tremble in her sleep.

"Yes, that's it," Old Molly slurred in anticipation, as if drunk with ale. "Now, let's pour ice water in 'er ear, just a few drops! The music is just right."

It was only when Molly broke the circle to fetch the ice water from the teacup that Fin noticed the piano tinkling in the other room. Shanny's father crooned a slow tenor blues rhythm accompanying the keyed notes. The raiding band of fairies ignored the music—everyone but Fin, that is. The sound was distant and difficult to make out. The accompaniment's discordant arpeggio was as strange as the wordless lyric that followed it.

The fairy dust still glowed on the little girl's cheek, ear, and exposed neck. Raz thought greedily, *If only we had our bigger kin's fangs, we could all bite through the skin and suck the life-giving blood right from the child's veins.*

Alas, their little fangs were too limp and short to penetrate the skin. Graced with uninvited access to residential or holy ground, fairies were limited to drinking untainted, virgin blood from an open source. Jilted teenaged cutters were the best, but they almost always had layers of heavy bandages over open wounds by the time the fae came a-calling. Teens who were seldom serious about suicide slit shallow. The cutters left just enough blood-quickening to tease, not satisfy.

Shanny's distress reached a feverish pitch. The singing stopped, but the tinkling piano continued to resonate into the living room. Hilde moved to divert the girl's father. They didn't need him coming in and spoiling their carefully cultivated nightmare.

Mr. Prentice had risen from his piano seat and just made it to his easy chair when Hilde doused him with a generous portion of fairy dust directed by her wand. As his eyes grew heavy, Hilde smiled. Hovering over him, she cut across the piano's air space, intent on rejoining the group, when she realized that the piano was still playing with no particular tune or rhythm.

Hilde hesitated only a moment, just long enough for the cat to leap off the keys and grab both her wings. As the cat dove down behind the furniture clutching its prey, none of Hilde's kin saw the horror grip her face as the feline devoured her. Hilde was gone before the cat landed softly on the carpet.

Raz, Molly, and Fin were dumbfounded. One would have thought they were paralyzed, too, for their lack of action.

Shanny awoke with a start. "Rusty!"

Fin broke first, heading for the window. Finding the crack in the glass, he beckoned his surviving comrades to hurry along. Raz and Molly were cut off by the calico beast.

The puss could see them!

"No wonder that mongrel smelled so funny," Fin muttered to himself. "All that musty dander masked the feline scent." Before mounting his firefly, he sought his comrades.

Raz and Molly disappeared under the sofa to evade the furry hellion's onslaught. They both emerged from beneath the far edge, just ahead of razor-sharp claws. Fear gave gossamer wings strength like never before, and they reached a zenith near the chandelier.

"Fin, go. Leave us. The town must know to stay away. Warn them!" Raz shouted the orders as the cat leaped off furniture from every angle to gain altitude, paws swinging wildly. The chandelier swung gently, an asylum yet just out of reach.

Adrenalin waned, and the fairies lost elevation. Finally, Raz and Molly stole refuge in a narrow-necked wicker basket. Rusty followed, hissing and winding his way as far down the basket as his lithe body would allow; then he was stuck. Barely out of reach of those claws, Raz used his staff to pry through the reeds.

"Hurry, Raz." Old Molly cowered from each swipe. "The beast is close!"

Raz cringed at the sickening crack below him. The reeds parted, but only at the cost of his staff. He got Molly out first.

Shanny raced to rescue the distressed Rusty from his predicament. Raz led Molly on foot under a closed door to another room.

"We need to find a window," Raz commanded. He saw the only window in the room even as he said it.

"Give us a minute, Raz," Molly pled. "These old bones don't move like they used to, you know."

Raz climbed the bedpost, huffing and puffing, nearly as exhausted as Old Molly. He reached the sill in time to witness Fin's fate.

Fin must have resigned himself to his doom when he saw the mosquitoes wrapped in sticky webbing in the dull, pulseless glow of the fireflies. Still, steady, dead glint. Their mounts were as dead as any chance of escape for Fin or his friends now. Stuck fast to freshly spun strands, Fin felt a gentle tug on the web from separate corners.

Knowing he would soon share their fates, Fin reached out to caress the two nearest firefly corpses. The three spiders, giants by arachnid reckoning, closed in on him. They must have driven off the old spider and roamed, surveying the territory before weaving webs of their own. Fin's body was divided evenly between the deadly triad without fuss.

"Don't look, Molly," Raz turned to hug her neck as she reached the windowsill.

Although the youngest member of their party, Fin may have been the bravest. Both Raz and Molly remembered when he was just a sparkling mote of fairy dust in the night.

Molly wept into Raz's shoulder. "What do we do now, Raz?"

The cup came down over the two of them before he could answer. Red Kool-Aid droplets splashed them both as a bingo card slid under the cup, trapping the fairies. Movement jostled them off their feet before they tumbled into a clear glass jar that smelled faintly of peanut butter. Old Molly clutched her leader as the grinding sound of a lid screwing on tightly dashed their hopes.

"Don't worry Molly, I'll think of something." Raz's fingertips began exploring the walls of the jar for a defect he knew would not be there.

A flashlight's beam danced through the jar as Shanny assessed her two new pets. "What shiny wings! I'll take you in to class on Monday for Show-and-Tell. Maybe Mrs. Walcott can tell us what kind of bugs you are." She smiled. "She's my science teacher."

The little girl set the jar on the floor beside her bed and climbed under the covers. An uneasy peace settled over the room.

"This doesn't look good, Molly," Raz said. The strawberry Kool-Aid became sticky as he smeared the glass with his hands.

"It's cold, Raz," Molly said and sat on the floor of their new home. "I don't like being cold. I can still feel the breeze of his claws when that beastly cat swiped at me."

"You've had your rotten old feet soaking in that icy drink for hours. Your back is soaked with it now," he said, looking at his hand.

"You must be right, Raz. Look at me sweater. It's dripping wet. But doesn't the drink feel warm to you?" Molly yawned as she palmed the carmine pool collecting around her hips. "Feels warmer than I do. This cold must be making us sleepy..."

Molly tumbled over on her side.

"Molly!" Raz shouted.

He tasted the goo on his fingers. It didn't taste like strawberries. For Raz, this was the first time there was no quickening at the flavor of blood.

He knelt by old Molly and cradled her head gently. His moment of silence was torn asunder by the ferocious clawing and hissing of Rusty, the tormenter.

"Can't I even mourn in peace, beast?" Raz shouted.

The jar rose out of reach of the cat, only to meet the curious eyes of the waking child.

"I'll put you up where old Rusty can't get at you, okay?" Shanny pressed her lips to the side of the jar nearest Raz and Molly, then placed it on the top shelf of her bookcase. "Sleep tight. Don't let the bedbugs bite!" she said, yawning and pulling covers over shoulders once again.

Raz was alone. He had failed his mission and lost his entire hunting party to a little girl.

"A girl named Prentice," Raz nearly laughed. "Prentice, a classic witch's name. One of the original twelve. Why hadn't we seen that?"

Fin had done his diligence. There were no witches in the house, but witch-blood must run in this girl's veins: Enough to attract a familiar.

From a tense crouch, Rusty glared at Raz from the corner of the room.

"Now she's going to take me to this Walcott woman. What are the chances that a science teacher named Walcott is the leader of a coven?" He had already concluded the value as close to 100%.

"The Vampyr will go on the rampage when I fall into witches' hands." Raz began to pray, "Beelzebub, get me out of this mess, save my village, and I'll never lead another tooth party for as long as I live."

He hung his head only to see the dawn creeping through the window below him. It promised to be a bright morning. The sunshine waxed and climbed up the bookcase to the top shelf. Raz watched the gleam reach his feet with blinding intensity and no shade in sight. It would seem that Beelzebub indeed had a wicked sense of humor in the granting of wishes.

As the sun had its requisite effect on any vampire, big or small, Raz muttered to no one in particular, "Bloody fudge."

Every vestige of Raz and Molly was gone in a puff.

—⟨●⟩—

"Shanny, breakfast," Mr. Prentice called from the kitchen.

Shanny stretched and petted Rusty, who'd settled in her lap in the wee hours. Her eyes opened wide and she sprang from her bed, sending the cat sailing. She grabbed the peanut butter jar and sprinted to the kitchen. She shimmied onto a barstool next to Tommy.

A sidelong smirk at her little brother, already halfway through his bowl of cereal, prefaced her offer: "Want to see my Angel bugs?"

Tommy dropped his spoon with a clank, "Heck yeah!"

General Lee, the old Labrador, licked at the spoon.

"Hey! No bugs at the table," their father said with a stern look at both children.

"Daddy, you've got to see them." Shanny beamed. "They're sealed in this jar. It's safe, see?"

Her glee turned to disappointment when she looked inside.

"Cool, sparkly dust." Tommy said. "What's it made of, Daddy?"

"It's magic glitter, Tommy," their father said, "but it's your sister's, so you leave it alone. Deal?"

"Sure." Tommy folded his arms and sulked. "I don't want any old girly glitter anyway."

Shanny had the jar open now. "It used to have Angel bugs in it," she said glumly, climbing down from the stool and walking to the windowsill.

"Sweetie," her father asked, "whatcha' doing?"

"I'm going to sprinkle this on that big old spider web outside the family room. Maybe it will warn other Angel bugs away from that mean, sneaky spider." Rusty leapt into her empty arms, anxious for a petting.

Shanny frowned, looked down and spoke to Rusty, "Now what am I supposed to take in to Mrs. Walcott for Show-and-Tell?"

— GLAMOUR —
by Grey Yuen

T he first sign the morning was going to be rubbish was how early the paparazzi were. They had beaten Jack to a crime scene before, that was true, but never without the whole world already with them at the playground, and most certainly never at 4am. Sergeant Hilton was at the tape line waiting for him, looking paler than usual and just about as cheery for the hour.

"I saw the name," Jack said, waving his handphone before putting it into his back pocket.

"I didn't mean for it to be dramatic. I just thought a little advance warning would soften the shock."

"But isn't her house on Notting Hill? Whose apartment is this?"

Hilton nodded. "Hers as well. According to the razz, this is her workspace, like a home away from home where she writes her songs and whatever."

"Boggles the mind, doesn't it, that the children these days have another term for an 'office'?"

He thought it was a fair enough association, as the 'razz' he saw were just two girls—he couldn't think of a better word for those no older than his own fourteen-year-old at home by a couple of years— sitting on the curb with their camera and huddled together like brats after a roller-coaster ride. They didn't look like they had come here for this. One of Hilton's constables stood a few feet away, the round-faced young man whose name Jack always forgot. He remembered calling him "Wilhelm" before but guessing it wrong here would be embarrassing.

Past an arch of brass, they came up to what remained of a fine wooden door. It could have been a mahogany antique if they could ignore the dozen or so slashes added to the facade, all fresh and apparently inflicted by something sharp and heavy. The turn-latch lock itself had been shattered in one or two strikes, the pieces still twisted in the locked position from within. Leaning against the wall close by was the instrument of destruction—a red-painted axe taken from an emergency glass case somewhere.

"So the Big Bad Wolf failed at huffing-and-puffing and decided to try a battering ram?" Jack went for the obvious and wrong with a slight sing-song tone, a lead-in for their own little Punch and Judy routine.

"Not quite like that, boss," was the reply, as always. She tipped her head back toward the two on the curb. "Somebody did try to get the door down, but lacking the expertise, failed, panicked and called us, all the while screaming about how someone was in trouble inside. That bit—" she indicated the blow that actually destroyed the lock "—was me."

Jack nodded his approval, but his gaze remained on the girls. "They know something?"

"They think they do, but you might want to take a look inside first." She hesitated before they stepped in, dropping out of their usual exchange pattern. "Don't mean to be naff, but you're not a fan, are you?"

"Oh, Sergeant, how I wish I were that young."

Like everything on the street, the apartment was an old relic with a new skin draped over ancient bones, except this one had nothing in between, no meat, no substance. Jack felt his mouth fall open standing at the doorstep. The living room was bare beyond what the lads nowadays would call "uncluttered" and "minimalistic," two nonsense words he knew were invented just to avoid calling someone's house "empty." A single yellow tungsten lightbulb lit up the place as vacant as any up for sale.

"The blazes! They nicked this place clean?"

Of course it couldn't be a burglary. At least not of such a scale and this close to the main road without drawing the wrath of the entire neighbourhood. The floor was clean, practically dust-free and without the usual marks of heavy furniture dragged across it or shapes that outlined where they could have originally stood.

A flash bounced off the walls ahead, followed by a high-pitched whine. Anderson the Mannequin was already here and waiting where the action was. The bedroom was small but not cramped, enough space for the only piece of furniture they could see in the apartment—a bed, befittingly queen-size. Hogging it like a stage, even to the very end, was the still figure of the Queen of Glam—Darling, Princess, or Goddess, depending on who was asked—Green Maeve.

Jack took in a deep breath and blew it out slowly. "This is going to be a spritely day."

Music, as he always told those around him enlightened enough to listen, ended after the reign of the Beatles, and people these days were only swaying along to the echoes that lingered before they died out completely. On the rare occasions he could tell any of these new pretenders apart from another, he'd more likely get the wrong song to go with the name.

Yet here he was looking at someone he had seen countless times on the telly, on the Internet, on magazine covers, and whose songs, if he was honest about it, he could at least hum. The dozens of headlines from the past two months alone gave him no doubt he was looking at the winner of eight Grammys the year before, with two debut albums hitting triple platinum. For any radio station to go two hours without playing anything from her was sacrilege. What she wore one week practically defined the dress-code for the next, and it wasn't uncommon to see boys putting on mascara to get the "Maeve Eyes" when they could get away with it.

"Indeed," said Anderson without lowering his camera. "Come morning, the razz are going to feast like crows."

Jack never appreciated the cliché of comparing the dead with the asleep, but he had to admit it was difficult telling the difference this time. There was no visible wound, no blood, no sign of violence. Even without makeup or the tricks of studio lighting, the Princess of Pop looked divine with her perfect features, as if only her breath had been taken from her and nothing else. She was just lying down for the moment, waiting for her Prince.

"How goes the tale, Anderson?"

Jack never liked calling the man by his nickname, largely because nobody remembered the history behind it at the Yard, but he agreed "Mannequin" was pretty much spot on about Anderson's emotionless on-site demeanour. He hadn't always been like that, so they said, and the word from Forensics seemed to be that if you could arrive on the scene earlier than him, you could ask. Nobody ever did that. Professionalism was its own reward.

"I'm still reading the book, Inspector, but you can skip ahead to see the ending. Spoiler warning: it isn't a happy one."

Unnatural death was a certainty, but how the boys and girls would cry was going to depend on whether it suicide, homicide, or a drug overdose.

The big question. "Foul play, you think?"

"Two hours from the body temperature and iris response, but we aren't seeing any rigor mortis, yet. It's... a tad unusual. Give me a few more minutes." Anderson turned to give him a long look over his glasses. "If you want another plot twist for this tale, you might want to look at the next room first."

There was only one other, and Hilton was there like an American game-show presenter leading him into the bonus round. He saw no bed within, only a heap of what appeared to be unwashed laundry. Lying on it was a sight that stopped him at the door. Memories flashed from the moments years ago when work still kept him late, and all he could do spare every night coming home was a minute or two by the crib to check in on his Pip.

"Oh, crikes."

"I wasn't trying to be coy, boss," said Hilton, "but this isn't something I could text."

Like every other vacuum, the one in his mind lasted barely a second before the laws of physics collapsed it with questions and thoughts and guesses to fill the void. But Hilton was whispering to him, and it was reason for a sigh of relief.

"Wait," he said, repeating it aloud a few times to be sure. "Green Maeve has a little sprog no one knew about? Was she moonlighting as a nanny?"

"We don't know. Nobody knows. Sorry, I mean I have never heard of this and I don't think anyone has."

"No." Jack's hand was up. "No. The first thing they teach at the Yard, Sergeant. Somebody knows. Somebody. The tabloids must know, and those two outsi— uh, hullo! And what do we have here?"

They had missed something right by the door and in the hard shadows under the single light-bulb. The strap gave it away: a messenger sling-bag, leather brown and stylish and wrong. No woman would be caught on the streets carrying that unless they were itching to be lectured on the existence of the Yard's elusive but highly influential fashion department. They lifted its flap without using their fingers and slid out the contents, and the first to do so from between stacks of contracts and musical score sheets was a tiny pill bottle. It was plastic and empty, with remnants of a torn label on the side, the writing gone.

Jack took out a ziplock bag and put it in. "We'll have the boys at the lab look at this."

They dug out an organiser with a name embossed on the faux-leather cover, one that also appeared on all the documents as either the signatory or the addressee.

"Thomas Lin."

"Tommy Lin," Hilton corrected him with a nod. "Her manager."

"Brilliant. At least we know people still use these archaic things." It did what an electronic tablet couldn't, like keeping stuffed between the pages numerous pictures of Green Maeve in various photo-shoots, along with spreads cut from several entertainment magazines and album covers. There were also receipts and name cards of makeup artists and photographers. Out from the stack dropped a piece of thin card with a serrated torn-off edge.

"A bus ticket stub..." Jack stepped closer to read the details, "from Yorkshire just earlier today." He stepped back and began looking around. "He was here? And straight from Yorkshire?"

"Ah that," said Hilton, "you might want to talk to the two reporters outside first. They have not stepped in past the door yet, and I haven't told them anything."

The pair looked like they were still trapped in a state of limbo and tears, their makeup ruined with mascara running down their cheeks. Another night and they could well be in some Shoreditch club having their age checked for drinking. The ginger was Joan and the brunette, Rachel, and they were keeping each other warm by the side of the road and under the watchful eye of Constable— Wilhelm? Or was it Jacob?

Jack showed them his ID. "I'm Inspector J. B. Nimbell. I would say 'good morning' but that is hardly appropriate now."

"Wait," said Joan, catching his printed name. "That was Sergeant Gillian Hilton. So that makes you two—"

"An inspector and a sergeant, yes." Hilton was the most competent sergeant he knew, and it was only the obsession of people finding humour in the coincidence of their names that made their rapport a bad thing. More than once at the station he had taken pains not to be seen with her at the water-cooler area. Still, the keen observation from the ginger was what he needed. "Can you tell me what happened earlier? You called us about some trouble inside."

"We are, like, her biggest fans, you know? Sure, we're working for the *Tinker Belle*, but it's a dream job to cover her pics, to just be there. Tonight was, like, the biggest news ever, 'cause Tommy was coming over—"

"Tommy Lin? You mean the PA?" Jack could have sworn the two rolled their eyes were it not for the mascara smudges.

"Her manager. Ariel's her PA. She's really alright, but Tommy is the one behind, like, all her records and MVs and awards and stuff, and... and practically her Prince Charming." Jack blinked, but took everything down without interrupting. "I mean, everyone knows they're made for each other, just never, you know, *caught together*, right? So tonight we caught them coming here together, finally. They have never done that at night before. We came here and waited, you know? Not to, like, bust them, but just to be happy for them."

"They arrived here together? What time was it?"

"It was after midnight. I remember because it's a big thing to catch her out of the house after midnight. It's like her personal curfew or something. More importantly, it was with Tommy this time."

Jack made eye contact with Hilton again before asking the next question. "Was either of them carrying a bundle? By which I mean, like, cradling something in their arms?"

"Cradling?" The two looked confused. "I don't think so. We were both trying to catch them finally holding hands, and they weren't. But they couldn't be carrying anything in their arms."

"So you saw them going in, and they didn't see you. And you just went on waiting out here?"

"I don't... I know it sounds like we're stalking her, but... but we *had* to stay and wait. Something was going to happen, and... and something was... making us know that. And then... and then..."

Rachel cut in with a gasp, suddenly shaking from the memory. "The door! We saw the door. I swear it! It had a mouth and it screamed! Because she was dying. It screamed because... she was dead... we were just out here! It was—"

"Rachel! We just talked about this!" Joan snapped out, and they both fell silent.

Jack held back. He kept still and waited for them to compose themselves, and again, it was Joan who finally spoke.

"You think we're crazy, don't you? You think we're on drugs or something and that we killed her somehow."

"I didn't say she's dead."

"We *felt* it, inspector! That's why we grabbed that axe from the lobby and... Look, I even chipped my nails. We couldn't... we had to call you. That's all we know." Joan was crying again, and Rachel joined in. "Please, Inspector, tell me you got him. If we couldn't save her, at least tell me you caught him. Was it Tommy? Was it him?"

With that, they were bawling their eyes out again and there was nothing more they could say. Jack strode back past the ruined door, past Hilton and all the way to the kitchen. It had no stove, no refrigerator—nothing, but the windows had a grill across, secured with a tiny padlock that was practically a lump of rust. Nothing here had been opened for years, let alone had someone snuck through without leaving a trace.

What draw could a place like this hold for someone like Green Maeve? Or was it just more of what he called "tosh of the posh"? Fame on this level was different from being merely recognisable as someone on the telly. Beyond a certain threshold was a way of life quite unfathomable to the hoi polloi of Nine-to-Five Land, and she happened to be the very icon of it for her generation. Even her most ardent worshippers could do no more than guess at her likes and dislikes, her motivations, her reasons for doing anything at all.

"I'm surprised they didn't leg it before you arrived," Jack said.

"Do you think they're lying?"

"I think we'll need more questions for them at the station. If they're not, they present an interesting obstacle to the only exit here."

"And before you get to asking, boss," said Hilton, "no one got out behind me. I'm sure of it."

It was hard to argue against that, considering there was obviously nowhere to hide in the living room, and the lack of cover made it impossible to cross it without anyone's notice. They returned to the baby room. The little fellow was still asleep, and they stood in quiet thought listening to the clicks from Anderson next door. Jack's attention fell to the organiser by the bag, staring at the name for several seconds before it came back to him.

"Twenty years," he whispered.

"I'm sorry?"

"Yorkshire. I remember now. He was big news twenty years ago." He resisted looking at Hilton and adding *before your time*. "A six-year-old boy found abandoned in the middle of a field, dazed and unable to speak for weeks. He matched none of the missing children reports. I was fresh in the Yard, then, a rookie bloodhound given a scent and a quarry. And we found bloomin' *nowt* about him in the records. No identity, no information. Drove everyone mental. The case took months to fade from the limelight, and when it did, a migrant couple from Asia adopted him, proper legal and all. It explains his rather distinct last name for a Yorkshireman."

Hilton arched a brow. "Nothing wrong with that, boss."

"Nothing wrong with that." Jack nodded. "And then two years ago I read in the papers that the couple died in a car crash. Tragic is what it is. And Thomas. Did he grow up to have a son with a singer? And then chickened out of a suicide pact?"

"Suicide pact or something more malicious."

Neither of them would say it. Even the cleaning lady who worked at the Yard could see the impossibility of either scenario. But there was also no third option, no other way things could have gone. No other way *he* could have gone.

"We've tried calling him," said Hilton. "His phone is off."

"That's right!" Jack's eyes lit up. "And where is it, Sergeant? If his bag is here, his phone should be as well. Where is it?"

Someone was shouting. Jack's reflexes kicked in so fast he was reaching for his weapon before realising it was Anderson cursing and screaming from the bedroom. Before anyone could say a word, the Mannequin stumbled out like a man running for his life, his face bloodless and eyes wild.

"She's—she's gone!"

Hilton was the first to rush past him into the room and she stopped so quickly Jack almost crashed into her. There was no trick of the light, or smoke or mirrors, but Green Maeve's body, on the bed just moments ago, was missing.

"I just looked away for two seconds, had my back to the bed," Anderson said as he retreated to the wall and slowly sank to the floor. "And then she just... vanished."

Silence washed in like a tide and for almost a whole minute no one made a sound. No one knew what to ask or say; everything they needed to see was there without any room for tricks. Jack's mind grasped for something amusing to tamper the shock while his thoughts escaped his rein and raced down every line of reasoning in every direction, failing at every turn.

Anderson remained glued to the screen of his camera, his face twisting into an expression few had glimpsed before. The Mannequin had no fear, that was the rule. Now everyone was breaking all the rules. He lowered the screen for them, his trembling finger toggling between one picture and the one after it. "I always take two sets of pictures. With flash and without. They bring out different things, different perspectives."

The camera was good. Even on its tiny screen, Green Maeve remained in vibrant colours, picturesque and serene. The other picture was different.

"Wait— What?" Hilton jerked her head back on reflex. "That's... not... her."

It was some other woman, someone too thin to be healthy, with nothing more than skin stretched over bone. Her facial features were unlike anyone Jack had ever seen, as if some deranged surgeon had put together a human visage from a blank slate based solely on descriptions of how a woman should look.

Hilton's breathing was becoming short and choppy. "What is happening, Anderson? What did you do to her?"

"You were just there, Sergeant!" Anderson shrieked. "What do you think I could do to—"

"People!" Jack said in his normal voice that somehow hushed them both. "We have a sleeping baby next door."

They were the audience of a magic routine gone wrong, now left gawking on the stage to wait and see if the illusion would break under their glare. But without the body, they had nothing—no case, no incident. Was there even a way to proceed forward? Jack picked up a new smell, one so far removed from those of the city it threw his memories to his childhood decades ago. He remembered flowers. He remembered summer afternoons. It was the smell of honeysuckle and yarrow flowers rotting in the wide fields on the countryside.

He moved closer to the bed to examine the shadow left on the sheets, the dark silhouette that still vaguely described the shape of a body. He had seen blood and this wasn't blood; blood didn't dry like this. It was brown—no, not brown. It was rust.

"This is some kind of trick," said Hilton. "Like a magician's sleight of hand illusion."

"A trick, yes. But not an illusion." Jack looked outside where the sky was slowly lighting up. "It's sunrise."

The chaos swirling within began to settle, some fragments of thought falling into place. None of it *made sense*, but everything was leading *somewhere*. He took out the ziplock bag from his pocket, opened it and took out the pillbox. Hilton's eyes widened like she was staring at an oncoming train.

"Boss, are you sure—" she started to say but he was already easing open the cap to take a whiff. Certain poisons can kill in amounts less than what is needed to generate a scent, most of which have been romanticised to no end in novels and movies. But what once filled the container was neither odourless nor toxic, just something he hated with a passion.

"Blood supplements," he said. The coppery smell brought back all the familiar pain.

He dashed back to the organiser and tossed out all the other things between the pages. Aside from the photographs and cards, there were newspaper cuttings, all yellow with age, all that he now saw were stories of kidnappings and disappearances of children. Every one had names scribbled on the side but most were crossed out as if they had been rejected. On a page torn from another notebook was a list of book names along with their authors, with one of them circled multiple times titled *The History of Changelings.* An arrow led from the entry to a comment lower in the margin:

No writing of names. They know when they've been written down.

He kept going back to the word in the book title, staring long at it before flipping to the last entry made just the day before. The last was also the longest, and while the handwriting was no school teacher's pride, it didn't look like something penned in a hurry.

Plan B: There is none. I have no backup. It is hard to accept that for all this planning, there is no contingency, but revenge has never had that luxury. This is the last and only prep/check before going forward. They may not acknowledge good or evil, but that means nothing to those who suffer the consequences. This is for my family. I no longer remember what they sounded like, but I remember all their faces. It is late, but it must be done.

The word "revenge" was the third one used in its place, with "justice" crossed out before it and another, earlier "revenge" in front of that. Every page after that was blank but the next one held an envelope. Thin and unmarked, it was sealed with letter wax over the glued flap, complete with a stamp that read "TL." It was a classy touch no one did anymore.

"Boss!" Hilton shouted from the living room. "I found the phone!" She was clanging away at something metallic and hollow like a percussionist gone mad. "It's between the blades in the radiator."

The radiator. Like the lights, the windows, the grills, it came with the place sans the furniture, and there was no stealing or removing it. He remembered seeing it on the way in, black and traditional cast-iron.

Jack almost tripped springing to his feet. "No, Sergeant! Wait—"

He heard her yelp out, and something dropped to the floor. She was holding her hand close to her chest.

"It... it's burning hot!"

It landed face up, its screen just lighting up with a call coming in. There was no picture but the name displayed was clear: Ariel. Hilton took a step forward despite her hand and Jack stopped her.

"Don't answer it!" he said. "Don't touch it!"

"But it's her assistant, and she might know what's going on!"

Jack never learnt to explain it like his grandmother, possibly the reason he never came to understand it, either. But the truth was he never really believed.

"Don't touch it!" he kept repeating in case Hilton thought for a moment it was safe. How many ways were there of dropping a phone in the radiator by accident?

Anderson peered out from the room now, drawn by the commotion. The phone was almost becoming animated by its vibrations, practically bouncing clear off the floor like a Mexican jumping bean in a cartoon. Of the four power bars one was out and another was blinking. Without anyone touching the answer button, a new voice screamed through the speaker:

"Release me, Tam! End your useless cantrip here and now, do you hear me? Your toy is tiring itself out, you little worm, and my patience wears thin. The Queen will hear of this and you will suffer! The Queen! Where is she? What have you done to her?"

Pulling herself up, Hilton reached for her weapon.

"No!" Jack shouted. "No, not that! Not with lead." It was the first time she ever needed more than a few seconds to understand what he was saying, but he was already running straight to the door.

He saw the girls still outside with the constable, all three staring at him with eyes wide and mouths open, frozen or entranced. But he wasn't here for them, or to escape into the city. He grabbed the weapon Hilton had left outside. It took to his hands well and was weighted perfectly, the head made from high grade steel to withstand repeated abuse. Steel. Iron and carbon.

The phone stopped jumping. It was still lit with the call connected, but had gone still and silent. Jack lifted the axe high over his shoulder.

"You can smell it, can't you?" he said. Anderson and Hilton fell back to let him talk. "You can feel it, wherever you are? This is cold, hard iron."

For a long while there was no reply. Then just as Jack was about to bring down the edge, the voice of Ariel came again.

"Where is Tam? Where is he? What has he done to the Queen?"

"Maeve," Jack said. "Green Maeve is gone. We don't know where Thomas is—"

The scream came with more power than anything the tiny speaker on a phone could possibly contain, stabbing right into the head like a knife and throwing them to their knees. Jack almost dropped his axe.

"Enough!" He slammed it down just inches from the phone, the blade cutting deep into the wooden flooring. His grip was trembling and his fingers were numb, but the screaming stopped. "That is enough! She is gone. Your queen is gone. If she was the only reason you are here, there is none now. No one has summoned you and no one binds you here."

"*Where is Tam—*"

"Thomas is safe and he is not going back with you. Not today. Not tomorrow, either. I don't know the right words to say and I don't know what names to invoke. I don't even have any real grievances with you. But I do have an axe in my hands and I can probably bring more men with axes if—" he hesitated, unsure if he should bargain or plead or intimidate, "—if we cannot come to an understanding here."

He kept his eyes on the last flashing bar; he needed a decision before it winked out and he wasn't sure he had the reflexes to make a difference. The others were of no help now in their struggle to deal with what they were witnessing. He yanked the blade free with a grunt.

Something in the air shivered and, as abruptly as it started, the call ended. The phone went still and dark. All around them the scent of dead flowers faded in a single breath, leaving the dank odour of a concrete cave left empty for years. Still no one moved, until Jack released the axe from his grip.

"Cheers, m'lady."

Hilton slowly straightened up.

"Tommy," she whispered. "You lied about Tommy. We don't even know where he..." She trailed off as Jack slowly shook his head, then her light of comprehension shone through her face. In unison their gaze shifted to the only place Tommy Tam of the Lins could be.

The mess from everything they dug from the bag lay scattered across the floor but they were not going through Tommy's possessions anymore. They came to stare at the baby. Hilton began muttering nonsense words to herself before biting down her lip and turning to Jack.

"No, boss. You don't get to say it." She was speaking very slowly the way Jack did himself at home whenever he needed to stop someone's tantrums carried too far. "No disrespect meant, but I think you've gone barmy. Mad. Insane. Off your damned trolley. And... and the only issue I have with that is, so have I."

"No disrespect taken, Sergeant, and I would happily agree with you, except, as you can see, Anderson isn't a white rabbit and I am not wearing a hat."

Anderson had slipped in the room with them after regaining much of his composure. His hand was barely trembling when he straightened his glasses. "I don't have a better explanation, Inspector, and I'm going to sound like a broken record if I keep asking what just happened. But that... what you're saying... it can't be real. They can't be real. What you're saying they are, they're... they're children stories!"

"I'm not good with stories," Jack said, wondering how else he could say this, "and I can only tell you what my Nan told me. She used to talk about her childhood and how our family was kept safe during the War. How none of the bombs fell on our town and why the Nazis never crossed the Channel. For that, she always left some milk and bread out after everyone had gone to bed. She told me that's how neighbours take care of one another. Good neighbours. But they are not the stories we made up about them. They have a darker side, something they'd remind us of every now and then, in case we were getting too comfortable, too familiar. They take from us, as well, children, in particular."

"No, wait! Stop. That was a euphemism for the high infant mortality rate during the Middle Ages."

Jack nodded, but not in agreement. "Except when you have a straggler find his way back somehow, or brought along in one of their visits. Maybe it was his plan all along, or maybe it only came to him after seeing the place from which he'd been taken as a babe."

"You mean murder?" Hilton cut in. "That's proper mental! They can't be... that is ridiculous!"

"More than what we've seen?" Jack smiled this time, finally hearing something amusing. "I don't know how he did it—could be a wager, a trick of gobsmacking proportions, an outright spiking of the drinks— no idea. But I know he used this." He held the empty bottle up to the light. "My boy Pip was anemic, if you remember. And what's the worst we get from overdosing iron tablets? Possibly less liver damage than my weekends at the pub."

"Even if that works, you are talking about murder, first degree. This is something *we* do, not something that happens in... in the stories."

It wasn't murder. Not to them. They would never understand it as murder any more than they could call what they did 'kidnapping.'

"But stories change, Sergeant, even if *they* don't. My Nan used to call them the very embodiment of splendour and glamour and brilliance. They are timeless and unchanging. If they were even created at all, they were made to be envied. But look at where we are now, just look outside. See the neon lights and listen to the electric beat coming out our car stereos. The stories aren't the same anymore."

They were all looking at the baby when he woke up, who surprised them by not crying at the sight of the three strangers, instead choosing to study them one at a time with his deep blue eyes. His little mouth curled up in a smile and that shattered something between them, a tension that had locked up a part of their breath. Hilton stooped to touch him and brush a lock of hair from his face.

"This... can't be *him*. You mean his life—his whole life—was a lie?"

"Glamour," Jack corrected her, "is more than a lie. But that's just like the old stories, isn't it? The house of bread disappears, the hoard of gold vanishes. And twenty years of his life..."

"But who is... was... he?" she said.

Jack picked up the envelope and broke the seal. Inside was a single A4 photograph of a gravestone in a cemetery somewhere, taken on a sunny day and blown up in high definition. The years were clearly 1679 to 1680 but the family name was obscured by lichen and moss. Inscribed were the words:

Our treasure taken too young from us and from the Lord. Would the Good Folk be kind to return him to us.

"Someone who has spent a long time looking for an answer to that question," he said. He bent down and picked up the baby in his arms without startling him. His two monsters at home had given him good practice.

"What are we going to do with him?" asked the Mannequin.

"I'm just an old Dibbie and not one to judge what he did," he said. "But I know every little boy needs to start the day with some breakfast."

— SEE A FINE LADY —
by Seanan McGuire

T he issue was not—entirely—the fact that the woman was riding a horse into Target. That was *an* issue, as the store had a clearly posted, firmly enforced "no pets" policy, and while there were probably some arguments to be made for the horse as a form of service animal, they weren't really going to hold up well in court.

No, the real issue was the fact that no one else seemed to notice the woman on the horse.

It wasn't a small horse, either. Frankie had never really been a horse girl; while she'd liked them well enough, her family hadn't been exactly well-off, much less rich, and so riding lessons and stable fees had been outside her reach before she'd even known she might want them. But she'd been an ordinary girl in a school filled with horse girls, and she'd picked up a few facts in self-defense.

This horse, this horse was probably some sort of draft horse, taller than the average man, with thick, muscular legs that ended in broad hooves that looked like they could dig in and drag a boulder up a mountain. It was snowy white, from the tip of its muzzle to the feathering around its ankles. Its mane and tail were long, lush, and flowing enough to have caused fits of jealous rage in every hair salon in the world. It wasn't the sort of horse that went unnoticed. It wasn't the sort of horse that went unremarked. It certainly wasn't the sort of horse that belonged in *Target*. Big box stores and glorious white stallions didn't belong in the same sentence.

Then the horse turned to look at Frankie, as if it could somehow sense her increasingly jumbled thoughts, and she was forced to amend all her thoughts about the suitability of horses in Target.

Somehow, "unicorns in Target" didn't feel any better.

The woman on the unicorn's back was thin and dreamy-looking, with a crown of blackberry thorns topping her black curls and a distant look in her dark brown eyes. She was wearing torn jeans and a T-shirt with a faded logo advertising a band whose name had been lost to cheap ink and harsh detergents. She wobbled slightly as the unicorn walked toward the women's wear section, looking as if she might fall off her mythological steed at any moment. She was not, Frankie noted, wearing shoes.

Frankie couldn't decide whether this was better or worse than the part where the woman was *riding an actual unicorn*. It was definitely more directly against store rules, which didn't have anything to say about equines that didn't exist, but was very firm on the idea of "no shirt, no shoes, no service."

"Excuse me?"

The question itself was polite. The tone in which it was asked, well, wasn't. The tone turned it from a simple inquiry to an implicit threat, dripping with "do I need to speak to your manager?" and "people like you are the reason I can't support raising the minimum wage." It was the tone of impending doom, and Frankie's attention snapped instantly back to the woman on the other side of her register, who was watching her with undisguised disdain.

"I am *so* sorry," said Frankie, and began swiping the woman's items double-quick across the scanner, hoping to make up the time she had lost.

The woman didn't say anything.

Frankie seized on the escape silence offered her, finishing the transaction with a speed that was equal parts practice and panic. When she read off the total, the woman sniffed and fixed Frankie with a steely eye, clearly waiting for some discount to be offered as apology for the offense of waiting. Frankie smiled blandly back. In this, at least, she was in the right; even if the woman went to Customer Service with her tale of woe, Frankie's equine distraction hadn't lasted long enough to take the length of their interaction from "acceptable" into "unacceptable." Discounts weren't offered for acceptable service.

Discounts weren't offered for much of anything. The corporate bottom line was more important than anything a mere associate might be able to screw up in their brief interaction with a customer.

The customer, looking disgusted, finally moved on. Frankie looked at her empty line, and at the three customers pushing their red carts toward her as fast as they could without actually running, and clicked the "on" light above her register off. All three customers shot her venomous looks. Pretending not to see them, she turned and walked after the unicorn as casually as she could.

It wasn't difficult. The unicorn was, after all, remarkably large, and it didn't appear to be in any hurry. The fact that no one else seemed to see it probably helped. Why hurry when you were apparently invisible megafauna?

Frankie had seen a moose once, by the side of the road in upstate Washington. It had been casually munching on a bush, watching the cars go rushing by with a vaguely malicious air, like it knew it could ruin a whole lot of peoples' days just by stepping into traffic. The unicorn was sort of like that, only potentially meaner.

Frankie was pretty sure the unicorn could take a moose. Maybe two moose. The lady on the unicorn's back might look like the kind of airy, dreamy girl who would try to feed a moose carrots because it looked sort of like a horse, maybe, but the unicorn? The unicorn looked *mean*.

As Frankie watched, the unicorn lifted its tail and dropped a massive pat of unicorn crap in the middle of the aisle. Unlike the half-joking unicorn-related T-shirts she'd seen in the kid's department, the unicorn crapped neither rainbows nor glitter. The unicorn crapped, well, crap. Big and brown and wet-looking. Frankie looked from the unicorn to the crap and back again before making an executive decision and fading back into the racks behind her, waiting to see what would happen.

What happened was a customer, not looking where they were going, driving their cart directly into the giant pile of poop, splashing it over the surrounding linoleum and onto the edge of the carpet that went under the clothing aisles. There was a momentary startled pause before the customer actually screamed, a deep guttural sound of shock and disgust and sheer indignity, like they couldn't believe this was happening to *them* while they were out shopping at *Target*. The scream managed to somehow imply that this was a classy establishment, above random piles of horseshit in the aisles, and a tawdry den of filth where such things should absolutely be expected, at the same time.

It was very impressive. Frankie was very impressed, even as she faded further back into the shelves, out of view of both the customer who'd suffered the unicorn poop encounter and the uniformed crew members who were now rushing to assist with the unexpected cleanup.

Technically, this was an emergency, and as she was still on the clock, she should have been hurrying to help mop unicorn poop off the floor, the merchandise, the cart, and the customer. But she had more important things to do, and so she quietly turned and walked away, following the unicorn's most likely path through the store.

It was interesting. People couldn't see the unicorn, or the woman on its back. No one had seemed to see the pile of poop—and it had been a quite considerable pile of poop; Frankie was reasonably sure no one could have overlooked it without really trying, if it had been visible—until someone actually interacted with it. After that, *everyone* had been able to see the poop. The poop had been, as it were, announced to the world.

So what would happen if someone interacted with the unicorn? If she were to, say, put her hand on its pearlescent flank, to feel the silky brush of its fur against her palm, would it appear to *everyone*, or would it continue to be visible to only her? And did she *want* it to appear to everyone, or did she want it to be her secret, shared only with the dreamy girl on its back, who didn't seem to appreciate, or care, that she was riding an actual unicorn through a large retail store?

All these questions were more important than getting back to her register or, hell, holding on to her job. Anyone could fill out an application to work in retail. Sure, the market was competitive, but one bad reference wasn't going to knock her completely out of the market. Seeing a unicorn, on the other hand...

That felt like something special.

Frankie worked her way through the merchandise as quickly as she dared, ducking behind racks and using shortcuts through the least popular areas, struggling to avoid customers. She could desert her register. She could avoid cleanup calls and even "forget" to check in with her manager. But if she blew off a customer who genuinely needed help, her ass would be grass, and like all grass, it would get *mowed*.

She was almost successful. She had managed to weave her way through clothes, kitchenware, and storage, and was almost clear of the toy department when a voice said, in that bright, cheerful, unconsciously imperious tone used by customers everywhere, "Excuse me? Miss? Do you work here?"

No, I wear a red vest and a nametag for fun, thought Frankie, but she was already smiling as she turned, ready to be a good associate, Ready To Help. The capital letters were key: they reminded her of the fact that in this moment, during this interaction, she wasn't fully human. She wasn't equal to the needs of the customer.

The customer, who was had somehow traded jeans and T-shirt for a gauzy, flowing dress, although she still wore no shoes, who had a crown of blackberry thorns resting on her curls. She smiled blithely at Frankie's obvious confusion.

"I'm sorry, but I need grapes," she said. "Big green grapes, the kind that don't have any seeds in them. Do you know where those would be?"

"The produce section," said Frankie. She felt faint. The world was spinning slowly around her, and she was fairly sure that if she closed her eyes, even for a moment, she would be woken up by the clanging shriek of her alarm clock telling her that it was time to get out of bed and get herself ready for work. This couldn't be happening. This *wasn't* happening. This ethereal woman wasn't talking to her; there wasn't an unattended unicorn somewhere in the store. There *wasn't*.

The woman's smile grew, wide and serene and trusting in a way Frankie had never seen in an adult human. "Can you show me?" she asked. "Kevin and I get all turned around in these places, and last time I tried to do it on my own, he ate a towel."

Frankie blinked slowly, twice. The woman continued to smile.

"Kevin is…" she said.

The woman's smile broadened. "With me," she said.

This had the potential to become a terrible comedy routine in very short order. Frankie nodded quickly, and said, "Of course. He's with you. I'll show you the way to produce." She started to walk. A hand on her elbow stopped her. Frankie turned, more confused than shocked. Customers *never* touched employees. It wasn't a fear of assault charges—at least not for most of them—or anything like that. More a seeming fear that if they touched too many associates, they'd wake one day to find a red vest in their own closet, like working retail was contagious.

"We need to go get Kevin," said the woman. "He's waiting for us at the end of the aisle."

"Oh," said Frankie. Then: "Why didn't he come with you?"

"Don't be silly." The woman dimpled. Actually *dimpled*, like she was something out of a Shirley Temple film. "He wouldn't fit."

This time, she was the one who turned away. Frankie trailed after her, too bewildered to do anything else.

They walked down several aisles, until even Frankie felt like she was getting turned around and lost in a store she knew like the back of her own hand. She'd been working there for four years, even though she hadn't been planning to stay for more than one. She'd started out as a seasonal hire, one of the bright-eyed, straight-shouldered newbies who thronged in the stockroom every time the holidays rolled around, trying to keep the shelves stocked with "the latest thing," whatever that happened to be. Most seasonal hires were let go at the end of their contracted term, released back into the wild to resume their lives. Not Frankie. She'd been too competent, or maybe not competent enough, and she'd found herself trapped, just comfortable enough to want to stay, not comfortable enough to ever quite relax.

They walked, and they walked, and then there he was: the unicorn. Kevin.

He was just as big up close as he'd been from a distance, maybe bigger, since now there was no way to pretend that he was an optical illusion. He wasn't an illusionary anything. He smelled of horse, that mixture of sweat and fur and hay and apples that Frankie had always found in the stables at the county fair. The woman had left him standing next to a display of house-brand granola, and he was occupied with munching his way through a box, sending bits of cardboard and organic nuts showering to the floor. No one seemed to have noticed them, yet. Frankie assumed that it was because the unicorn was still *right there*, blocking anyone from registering the consequences of its large, equine actions.

"Hello, sweetheart," said the woman, ghosting her hand across the unicorn's flank as she stepped up beside him. "I found someone who can help us. See?"

The unicorn turned to regard Frankie, snorting a hot gust of musky-smelling breath in her face. She held herself perfectly still, suddenly terribly aware that a unicorn was really nothing more than a horse with a large knife growing out of the center of its forehead. And because this unicorn was a really *big* horse, it was a really, *really* large knife. A sword, technically. A sword long enough to impale anyone who happened to get on the unicorn's nerves or be standing in the unicorn's way.

Frankie did not want to be either of those things. Frankie wanted, with a vehemence that was more than a little bit startling, to live.

The unicorn snorted again. The woman nodded solemnly, as if he had just said something very wise, or at least reasonably articulate.

"Exactly," she said. "This nice lady, she can see us. Isn't that wonderful? It's always so much easier to do our shopping when someone can see us."

Another snort, this time accompanied by a toss of the unicorn's long, pearlescent mane. Glitter sparkled in the air, hanging as if suspended on moonbeams. Frankie thought she might be sick. Maybe if she did it close enough to the unicorn, no one would notice, and she wouldn't have to clean it up.

"Yes!" said the woman, clapping her hands in obvious delight. She turned to Frankie. "Kevin wants you to put your hand on his muzzle."

"Kevin," said Frankie slowly. "You mean the unicorn."

"Yes."

"Wants me to put my hand on him."

"Yes!"

"My actual hand, on the actual unicorn."

The woman stopped clapping and looked at Frankie with some concern. "Yes. That's what I said. Are you feeling all right?"

"I don't think I am," said Frankie. The urge to sit down right in the middle of the floor was strong. She clasped her hands behind her back instead, to keep herself from touching the unicorn. She wanted to touch it. She didn't want to touch it. If she touched it, she was sure, it would be too late; something would change, possibly forever, assuming it hadn't changed already. Maybe seeing the unicorn meant that it was already too late. She should touch the—Kevin—and let whatever was going to happen, happen. It couldn't possibly be worse than retail.

"Did you still want me to show you to the produce?" she asked, and the unicorn snorted again, nodding its head up and down in what she could only interpret as vigorous agreement.

"Sure," said the woman. "You can touch him afterward. It's okay. We have some time to shop."

None of this was within Frankie's normal frame of reference. She didn't want to think about it any harder than she absolutely had to, and so she slapped a glossy smile across her face, turned around, and started walking toward the groceries. Once the unicorn had his grapes, surely he would take his confusing barefoot woman and get out of the store. Yes. This was how everything became normal again, and how she got her store back.

There were already people in the produce section. Of course there were people in the produce section. This was where you came if you wanted produce that was cheaper than Safeway and better than Grocery Outlet, and not a single one of those people turned to look when the unicorn came trot, trot, trotting into their midst.

The dreamy woman picked up a bunch of grapes and offered them to Kevin for inspection. The unicorn sniffed them daintily before consuming them in a single massive bite. No one said anything.

Frankie felt faint.

"Now," said the dreamy woman, turning back to her. "Will you touch him, please? We don't have all night, and the longer we spend standing around here, the higher the chances are that you're going to freak out and run away. If you do that, Kevin has to chase after you. Kevin *hates* chasing people."

Kevin turned to look at Frankie, grapes dangling from both sides of his muzzle. Once again, Frankie was struck by how impossibly large and sharp the horn atop his head was. This was a horse designed for homicide. Maybe multiple homicides. He was big and strong and sure, he had hooves instead of opposable thumbs, but would that really stop him when it was time to hide the bodies? Somehow, she didn't think so. Somehow, she was pretty sure this unicorn could figure out how to arrange a bathtub full of lye in no time flat.

Trembling slightly, tasting hot bile in the back of her throat, Frankie pressed her palm flat against the unicorn's flank.

Her first, somewhat nonsensical thought, was that Kevin—why did his name have to be *Kevin*? This was a unicorn. Unicorns were supposed to have poetic, ethereal names, like Mistwhisper or Rillrunner; they weren't supposed to be called *Kevin*—was exactly as soft as he looked. It was like stroking a kitten's belly, only about a thousand times better, and with the added bonus of not worrying whether she was about to find the kitten clamping down on her hand like a beartrap. It was like running her fingers through a cloud. It was also hot, and solid, and absolutely real. This was a real animal. She was touching a real animal, which meant this was really happening, which meant her window to run away and *not* be pursued by a heavily armed farm animal had probably already snapped rather conclusively closed.

Honestly, it closed as soon as you saw *me,* said a mild, amused voice, somewhere in the space between her ears and the front of her forehead.

Frankie froze.

She was well aware that her brain was stored in that general area, but as she never exactly *felt* her brain, she had gone through life mostly pretending nothing existed there except for air and the occasional migraine. That certainly wasn't a place where she ought to be hearing voices.

But you are, said the voice. *If you could please move past your understandable but tiresome human shock, I would be* ever *so grateful. This is a waste of both our time, and time is short. For you, at least.*

"Ma'am I think your unicorn is talking to me and it's sort of upsetting me right now," said Frankie rapid-fire, words spilling over each other like marbles rolling across a tile floor. She wasn't entirely sure they'd ended up in the correct order. She was absolutely sure she didn't care.

"He does that," said the woman fondly. She stroked Kevin's muzzle with one hand before offering him another bunch of grapes. "This part goes better when he takes care of it. I always get all confused and then nothing fits together the way it's supposed to, and anyway, just listen to Kevin, okay? Kevin knows what to tell you."

"Listen to Kevin," said Frankie faintly. "The unicorn."

"Yes," said the dreamy woman.

Yes, said Kevin, and pooped on the floor again.

Somehow, that was the thing that convinced Frankie that all of this was actually happening. Hallucinating a unicorn? Sure. That was the sort of thing she'd do. Hallucinating a hilarious unicorn poop incident resulting in a customer needing new trousers? Sure to that, too. Sure to everything. But a second poop? That was overkill. She'd never enjoyed it when a comedian felt the need to drive a joke into the ground. She wouldn't have imagined a second poop, no matter how mad she was at the store, or the customers, or herself, for staying in the company of both.

This was real. This was happening, and it was happening to her, and she reeled, hand almost leaving the unicorn's flank.

If you pass out, I will piss all over you, said Kevin sternly.

Frankie stood up straight. "That's disgusting."

It worked. Never question anything that works.

"No one here sees you except for me. Why is that?"

"You have the Sight!" The dreamy woman clapped her hands together. "It's so rare anymore, it's so special and hard to find, I wasn't sure we'd be able to find anyone at all, but then Kevin wanted grapes and so we came here and we found you, so I guess you really *can* find anything at Target!"

Frankie wanted to argue. She just wasn't sure where, exactly, she was supposed to start, and so she didn't say anything. Maybe if she stayed quiet, this would all be over soon.

Now that we've found you, of course, we'll be whisking you away to the world beneath the hills. It can't be helped.

"What?!" Frankie yelped. This time she *did* pull her hand away from the unicorn's flank, taking two large steps back for good measure, as if some distance could change her overall situation. It didn't, but it made her feel a little better, which helped.

"Have you heard of the Gentry, the Good Folk, the People of Peace?" asked the dreamy woman.

"You mean fairies?" asked Frankie.

The woman winced. Kevin snorted and pawed angrily at the floor. "Yes, but we don't like to use that word. You've heard of us, though?"

"Yeah," said Frankie. "Everyone's heard of you. Walt Disney—"

"Was a good man," said the dreamy woman, voice going grave. "He did a very good job, considering that he was a construct of fruit and moondust and water stolen from a witch's well. We honestly couldn't have asked him to do any more than he did. Why, I have a gooseberry bush in my garden that was sprouted from one of his seeds! Isn't that just delightful?"

Frankie blinked slowly, and said nothing.

"I didn't plant it, of course. We don't *work*, exactly. Other people work for us. And of course, there's a balance to be maintained. For every construct like Mr. Disney that we place here, on this side of the hills, we need to remove someone, so that the number of humans—or supposed humans—in the world will stay where it's supposed to."

Frankie's throat was very dry.

"We try to take people who won't be too awfully missed. People don't really see us if they're happy with their lives, but 'not happy' and 'won't be missed' aren't the same thing, you know? You can have three kids and a happy marriage and still be unhappy, if your brain chemistry hates you."

Somehow the word "chemistry" sounded very wrong dropping from the dreamy woman's lips, which had been formed to shape poetry, not scientific terms. Frankie frowned. "You know what chemistry is?"

"We're the Fair Folk, not squirrels," said the woman. "We keep up with what you humans are doing. It's the only way to know what you're likely to listen to. We follow the trends, as it were. Only instead of tabloids and cinema stars, it's scientific advancements and what's bringing in big money at the box office. We need to know the schema of the stories you're telling each other in order to know which stories to start telling you on our own behalf."

Frankie blinked. There was a point tangled up in all of this talking, but it was getting harder and harder for her to see, like it was receding into a deep fog. "Why are you telling me all this?"

"Call it an introductory session," said the woman. "Or you could call it a recruitment speech, I suppose, although it isn't quite, since you've really already been recruited. It's all very strange and a little non-linear and humans don't usually understand it. But we need someone *on* this side, and that means we need to take someone *from* this side. You can see us, so you've been selected."

Humans. Frankie seized on that word like it meant something. "If you're fairies—"

"We don't like that word."

"—doesn't that mean you have to be either good fairies or bad fairies? Can I get someone to come and argue the other side for me?"

The dreamy woman cocked her head to the side. "Why would you *want* to? I'm offering you a world made of starlight and dreams, where the flowers sing and the clouds store up the sun, so that the night is never any deeper than we want it to be. Isn't that better than this realm of plastic and steel and working your fingers to the bone for someone who'll never appreciate you as you deserve?"

Frankie opened her mouth to object. Then she paused, looking thoughtful. "Okay, lady," she said finally. "One last question."

"Yes?"

"Do you offer medical?"

When her supervisor came back from his break—which had managed, as it often did, to extend for almost the entire second half of his shift—he found a pile of autumn leaves mixed with strange silver coins sitting on his desk. The leaves smelled of loam and wildness, of the good green places where people seldom went. He found himself almost overcome with nostalgia for the summer when he was twelve, the summer he'd spent roaming the woods behind his grandparents' house.

A single Post-It, incongruously pink, had been placed atop the pile. *I quit. —Frankie.*

The store was overrun by squirrels, rabbits, and other woodland creatures the next day.

Frankie Anderson was never seen again.

— OR PERHAPS UP —
by C. S. E. Cooney

I t was—I freely admit it—*stupid* to take the swan boat out for a spin. What had appealed to me more about it? The joke? The romance? All right, no, I know. The swan boat made me laugh out loud. And I hadn't laughed *ferdays*. Boyfriend issues. Well, ex-boyfriend.

I was following my map that late September afternoon through the Preservation Trust Town Forest. My "map" was in fact a picture of the map posted in the parking lot that I'd snapped with my iPhone, so it took some squinting. Several hiking trails snaked through the woods for the delectation of the pleasure walker: the colored lines on the map corresponded to colored dabs on the trees. There was the short green loop, the longer red loop, the yellow trail—which led to some picnic grounds—and the blue trail, which wandered right down to the bottom of the woods, to the river. Which was where I found the swan boat.

That scabrous, black-eyed thing flat-out delighted me. Too much Hans Christian Andersen as a child, I don't know. I was so delighted with it that I spent a good two hours excavating the swan boat from its muddy grave beneath a sweet pepperbush shrub. The wildly fragrant white flowers were falling away to fruit now, none of the leaves yet blushing yellow.

As I worked, digging away in the mud like a child, I wondered: who had the swan boat's original owners been? Had they thrown out this whimsical, this retro, this highly metaphorical cygnine beauty for some sleek new kayak, color-gel-coated for their pleasure? Had they tired of this vintage white two-seater's authentically distressed nostalgic novelty and gone in for a younger boat's radiant orange fiberglass velocity instead?

Poor unwieldy relic. It had my sympathies. Liam "the Rugger" Boyle had done me a similar turn recently. Now, not only was I experiencing pangs of fellow feelings for a swan boat, I also had an ex-boyfriend named "Rugger"—which was terribly embarrassing, really, and made him difficult to talk about, or even think about, because he was *just* like his name sounds.

But back to the epic saga of my stupidity that day.

Since I was already down there by the river, and already head to toe in mud, and it was an uphill hike back to the parking lot where I'd chained my bike, and I wasn't ready to go home yet, what did I do next? Well, having now entirely excavated the swan boat, what was there *left* to do but grab it by the grimy neck and drag it down the embankment for a test run?

(I know. I know. Choice by choice, inch by begrimed inch, there I was, Luz the Loser, cheerfully ticking off all five nomination requirements for my own personal Darwin Award. But wait. It gets worse.)

Even pocked with white petals and riddled with dead-and-otherwise bugs, the swan boat seemed a sturdy enough article. My final theory on its origins was that it had hailed from the Enchanted Forest, an abandoned theme park just a few miles down the road in Hope Valley. Mamita and I had stumbled across some overgrown signage for the park on an exploratory drive together and afterwards looked it up on Atlas Obscura. Apparently, the Enchanted Forest was very popular back in the '70s and '80s, with its kiddy rides and fairytale theme. Perhaps the park had once included in its full complement of attractions a goofily mawkish Tunnel o' Love, complete with a flotilla of swan boats, which, decades later, was thoroughly pillaged by various teenager raiding parties gone on the hunt for illicit keepsakes. Bet you anything Rugger would've done something like that in his high school days—and then, after burying it in the woods and sleeping off his hangover, would have forgotten all about it by morning. But that was something else I'd never know for sure.

You see, I should have remembered the Preservation Trust Town Forest literature. Swans, however beautiful, were—like porcelain berries or kudzu—an invasive species in these parts, unwholesome and unwelcome. I should have remembered that swans were aggressive and full of bluster, and recalling this, been a little more wary even of a simulacrum. Hell, I should've remembered all those aforementioned *fairytales* (of which mamita and I were both so fond): that swans nearly always show up where dead girls drown.

Last but certainly not least, I should also have remembered basic meteorology. Late August and early September had been hurricane-heavy. Now, at September's close, the Pawcatuck River was engorged like a well-fed tick. When the swan boat capsized, so did I.

It wasn't long before all of this and my life flashed before my eyes.

Mamita is a magpie for ephemera. When we first moved out east together, she immediately goes out exploring and comes home with bouquets of brochures, factsheets, flyers, leaflets, and pamphlets—whatever is on offer at the local tourist bureau. Whereas it takes me weeks simply to pop my head into a place and window-shop, feeling that I have no right to a place of business when I have no intention of actually buying anything, mamita will be on a first-name basis with its owners from day one. She's always been adventurous. When I ask her how she does it, she only beams at me and quotes me one of her happy hippy songs: "I'm a summer child, lost in love."

The year I turned thirty (last year), we'd decided to try living together for the first time since I was eighteen. I'd moved out of state for college and had been working in Minneapolis ever since. Between phone, internet, and annual visits, mamita and I had managed to stay close, but after twelve years of that, we were missing each other, feeling our mortality, and on the whole, ready for new horizons and new adventures. Adventures being easiest with a companion, we'd opted for each other, and settled on a date and a destination. Mamita left New Mexico, I left Minnesota, and we struck off for Rhode Island with a few thousand dollars in savings and not much of a plan.

Mamita is an ideal roommate. She loves cooking, does more than her fair share of dishes, doesn't mind that I randomly burst out singing at the top of my lungs and dress in outlandish crinolines and combat boots. I keep my bedroom tidier than she does, but she deep-cleans things I ignore for months on end. She's intensely project-motivated and forgets to take breaks; I'm really good at gently haranguing her when she's been working non-stop. I force her to lie down and put her feet up and read a book for pleasure, even though it always makes her feel guilty.

"Look, Teresita Floracita," I tell her, using her own nickname for herself from back when she was a good Catholic child and was totally convinced she would grow up into her glorious martyrdom and eventual sainthood, "you and I work whatever part-time jobs we can get, all at minimum wage, just to make ends meet. We'll never retire. That age has passed. Retirement is for rich baby boomers. So we have to take our *semi-retirement* wherever we can get it."

"Semi-retirement" is an optimistic way of viewing a work schedule wherein, if we are lucky, we are each given a couple of half-days a week. No one is hiring full time around here, not even fine women with English degrees and years of experience behind them. With the hours we're given, we have enough to pay rent—if we never ask our landlord for little things like repairing the leak in the roof or fixing the holes in our floor; and utilities—if we mostly do without light and heat; with a little left over to set against the ever-accumulating interest on my college debt. But it is definitely not enough to replace the Honda's transmission, which has just failed, or buy the next round of bus tickets, which are are running low, or buy mamita's migraine meds, which are so expensive she always cuts each pill into thirds to make the bottle last.

Heigh-ho, and so this week's grocery shopping will be done at the Pawcatuck Neighborhood Food Pantry, but they are always kind and generous and cheerful, and the pasta is abundant. And the library, we love to remind each other, is still free!

Corkers, unlike the library, is very much not free. It is the town's very hip (and only) café-cum-bar, where Rugger bartends and occasionally plays gigs with his band, the Flying Wedgies. When we are first eyeballing each other with mutual interest, he woos me by giving me drinks on the house. Later, when I am out of the picture, Rugger immediately starts dating a dark-haired poet girl who makes her own t-shirts and binds her own books. She gets the free drinks now, and I am cut off from Corkers and the society of my peers. Mamita never goes there anyway; caffeine and alcohol both bring on her migraines, and the music is too loud. But I miss it. I don't harbor any real rancor toward either Rugger or his new lady. Only, the idea of seeing them together irritates me, like willfully rubbing my eyeballs with nettles.

As I walk through the Town Forest—yea, verily, right up to the moment when I decide to take my newfound swan boat out for a little Lady of Shalott re-enactment!—I am just starting, very slowly, with the profound relief that comes from resentment finally lifting, to sweat off my sour attitude towards my break-up. That's what had sent me off on my bike ride in the first place. Mamita yet retains some of her childhood saintliness: she has a vast and compassionate patience for her beloved only child. I, however, heathen and atheist that I am—that *she*, in all fairness, raised me to be—have been more than a bit snappish with her since Rugger and I—politely, via text message—decoupled ourselves. And no adult should have to live of her own free will with another adult who snaps at her.

Despite our poverty, despite being two strangers come from the far west to try and scrape up a living in a small New England town, I *adore* cohabitating with her. I want her to love cohabitating with me too, in our bright, shabby, *darling* third-floor apartment, where we are within biking distance to all the woods and rivers and salt marshes and coastlines our too-long-landlocked hearts could desire. I do not want her to flinch at the sharpness of my voice or shrug off the fiery glare I am hasty to throw at her.

And so, I think, climbing into my swan boat: I shall go home directly after this, and apologize, and offer her oblations in the form of a foot rub.

And as I float further from the slippery pebbles of the shore, paddling away at the pedals of the swan boat, I start actually looking forward to the post-breakup peace and quiet. Mamita and I can go back to watching weird independent foreign films together on Friday nights. She has been missing that, missing our closeness, these last few months I've been dating Rugger. She's pretty cool and independent and all that, but we've always agreed that popcorn nights are better with two...

What will she do, now that I was drowned?

So, right. Yes. Yes, the swan boat, as I may have mentioned previously, capsized. Of course it did. The current was a sea-swift rush to the belly of the giantess Atlantic, and the boat—rotten, water-logged, unworthy—drifted a bit, overturned, and sank, taking me with it.

And where, you might ask, was *I* in all of this? What did I do? How did I act? Did I fight the mighty current? Did I thrash and rage and cry out? Was I pinned beneath the swan boat? Bashed in? Bewildered? Knocked out cold? Was my leg caught? My arm? Did I succumb to weariness or hypothermia? We must both of us be forever curious. I did not recall.

I *did* remember a certain topsy-turviness. A mirror-flip of sky. My world of air funneling as through an hourglass, emptying into a world of water. But I was aware that at some point transition had occurred. That I had gone from human person to *something else,* plonked right there at river's bottom. My scarlet frolic-in-the-wood frock, courtesy of the Groton Goodwill, dragged at me like plate armor, exerting a tidal pull and spreading around me like a dark stain. But I was not in any discomfort. Even the enormous wooden agent of my demise, with its DayGlo orange beak and unholy black eyes, which sat atop me, crushing my legs beneath it, did not so much hurt as *frustrate* me. There I sat, stuck, seething, contemplating everything that had brought me there. Silt and stone beneath me. Everything rushing by. Water in all directions.

But no direction was *up*.

What worried me most was this: I'd left my red Converse high tops on the riverbank, my bike locked up in the parking lot. Sooner or later, someone would find them and report back to my mother that they were all that was left of me. I could not stop imagining what her face would look like when they brought her my shoes.

I was down there in the rushing dark ferdays. "Ferdays" was a word that Rugger had taught me while describing my ass as "cake ferdays." I liked the word—the whole phrase, really—despite myself. It was almost Shakespearian in its poetry and vulgarity, and I have a weakness for the Sh'peare. (See above, re: English degree, college debt.)

To be fair, it wasn't really *days*. Or, okay, it might have been. Might have been forever for all I knew. I wasn't wearing a watch after all, and I'd lost my iPhone with its map of the woods—not that it would've worked underwater. I didn't even have a heartbeat to count by. They say you lose all sense of time in a sensory deprivation tank. They say the same about Faerieland. Wherever I was, it was a little like both. My katabasis tank. My fairy holding cell.

After some time, I realized I missed breathing, and I sighed, unhappily. Water rushed out of my nose and mouth. There was no air in me anymore. Then I heard another sigh, not my own. Like a new pressure on the ears, a new direction of current.

I turned and saw him.

His hair drifted around his head like several surprised squirts of octopus ink. Looking at the direction of all that floating hair, I thought to myself, "Ah, *that* must be up," but couldn't do anything about it, pinned as I was.

He was sitting not far from the swan boat: cross-legged, elbows on knees, chin on hand, all angles, on the top of a very slick, very green, very large rock. Watching me. A lifetime of deep current rushed between us. We were in no hurry to do much more than observe each other. He reminded me of a cormorant.

Cormorant, I recalled, meant "sea-raven." At least, that was what it said in the Preservation Trust Salt Marsh brochure, one of the plethora of brochures mamita used to bring back to our apartment (in those halcyon days of yesteryear or perhaps a minute ago when I had both a mamita and an apartment) and stuff into a basket, labeled in her best calligraphy-on-notecard style, "Ephemera & Realia, Tra-La!"

"Sea-raven," I'd told my mother, looking up from this newest brochure, enraptured at the alien etymology. "Isn't the very name thrilling and wonderful and wildly romantic?"

"Wildly!" she'd agreed. "I can't wait to see one! I'll have to dig out my binoculars!"

But when I'd confided our fond ambition of cormorant-spotting to him, Rugger just laughed and asked, "What, those armpit birds?" with the hard shine in his eyes of a tried and true Rhode Island tease. "They're ridiculous," he assured me, with the authority of someone who had lived in New England his whole life.

They were a little, maybe. The way those gawky black water birds perched on telephone wires or on rocks in sheltered coves, wings outspread, awkwardly drying themselves. But the look on mamita's face when she witnesses her first cormorant! The love beaming out from her. That bright grin. The unguarded eyes of a newcomer to the miraculous. She kept that look even after seeing hundreds of cormorants, hundreds of times. After her first encounter, she would always take the scenic Route 1A on her way home from work instead of the expressway, even though it added twenty minutes to her drive, just so that she could pull off to the side of the road and watch them dry their wings—proud and patient, like they were practicing for the day they would finally become heraldic achievements.

Mamita was a cormorant for last Halloween. We didn't have any money for costumes, so she dressed all in old black clothes, and made herself a plague-doctor's beak from old newspaper and flour and water, and flapped around our kitchen raggedly, joyously, armpits exposed and neck extended, making big, honking, cormorant-like pig grunts as I laughed and laughed and laughed.

You will know from having read such things that weeping underwater after drowning results not in tears but freshwater pearls. These baroque beauties were large and pinkish and irregular, and tumbled away from me, disappearing into the silt they'd disturbed.

When I blinked my eyes clear again, I went immediately back to observing my new companion. Our gazes met a second time, and he lifted his head as if surprised I could see still him. Maybe he always looked surprised; he had those kinds of eyebrows.

He was like a cormorant in more than just coloring. Raggedy and ridiculous, barely more than a silhouette. A Rorschach blot in the water. Shy and worn, with thin arms. Thin everything. My mother would have loved him on sight, loved him forever, adopted him as her own. Me, I didn't know what to think. It was enough, for the moment, not to be alone.

I tried out a smile. It was shockingly easy, as if my face had just been waiting for me to ask.

He smiled back, dazzlingly. His teeth blazed. Small white stones. Quartzes. Ground to smoothness by the running water. Immediately he pushed himself off his rock and launched himself toward me, hooking his arms beneath mine the minute we made contact, and heaving. The swan boat toppled.

Up we went. Straight up and fast. An eruption from the riverbed. A geyser. Up.

Or maybe down.

The riverbank we ended up on wasn't the riverbank I'd left. Not the bottom of the Preservation Trust Town Forest in our small Rhode Island town. Nor was the river water I was puking up the Pawcatuck river. It was not even really water but mouthfuls and mouthfuls of small white stones, water-worn glass, ammonites. It occurred to me that maybe I was only puking because I thought I had to. As soon as I was ready to stop, I did.

The man—or whatever, *thing*—my companion from the river bottom was still there, crouching near me, watching, just as he had been when we were underwater. All knees and elbows and worried forehead, with eyebrows that rose so far into his hairline they kept winking out of existence. His face was absurd, sort of scrunched and whimsical, like a long-eared bat or a baby monkey. Heaps of wrinkled shadows piled on top of the other, black-on-black, smoothing out like onyx cabochon or contracting like crumpled crêpe depending on his expression. It was more like a dozen paper puppets all collaborating to form features than an actual face. Eyes as crystal-white as his teeth.

I realized my hands were shaking. Or perhaps the right word was *rippling*. I held them out and examined them. I had known, when pinned under the swan boat, that I had changed, but now I saw *how*.

My skin was become all the colors of hurtling waters: clear, silvery brown, with flecks of sunlight, glints of sky and tree, and deep cold shadows the farther down I peered. As soon as the ripples calmed, I watched a rainbow trout swim up my left elbow and into my left shoulder, where it disappeared behind my clavicle.

I looked up from myself. My companion was still watching me, intent on every expression I didn't know I was making, every small sound of astonishment I unconsciously uttered. I wondered if he could talk.

"Shake hands?" I offered, sticking out my right hand experimentally.

He automatically stuck out his left, a mirror image. We did a funny sort of hand clasping, all backwards. His ink-puppet hand didn't pass through my river hand but rested atop it, light as a water strider. I was aware of his touch but not as pressure—more like an event, a series of infinitesimal ripples spreading from the dimples his fingers made on the surface of my fingers. I sat as still as possible, feeling the repercussions of contact for a very long time.

The bank where we were sitting was ankle-deep in white stones, like the quartzes of his strange teeth, or the stuff I had been vomiting. The white incline rose steeply to the woods. These were not the woods I'd left, with those four clear paths marked by paint and tamped down in pine needles. The Preservation Trust Town Forest was small: mostly birch, hemlock, and beech. Some swamp maples, not many, drops of scarlet in the garish gold like grenadine in orange juice. When I'd left those woods, they were only just starting to shake out their summer clothes, folding them away to put on autumn, becoming what mamita calls "The Yellow Wood." Enough leaves had already fallen to make a lacework of the upper canopy, white diamonds of sunlight twinkling in the gaps.

Here, I wasn't sure that the sky *was* the sky. It might have been the surface of the river, high above me. The trees were white-on-silver, or conversely, silver-on-white, like trees etched on plates of glass, pressed between other plates of glass etched with more trees. Things darted through the branches, but they were not birds.

I blinked. An eel slithered across the thin water-skin of my closed eyelid, tucked itself shyly behind my ear.

"Am I a ghost?" I asked my companion, who shook himself like the glass-etched birch above us was doing. He seemed pleased to be asked, and answered immediately.

"No," he said. Then, "No, not *ghost*… precisely. Not *'ghost'* like we'd once thought, when we were alive. What is *ghost*? A malfunction of memory, doomed to repetition, utterly dependent on a living—or rather *untransformed*—witness for validation of its existence. No, we operate independent of those strictures. We have passed beyond any need of witness. So we are not *ghost*, I think. Spirit, maybe. Yes—a spirit—a sprite, a wight... *Spirits to enforce or to enchant?*" He opened the inkblots of his palms, half sheepishly. Finger-like shadows unfurled. A many-winged moth. A horned sumo wrestler.

Ah! I thought triumphantly. The gentleman—or gentle*thing* anyway—hath quoted the Sh'peare! So he *as well* must have been human once, whatever he was now. Like me.

I asked, "Did you drown too?"

His flyaway eyebrows flew away from him again. His mouth opened in a clown's O, then pronounced the "Oh!" out loud as an afterthought.

"Sorry," I said quickly. "It occurs to me that that may be a very personal question?"

His shoulders heaved, instigating a vast, full-body shrug. "Drowned? I don't know. We seem to have, with practice, an ability to curate our memories here, and I'm afraid I...curated my own rather too vigorously the last time I... So, as to drowned, I cannot say. But dead..."

I waited.

"Dead, yes," he said. "Or something else." He shook his long-eared head. The ragged crest of his hair-feathers whipped to and fro. A look of disquieting tranquility settled over his face. "Can the dead do what we do?"

Then he sang something in a voice that came not only from his throat, but clapped out from him bodily. A sharp shockwave. The white pebbles—or crystal teeth—upon which I sat rose up beneath me and formed a throne. There were little armrests and everything. Delighted with this turn of events, I applauded enthusiastically. Between the splashing wetness of my palms, a tiny rainstorm played out.

"Did you always know how to do that?" I asked. "Or did you have to learn?"

"I learned. When I came. It took me..." He waved a hand. "A while."

"It's so cool! I never expected it. And now I don't know what to expect!"

He nodded. "That is a good start. Strong. First, to shed assumptions. And then..." A starry, tar-black flush stood out upon his cameo-cut cheeks. But he also smiled, bold as a little boy who having drawn something in crayon that pleased him, knew full well that praise was his due. "Then," he said softly, "to commence invention!"

I patted the armrests of my throne. "Well, *this* invention is so totally faboosh!" I used the word mamita had invented for my more outrageous outfits. "A throne suits me, don't you think?" He nodded vigorously. I went on, "Mamita says I have an imperious nature. She doesn't mind—although she does refer to me as 'Lady Jane' from time to time, whenever I take too much to the tyrannical. The threat is implicit," I reflected, "as Lady Jane was eventually beheaded."

My companion snuggled down at the foot of my throne, leaning against my thigh to listen contentedly. Minnows swam up from my feet and ankles to explore the contours of our connection. I began petting the shining oil slick of his hair until it gleamed wetly. He practically purred; I knew the feeling.

"Mamita likes to pretend she's my lady-in-waiting. Helping me with buttons I can't reach, painting my nails, braiding my hair—I get so impatient with hair—things like that. Zippers. Mending. You know. Everything I'm not good at. I'm better at *time*. Organizing. Herding. Planning ahead. Making snap decisions."

I looked around, remembering the swan boat: my last snap decision. Some decisions, I thought, were better left to rot under the sweet pepperbush tree where they'd been sensibly buried. And some realizations came too late.

If we could indeed curate our memories in this place, I could probably just forget about the swan boat. Right now. Forever. It would be less embarrassing that way. I wouldn't have to spend the rest of my life, or whatever this was, with bruised pride and a smarting dignity. I toyed with the idea of erasing the events leading up to my death, starting with Rugger and the Flying Wedgies and ending with my last revelation in the middle of the swollen Pawcatuck.

But almost as soon as I considered it, dread at the thought of discarding what so closely concerned me caused a small quake at my epicenter. Quick as tossing salt over my shoulder, I scooped up a handful of small white stones (or teeth) and flung them back into the river, thinking that they could join the swan boat there, at the bottom—as assurance of my continued remembrance. But they merely clattered and skipped across the water's surface, went skidding and sliding, stopped at last at the far side of the embankment. Never sank below the foam. The river rushed solidly by, as if its surface were covered with a thin sheet of glass or ice.

I brushed a few more baroque pearls off of my face and lap. They joined the white stones, slightly pinker and shinier. My companion's hand came once again to rest on my arm in gentle understanding.

"I... I had a tower, once. I built it with my... She was... I was..." Another of his shuddering shrugs. "Someone else was here. I forget her name. I remember she left. So I made the tower fall."

"Hm." I splashed a smile his way. "Exile," I said with great wisdom and greater pomposity, "is often a common denominator in friendship. At least, if my memories of surviving parochial school still serve me."

He looked up hopefully. I bent down and reached for his hand. "So is kindness. You were kind to me first thing. I won't forget that."

"I won't forget this," he said.

That was the first promise we made to each other, the shadow of his hand under mine, my fingertips flickering with the silhouettes of tadpoles. He opened his palm, and I rested my current upon it. My hand held its form, only sometimes over-spilling the edges. He let me pour over him, and I heard him breathe out, breathe in. If you can call it breath. Like a desert breathes after it rains.

"Let's build another tower," I said. "I like to live high up."

The tower he sang up from the ground was drawn from a substrata of black rock deeper down than the toothy white quartz of the riverbank. Where it arose, it left a trench in a wide circle all around it, which dove down bottomlessly. While he rested—which he needed to do from time to time—I took over, singing tentatively. At first, I only spat out more pebbles, more shards of smooth glass. But as I grew bolder, better results attended my efforts. The first time a whole sun turtle crawled out of my face, it headed straight up one of the incomplete walls of the tower, where it settled in and became a small, translucent, turtle-shaped, green window that seemed not only to let in light but to produce its own luminescence. Encouraged by this, and by my companion's delight upon waking, I sang louder, with even more vigor. I sang like I used to sing Sondheim in the kitchen while making popcorn for weird indie movie night. I sang Leonard Cohen (everything) and Joni Mitchell (likewise) and *Hamilton*—well, everything but Lafayette's rap from "Guns and Ships," which I'd never managed to memorize and couldn't now recall—and random AC/DC lyrics I remembered from my Zombies, Run! workouts, and "O Mio

Babino Caro" and Pete Seeger's "One Grain of Sand," which I'd come to via Odetta.

Soon our tower had many window-lamps of varying shapes and sizes. There were otters, crocodiles, boas and beetles and bats, calla lilies, cranes, frogs, toads, one hippopotamus, one pink freshwater dolphin—all of which had tumbled out of my watery integument and made their way up the walls, where their forms froze into something like glass, something like light. Later, when I was more confident and precise, I made windows even out of the very water that rushed over and through me, falling sheets of water that was as much *me* as the shape I was walking around in. I made walls of water. Floors of it. Water was the bed we slept in. It spilled down the edges of the tower into the trench below and filled it until we had our own moat, as turquoise-green as the canals of Venice.

When the tower was several stories tall and beginning to feel like home, my companion and I ventured together to the riverbank to explore. That was when we began our "mudlarking for spirits"— trying to find others like us, who might be trapped, either under objects, or inside them, or who had become such strangers to the way they remembered themselves that it took an outsider to recognize them for what they were.

There was a spirit we found in one of the silver-on-white trees that looked like a bird, but when my companion coaxed it into his hand, it had a human face and spoke with a human voice. Its name was Dhanvi. It did not want to live in our tower with us. The forest was its home; it had built many a palace nest among the glass branches, and had friends enough like itself. But it would, it promised, look in on us from time to time, and introduce others to our acquaintance, if we wished. We did.

There was a spirit caught in the frosty cattails who looked as desiccated as a dried sunflower, but when we extricated her and brought her home, she filled out as golden and sweet-smelling as harvest wheat, and remembered her name: Mahalia. Mahalia loved our tower; it was shortly as much hers as ours. She proved a master mosaic artist, laying down makeshift tiles that she had plucked from the tidal shallows of my belly and thighs and spine: pottery shards and old doorknobs, miniature brass muskets and tiny clay pipes and broken bone lace bobbins and false eyes and ancient shoe buckles and free-blown bottles and rare silver fanams and many more objects which she lured forth by touch and call.

More joined us. Some stayed only a while. Others merely looked in. Others kept well away from us, hidden and flinching and burrowed down. Sometimes I thought we were surrounded by invisible towers just like ours, that we were not permitted to see, and from out of a hundred invisible windows our neighbors were watching us in secret, their oyster-scraped shyness such a repelling force that it felt at times malevolent. But even these secret watchers we hoped to win over by and by. There was time. Or maybe not. Maybe there was just the memory of time, which some forgot.

My companions and I did not attempt to hide our own tower. When I'd lived with mamita we'd tried to keep an open table, for all that none of our chairs ever matched and we'd curb-picked the table itself from a neighboring house on trash day. We'd re-labeled all traditionally "family" holidays as "Feasts of the Forsaken," in which any friend estranged from blood-ties or too far distant to claim them could come celebrate with us. Mahalia told us that when *she* had lived, she'd shared a house with four generations of women, and during the brief time she had lived alone, after illness and accident had claimed all of her progenitresses, she couldn't seem to cook for fewer than six people and would always end up with a week's worth of leftovers.

Our third companion could not remember his time from *before;* his "vigorous curation" had assured that. But anyone could see he thrived in company and grew more cheerful with every service he could perform on our behalf.

As we built our tower, therefore, we sang it visible, we sang it useful, and motley, with more rooms than we could possibly use, and in memory of the families we had left behind, and of those who had gone before us, we kept an open table, and we sang it home.

"Corazón!" I called from my seat by the window. "Come look!"

As our third companion could not remember his given name, Mahalia and I lavished him with endearments that made his silhouette-self blossom like a night-blooming flower. "Corazón" was my favorite and had taken the place of a name in my head. But "Sweetling" and "Loveliest" and "Noggle" and "Flittermouse" were also standards of address, along with several of my mother's favorites: "Cariño" and "Mi Vida" and "El Aire Que Respiro," and some in Mahalia's Tagalog, like "Dayong" and "Irog"—though she says "Irog" is old-fashioned, and only poets use it anymore.

Today, Corazón was immersed in his new project and did not seem to hear me the first time I called for him. Recently, Mahalia had mentioned wanting a chair-and-a-half for her bedchamber. So, of course, our beloved Corazón had at once thrown himself into constructing one for her. Right now, he was crouched near my feet— his preferred place of rest—busily plucking out his wild black hair to stuff the chair's cushions with. There was no lack of stuffing: the more he plucked, the wilder and wilier his corybantic crest of cormorant fluff did spring. If I looked long enough, I could see black wings of feather-hair growing and flapping out from the sides of his skull. Corazón's mobile face expressed a reverential pleasure in this self-de-racination; he looked like a dog scratching deeply at an everlasting itch. I could observe him for hours and often did; there was leisure for distraction here. But the scene outside our window tugged at me.

"Corazón," I tried again, running a few fingers of cold current through his hair.

Grinning and shivering at my caress, he glanced up. "Yes, Luz?"

"There is something in our moat."

"Huh."

"It's sort of... I can't tell what shape it is. Do you think it's a new spirit?"

He leapt up with that glad gawkiness I loved so well. "Maybe. They don't usually come into the moat, though. It's always via the river, or near it. I will look."

I was sitting near a large, silvery-green window the size and shape of a giant manatee. Corazón came to stand beside me, peering through the paddle-shaped tail. He peered and peered. Squinted. Pressed his face to the pane. He opened the pane outward and stuck his head through.

And then he started to wail.

"Oh, no! Oh, no, no, no!"

Abruptly, he withdrew his head and slammed the window shut, as if sealing off our tower from an oncoming hailstorm. But nothing was falling from the sky—which may or may not have been the sky. However, small white stones did come tumbling from his mouth to clatter all over the floor.

"No, no, no," he pleaded with me. "It is too soon! It's too soon, Luz— we haven't even—please don't..."

At the continuing noises of his panic and distress, Mahalia glanced up from her workspace on the other side of the room. She was finishing a new mosaic today: a table-top made up of found objects:

memento mori love tokens, crinoid fossil stems, marbles, broken teacups—all items that had emerged inexplicably from the region of my kneecaps. It was close, intensive work, and she tended to focus on her projects to the exclusion of all else, but for Corazón's sake, she deserted it immediately and came to investigate the new wrongness in the room.

I had thrown my arms around Corazón. He was shaking, spilling splotches of anxious ink and flakes of shadow everywhere like scattered ants. "What's wrong?" I begged him. "What is it?" But even as I spoke, I glanced out the window again, trying to see the thing in the moat.

"Don't look, Luz! Please." His face was buried in my shoulder, sunk puddle-deep, as if he wanted to dive into me completely. His hands splashed into my waist like striped bass at sundown.

Mahalia enfolded us both in her large golden arms, wrapping us in bands of sentient sunlight. "Gently," she murmured. "Gently."

"It's the strangest thing." I craned for another glimpse as Corazón clung to me tightly. "At first, the shape of it beneath the moat was barely visible. But it keeps getting bigger."

"Not bigger," Mahalia told me sadly. "Just closer. I've seen this before." She pressed a kiss to Corazón's forehead, leaving a brand of golden lip-marks upon his lustrous blackness. "So has he." She sighed. "It happens from time to time. It's always so disheartening—and after all our work! After all this... happiness." She sighed a second time. "Last time, I didn't have the heart to try again. That's why I fled to the riverbank. To dry up. To forget. And I did—I forgot why I fled in the first place. Because this, *this*," she squeezed us both harder, like an angry Corn Queen or a cloud of swarming bees, "is unbearable."

"But what," I asked, "is this?"

Corazón at last emerged from the shallows of my shoulder, the woeful quartz of his eyes like heartbroken stars.

"Someone," he said, "loves you more than anything. Someone loves you *enough*."

The moat was a glassy flatness of circular momentum where no drowned thing could drown again. I could walk atop it—we all could—but as with the river, we could not pierce the surface without a great deal of effort. We walked in this world with the lightness of damselflies.

Inside the moat, the object that had first caught my eye was still growing larger. It had been the merest speck when I'd first laid eyes on it, a pale blot in the surrounding green. Now that indeterminate pallor was taking shape.

First a head emerged. Orange beak, black mask, black eyes. The rest of the head was white: a dingy, dirty, muddy white, the white of maggots and mushrooms and wilderness abandonment. Then the neck, carved into that signature S curve. No wings, just the bulbous body of a one-time pedal boat. A two-seater for lovers, or best friends, or a parent and child. It sank slowly upward until it broke surface and began bobbing heavily on the water.

I stood on the bottom floor of the tower, the coyote-cut glass door flung open right over the moat: no deck, no steps, no footbridge. The water lapped at the water of my toes; we were all the same river. The swan boat was only a few feet from where I stood.

And so was mamita.

"Luz!" Her voice, like the cracked-open sky. "Luz!"

"Mami," I whispered.

"Luz," sobbed Corazón, pressing against me from behind.

Mahalia, who stood next to him, told me, "Go to her," and tenderly peeled Corazón from his desperate embrace of my waist, cradling him in her beams of summer, her sheaves of wheat and daisy fields and dandelions dancing. "Go on, Luz. She came a long way to talk to you. They always do."

"Don't go!" Corazón begged me. "Please! Don't leave us! Don't let the tower fall! Don't leave us like…"

Mahalia set her forehead against his, sunshine to midnight. "Her decision, kabagong."

My decision. My mother.

I threw myself through the open door, and fell upon mamita like rain.

She is wearing my old red Converse high-tops. Her feet are bigger than mine by a whole size—"whopping elevensies" as she likes to say—so she's had to chop off the round rubber toes to make the shoes fit. Her Solmate socks stick out the ends, bright and mismatched, like crazy quilts that keep only your toes warm. Her hair is… different. Frizzled. Undyed, undark. Like the silver-on-white wood. Like rain-clouds. It is much shorter than I remember it, as if she cut it all off at some point. There is a child's vulnerability in her skull; it gives her a priestly cast. The veins stand out on her hands. Shadows like too-full trash bags bulge out under her eyes. The delicate sparrow-feet lines I recall around her mouth and nose are now carved chasm-deep.

"Hi, Mamita."

Once I am in the swan boat with her, I stand back to gather more of my shape. I want her to recognize me. But I do not think she can hear me when I speak. Not all the way. Or see me either. Not properly. She leans forward, like someone staring into the depths of a dark pool, trying to hear whoever is shouting at her through several thousand tons of water.

"Luz." She is staring. I wonder if she can see her face reflected in mine, which, when calm, can become like a pond or a mirror.

"I'm so happy you're here!" I tell her, raising my voice to shout. Something on her face wavers, as if she has caught just the gist.

"I... wanted to see you again," she says, and her voice is harsh, like she has been wailing a whole year without surcease, and would be wailing now, except her throat has failed her. Her voice is like dynamite to a fall of boulders. Everything in me falters, cut off at my source, severed from the thing that feeds me.

"I..." I pause, uncertain. Try to smile. Raise my voice to bellowing again: "Do you want to see our tower? Come on in!" I wave an inviting hand toward the coyote door behind me, but I do not turn away from her. "We're still under construction—so much to be done! You have to meet Mahalia. And Corazón! You will love th—"

"Wait." Those words, the dry rasp of tears wept out. "Luz! Don't go."

Her words remind me of Corazón's. I wonder if he is still there, behind me in the doorway, waiting, watching me. I do not look. I do not dare. My mother is lifting a shaking hand to my face, her fingers practically translucent with thinness. The skin sags from her arms, robbed of all jolly surfeit. Her feet shift in the boat as she tries to keep her balance. The red canvas of the sawed-off Converse high-tops is wet. That makes no sense, for water *here* is not wet.

"Are you," I ask, uneasy, "drowning?" But I do not say it loud enough for her to hear me. The thought is filling me with a suffocating melancholy that even my own drowning had not merited. "Don't do that," I whisper, shaking my head. "Don't do that, Mamita. Not for me..."

"I need to ask," she says in a low voice, the knees of her jeans now soaking wet. "What is lost in the river... it comes here, in the end? If

I... if I direct them to cremate me, and bury my ashes in the riverbank, or scatter them on the water, will you find me—after?"

I imagine Mahalia reaching into my belly some bright morning to scoop out more objects for her mosaics. But instead, her massive midwife arms, slick as summer sunlight on a stream, pull my own mother out of me, strange and silvery with scales. The reverse of birth. Mamita, bare and barefoot. No red shoes. No swan boat. Here to stay.

But this is fancy, not fact. And since I do not know the true answer to her question, and do not think she would be able to hear me anyway, I lift my arms and shrug helplessly. Her face falls. The brine of her eyes falls. But she nods, decisively, and shakes herself out, even though her T-shirt (an old one, practically cobwebs, a favorite oversized nightie that reads: "1987: I survived 120°!" sold everywhere in the southwest after a particularly deadly summer), is soaked up to the armpits.

"Never mind. I'll take my chances, Luz. I'm putting it in my will that I'm to be cremated."

She takes a deep breath. But what is she breathing, I wonder, when this air is not air? It is difficult for her; I can see that. Like sucking oxygen through a noxious cloud. There is a red strain in the tiny capillaries of her eyes. The effort to ask the next question darkens her dear face, as if she was bending to lift a barbell twice her body weight.

"Luz. Mi vida. Can you come back with me?"

"Come... back?" Where my heart used to be, a frog leaps. "But I—" I want to glance over my shoulder at our tower, at my beloveds. But mamita's gaze fastens me, dry and red-rimmed and desperate.

"Come back. In this boat. I can lead you back. The red shoes will help. I will give you half my heart. One of my lungs. I would live half a life to take back half your..."

She cannot say the word. And, I? I do not know how to tell her that dead is not dead like we thought. That I am just... rivermade. Remade into a rivermaid.

This time, I lift my voice to decibels that could take on a storm, compete with a tidal clash of water, give the thunder a scolding: "What if you stay here instead?"

If I wait a few more minutes, she will no longer have a choice. The water-mark has crept up to her throat: the wet water of another world. She is like the betrayed lover in a Childe Ballad, sinking slowly in a rising current I cannot see. I offer my hand. If she touches me, maybe the waters will rise faster, and we can get this all over with, and she can come inside our tower with me.

"Luz!" Mahalia's voice pops in my ear, makes me flinch. She must have crossed the water to stand right behind me. "Family does not pull family under. We pull each other *out*."

I snatch my hand back from mamita, just in time. Mahalia is right. Of course she is right. And yet, if she were not watching me, I would do it. I would.

"But you can go back with her," says Corazón, from my left side.

He is standing right beside the swan boat. But he is not walking lightly on the water; he is hip-deep in the moat. The water does not wet him; it vivisects him. Traps him in its green glass ice. He treads, but he is sinking, like mamita is sinking. I wonder if this is how he had come to dwell at river bottom when I first met him. If he had sunk there for sorrow. For loss. When his last companion left, and he let their tower fall.

"You can go back with her," he repeats, his voice now calm though he is crying steadily. White stones tumble from his eyes. Quartz. Teeth. Freshwater pearls.

"She offered you half, which is fair. Half of everything. You can go back—at least halfway. You will not be the same. Neither will she. But you will be together. Half-enchanted. Half-haunted. And then, at the end..."

His fingers tighten earnestly on the edge of the swan boat. "I do not know if there will be enough of either of you to come back here. Maybe you will go elsewhere. I do not know. But I know that if you let her leave now, without you—and she does as she says, with her will, with her ashes—then you *will* see her again. We will lift her ashes from the riverbank, or from the weeds, or from your left shoulder, and we will re-kindle those ashes in the flame of our hearth. She will take for herself the freedom of a firebird, and you will never be parted again."

I look at mamita with longing, but I do not touch her. The water is up to her mouth. I want to embrace her. I want her to live in my tower with me forever, with new wings of fire, a new flamelight in her once-red hair. I want her to grow strange gardens on the riverbank with her long green hands, and braid the river of my hair until the currents flow three ways at once.

I also want to go back to our little apartment. I want to make abuela's tamales in our kitchen together with groceries we've picked up from the food pantry. I want our movie nights again, and trips to the Groton Goodwill, and all the free library events on the bulletin board, and all the Town Forest foraging walks the Preservation Trust can offer. I want it all, and I cannot choose.

Mamita, of course, sees this. Somehow, she can read my riverface like she used to read my frowns, my ups and downs, my sighs and grumbles and sudden fits of giggles. The lines on her face shift, lighten, brighten. She even seems to smile, and tells me, her words spluttering through unseen waters: "Never mind, cariña. Never mind. Entiendo perfectemente."

And then, suddenly, her hair is floating all around her head, and she is drowning in water from a different world.

"Push her back!" I shout to my beloveds, to Mahalia and Corazón. "We've got to get her back!"

Mamita begins to struggle in the swan boat, to fight, to thrash. Her movements are slow, weighty, languorous. This, more than anything, tells me what I must do. She is not ready. She must not come here now, not like this.

"Te amo, Mamita!" I whisper, and for once, for once, she seems to hear me with the clarity of a hard-struck bell. Her eyes meet mine.

Leaping from the wobbly wooden deck, I crash through the green glass water until I am shoulder to shoulder with Corazón. Mahalia is there too with us, treading the quickwater current, strong as summertime. Together we three grasp the edges of the swan boat, and push, push, *push* the boat with all the mightiness in us, back down to where it came from, down and down and down,.

Or perhaps up.

— DON'T LET GO —
by Alana Joli Abbott

The music at Carter's left something to be desired, but Rain danced to it anyway. She had never particularly been a fan of what she thought of as "thump-thump dancing," but being out on the dance floor meant not having to watch Brianna and Cole get snuggly again, which she got enough of at the house, and meant she didn't have to play second fiddle to Jonas, who was yet again picking up more offers for dates from men than she was. None of the brochures she'd read about the Isle of Man had prepared her for being out-dated by her gay roommate, which just went to show that either you couldn't believe everything you read in tour books, or that Jonas was the god of sexuality that he believed himself to be. She smirked, realizing she almost preferred the second option—at least then there was no commentary on her own lack of love life.

The bass shook her rib cage, music filling her all the way down to her toes. She was too close to the speakers for good sense, but she had always liked the reverb that seemed to push her cells out of place, seemed to infiltrate her entire physiology. Letting the music take over, she could stop wondering why she was still here, what she was even doing living on the Isle of Man, dancing at a club in Douglas she didn't like, failing at her independent studies, and generally wasting a year abroad. She wanted so much to not have to think about that, ever; to just be able to lose herself to the island, to actually study the history and read the books she'd meant to read, to have her papers materialize. But since none of those things were happening, she mostly wanted to go home.

The music slowed, incessant backbeat falling away to a ballad, and she moved to the edge of the dance floor, eyeing the bar. Two good looking men stood next to Jonas, neither of whom she'd seen before.

"Figures," she muttered, wiping away some of the sweat that drenched her forehead.

"What does?"

Rain liked to think of herself as reasonably laid back and in control, but the stress must have been getting to her. That was the only reasonable explanation for the height of her jump. The man who had spoken just laughed as she grounded herself. He looked down at her from his impressive height. His hair nearly glowed in the dim light of the club, and the piercings along his left ear caught the colored lights that flashed across the dance floor. Despite knowing that the Isle of Man had as much Nordic heritage as it did Celtic, Rain was always surprised when one of the tall, super-blond residents strolled her direction—natives of hundreds of years, rather than transplants from England like most of the population.

"What?" she shouted over the music, even though she'd heard him.

He gestured with his thumb over his shoulder toward a couch at the far edge of the room emptied of its usual wallflowers. She followed the gesture, still stuck on the idea that he must have been almost two feet taller than her—her shoulder was about the height of his waist!—before nodding and trying to find her usual grin. He started off toward back of the room territory and she followed.

Game face, she thought, trying to bolster her confidence. *First time a cute guy has approached you in a month, and you act like a complete dork.*

He grinned back over his shoulder, as though he'd heard her thinking, and the blush spread through her, starting somewhere near her shoulders. She hoped between the heat of the dancing and the dark of the club, it wasn't noticeable to anyone but her.

The stranger swung onto one end of the couch like it was part of his living room, and Rain perched on one arm, trying to give herself enough space to see his face. Even here, the hair and piercings glowed. Now that he was sitting, she could see his face better. He had smile lines at the edges of his eyes, despite being only a year or two older than she was, and his smile itself looked devil-may-care. But something about it was false. She glanced around the room again, spotting Jonas and the table where Brianna and Cole were snogging, planning an escape route if she needed one.

"You're safe enough here," said the stranger. "I'm Fin."

"I'm Rain," she said, taking his outstretched, and very polite, hand. He shook it, his grip far less tentative than her own. "I didn't mean to look nervous."

"Hard to know who to trust these days," he said, not sounding judgmental at all, "but less on the Isle than other places. Old fashioned morals and values here." His eyes flicked over to Jonas and he grinned. "Open minded though. We're good folk."

"I've noticed," Rain said wryly. "That's my roommate."

"Ah, so not a beau." Fin sighed in dramatic relief. "Here I thought you were pining."

"Nope, just jealous," Rain said with a laugh, watching his face to see how he'd react. He just continued to grin at her, carefree on the surface, but... "You're a native then?"

"Born and bred," he said proudly. "What tipped you off? Accent or good looks?" He must have seen her blush, because he rushed on before she could answer. "Hulking Nordic body on top of the traditional Manx charm, I bet. It's a sure combination. And you're American?"

"Yes." She wondered if he'd said all of that so quickly to save her embarrassment or to avoid hearing something that might not have flattered his ego. A bit of both, she decided. "I'm doing independent studies here."

"On?"

"Mythology and archaeology," she said. "You've got a fascinating hybrid of both stories and architecture here, part Irish, part Norse, a bit here, a bit there..." She stopped, feeling silly to be telling him about his home.

"You've been up to Maughold, then?" he asked, and she nodded, tickled that he knew one of the sites—the largest collection of crosses on the Isle—off the top of his head. She'd expected that everyone who lived on the Isle would be like that, but their landlady hadn't known about them.

"I wanted to stay up in Ramsey so I could be closer to the church," she said, "but Jonas and my other two roommates had a house rented in Port St. Erin, and they were looking for a fourth. It's not far from the hill fort at Cronk Moar, but otherwise..." She trailed off with a shrug.

The music changed again, and he moved off the couch like a wave crashing on the beach: fluid and swift. "I'm partial to this one." He put his hand out for her.

She took it, more confident this time in the way his hand felt around hers. His fingers were long, like a guitar player's. She hoped he wasn't. Nothing good ever came of her dating musicians.

"Never been good at any part of music but dancing," he shouted when they got out to the dance floor.

The music filled her up from her toes, and there was movement and chaos and electricity, and her thoughts vanished as she enjoyed the moment, enjoyed the tension in the space between them, the way he never let his body get uncomfortably close to hers. *Likely because our proportions are all wrong,* she thought to herself, looking up as he loomed over head. He winked down at her, looking as full of the music as she was, as though the drumbeat had become both of their pulses at once.

They danced through a second song, not talking, just being part of the music, two bodies on the dance floor. Thoughts floated through her mind, none of them sticking longer than a moment. She wondered what Jonas might think to see her dancing with a good-looking Manx giant, far too tall for her and with far more piercings than she would normally look at twice. It crossed her mind that Fin really wasn't her type, although it would be helpful to know a local who actually knew something about the Isle, which could, in theory, prevent her from failing her independent studies. If all she liked about him was the attention—*which is nice*, she admitted—she'd probably better make that clear from the beginning. A person could always use more friends.

But then she looked up at him, saw his eyes closed as he felt the music more than heard it, watched as the lights that sprawled across the dance floor caught in his hair and his ear studs. *Just a little while,* she thought as her stomach squeezed. *I'll pretend for just a little while.*

A claw grabbed Fin's shoulder and jerked them both out of the music as he spun, pulled downward so that his face was almost even with Rain's. Behind him was a middle-aged woman only slightly taller than Rain, her red hair streaming around her shoulders, and her face contorted in fury. Her fingernails dug into Fin's shoulder, and he hissed.

"Do not forget your place, above-grounder," the woman snarled. "Playtime's over. Get back to work."

She shoved him forward, and Fin stumbled off the dance floor toward a door in the back corner of the room Rain hadn't noticed before. As she watched, it seemed to fade, an effect of the swirling lights on the dance floor. Rain stood still, frozen in the presence of the red-haired woman who looked her up and down. Rain didn't breathe until, after a moment, the woman appeared satisfied. The anger bled away, leaving a brilliant smile in its place.

"He'll use you just like he used the others," she said, her tone confidential, almost pitying. "You can't trust someone like him."

"No," Rain said automatically, and for half a moment, she believed it was true. It had only been pretend, after all. He must have approached her because she looked lonely, because she was an easy mark.

"It's no fault of yours, dear," the red-haired woman said kindly, and her words wrapped around Rain like a shawl against the chill. "There are many evil people in the world."

"Hard to know who to trust these days," Rain said, and as the words left her, she remembered that Fin had said them before they danced, that he had told her she was safe. And as the woman left her, apparently satisfied, Rain thought of the sadness she suspected was lurking behind Fin's carefree expression.

Jonas was still at the bar, though he'd lost his companions. Rain stopped next to him, sliding a cocktail napkin in front of her.

"Looks like you caught a good one tonight," Jonas said cheerfully, "until that bitch snagged him."

"Tell me you have a pen," Rain said.

Jonas pulled a pen from inside his jacket—he never danced enough to get over warm—and handed it to her. "I hear he's a bouncer here," he continued. "Very pretty, if I may say."

"Mine," Rain warned him, handing the pen back. "No touch."

Jonas squeezed her hand as he took the pen. "You ready to call it a night?"

Rain looked toward the back corner of the room, where the door had been, where Fin had stood. "Am I ever." She slid the cocktail napkin across the bar to the bartender with a five-pound note and asked him to deliver it to Fin. She headed out with Jonas to the streets of Douglas to catch a taxi.

The National Folk Museum at Cregneash was hidden in the countryside on the center of Spanish Head, a long hike from Port St. Erin on a foggy day—and they were all foggy—but one Rain was used to making by now. It took less time to go straight there than it did to hike around the Head, like she'd done the first few times. There was supposed to be a stone circle somewhere along the cliffs below the Head, and she'd skirted the edge of the cliffs, looking downward, as much as she could through the fog without risking a fall.

Cregneash looked like a traditional village, rising out of the fog, surrounded by nothing with only one small road passing through it. A good half of the buildings had thatched roofs. The stone walls surrounding them fit together without mortar in the traditional fashion. Rain sat on the wall outside the museum entrance, waiting. The prior evening played over in her mind, the way that she had felt content dancing with a stranger, and how that moment had been stolen. She rubbed her hands up and down her arms, though it wasn't cold. Rain had decided that if there was someone not to be trusted, it was that woman, who reminded her of nothing so much as fire—beautiful but destructive, and quick to burn. She also thought she remembered a look of abject terror on Fin's face—something that could not be caused by a woman with good intentions.

When Fin drove up on a motocross bike, Rain was suddenly conscious of her legs, swinging back and forth against the wall because her feet didn't touch the ground. She shoved off of the stones—carefully so she didn't knock anything out of place—and approached while he was still removing his helmet. Even here, outside the lighting of the club, his hair had a metallic shine to it.

"Surprised to see me?" he asked, tentatively, watching her face as she watched him.

Rain shook her head, in part to break her gaze and in part because she wasn't surprised. "I had a feeling you were the kind of guy who couldn't deny a lady's request."

He tucked his helmet under one arm and offered her the crook of the other. "Lady, are we?"

"I don't know about 'we.'" She slid her fingers along his elbow, shivering at the touch, despite the fact that his heavy jacket was between them. It was leather, but not in the style that bikers in the U.S. wore—almost more like an old B-movie flight jacket. "I'm kind of hoping you're not."

He laughed, and the worry she'd seen lurking behind his expressions at the club was nowhere to be seen. They started forward, in tandem, through the museum entrance. "I thought you Americans didn't hold with titles."

"Figured it out, did you? Was it my accent, or my good looks?"

She snaked away from him and walked over to the desk, pulling out the exact change for a new four-visit pass. Janeice, an older woman who had probably been working at the museum longer than Rain had been alive, tapped the pass she'd pulled out as soon as Rain had walked in the door.

"Needing a new one, then?" the curator asked, in the process of taking the money and handing over the pass. "It's good we see you so often. You'll soon know more than me!"

"Oh, I doubt that," Rain said, holding the new pass out to be stamped. "Punch one for my friend, too?"

Janeice looked over Rain's shoulder and her face, already pale, whitened. She whispered something in Manx—which Rain had learned the curator spoke fluently—shaking her head. "Oh, no, miss. MacLeirrs never pay here on the isle."

Fin stepped forward, looking completely apologetic as far as Rain was concerned, but Janeice held her breath. Rain squeezed Janeice's hand, noticing for the first time how frail the older woman was. "It's all right," she said, though she had no idea what was wrong in the first place. "You can charge me twice or not—either way, it won't be him paying."

Janeice handed her back the pass with only one entry punched. Fin said something in Manx behind Rain, and she turned, staring. No one their age spoke Manx fluently, from what she'd been told. It was one of the greatest regrets of the island. He finished, smiled at Rain—again apologetically—and walked toward the outside door. Rain looked back at Janeice, surprised to see all the tension gone from the woman's face, her cheeks their usual rosy shade.

"I've not seen a MacLeirr here in years," she whispered. Rain squeezed her hand again and followed after Fin.

He was waiting for her outside, leaning against the wall and looking out on the thatched roofs. With his shoulders shrugged and his knees bent, he gave the impression of trying to make himself small—something that would be impossible for someone his height. Rain leaned next to him, purposefully not looking at his face.

"And I thought I had questions before," she said.

He snorted, shifting his weight in such a way that he gained three inches. "My family used to be very important on the island," he said tersely.

"Used to be?"

He shoved off the wall and strode forward; Rain had to match two of her paces to each of his. "It's a long story. Politics. Not as interesting as you'd think."

They wandered through the village, not really talking, just watching the workers—all in the costume of Manx villagers generations gone by—as they went about their speeches and demonstrations. The tension drained out of Fin as they walked, and soon he was joking with the parents and young children stopping to visit. Despite what Rain thought were obviously edgy looks, the parents seemed comfortable around him, and the children gave every appearance of wanting to use him as a jungle gym. Instead, he taught them the Manx words for grass and tree and house and sent them on their way to the next cottage.

"Does everyone like you?" Rain asked as they watched a family go.

"Not everyone." Fin stood his full height, hands on his back. "If everyone likes you, you're not being yourself."

"I wonder if Jonas knows that…" He looked down at her and she grinned. "My roommate. The popular one."

Fin nodded in recognition. "Surely there's someone who doesn't like him."

"He's terribly likable." Even when Rain was irritated with him, he was hard to dislike. "But so are you, Fin MacLeirr."

"Finbar, actually," he said, starting off toward one of the cottages.

"What does it mean?" she asked, hurrying to keep up with his long strides. "I assume it's Manx."

He nodded. "Wave crest."

"Finbar MacLeirr," she said, trying out the sound. "It suits you."

He raised an eyebrow as he looked down at her. "And how would you know, Lady Rain?" She just grinned. "Speaking of which, your own name is still a mystery."

Her grin fell. "You have to promise not to laugh."

"It can't be that bad."

"It is." She took a deep breath. "But you have to understand that my parents missed out on being real hippies by just a few years, and they were very committed to civil rights and equality when they got married."

He brushed some of her hair away from her shoulder, and she thought how drab her brown hair must seem when he looked at his own metallic, silver-gold hair every day in the mirror. But rather than moving his hand away, he tangled his fingers in her unspectacular locks. "I'll take it all into account," he said.

"Rainbow," she blurted. "Saltperson."

His lip twitched and she crossed her arms over her chest. "You promised not to laugh."

"So I did," he said, but his voice quivered just enough that she knew he wanted to. "Saltperson?"

"It used to be Saltman, but they thought that was too gender biased." She groaned inwardly. *And wanted to curse their children forever with explaining their last name. Thanks Mom and Dad.*

"It suits you," Fin said, letting her hair loose, slowly, so that it fell against her shoulder in clumps. She shivered.

"Thanks."

Fin ducked into the doorway of a cottage and stood at the back of the room, staying out of the way of a group of children crowded around a basket-weaver. Rain waved at him, just slightly, as he looked up from his weaving. He nodded back, continuing to explain the difference between the pattern in Manx baskets as opposed to

European or American Indian styles as he wove his fibers back and forth. The children were fascinated, and after letting them watch for a bit, the weaver set them up at a table with some fibers of their own to give a simple pattern a try. Parents loomed over their children and the weaver stepped aside, settling back on his normal seat.

"Nice to see you, Rain," he said. "On foot again?"

"Always," Rain answered, pulling up one of the small stools. "Thanks again for the ride to Castle Rushen last week."

"A pleasure." The weaver tightened the fibers in the pattern, pulling the bottom taught. "It's hardly out of my way."

"I suppose they put you to work there a few days a week, too?" Fin asked, and the weaver looked up at him, expression turning from annoyance at the question to delight in recognition.

"Well if it isn't Fin MacLeirr," the weaver laughed. "Glad to have you here, boy. Been too long."

"It has," Fin agreed, taking the weaver's suddenly outstretched hand. "I haven't gotten out much lately."

The weaver's face darkened, but just for a moment. "Well, since you're out, and in the company of my fine friend Rain, I should take the opportunity to invite you both to a bat barbecue we've got going on Friday next. Up at Billown. Caves up there are fabulous for it."

Rain blanched. "You don't eat them?"

Both men laughed at the question. "We watch 'em come out of their caves at dusk," the weaver explained. "Whole clouds of them! It's something to see. And then there's food, because what's a gathering without a bit to eat?" He looked from Fin to Rain, and then back to Fin. "You'll come?"

Rain looked up at Fin hopefully, knowing too well that she was showing all her cards. She wanted to go, and she wanted to see Fin again. Fin smiled and nodded, but the worry she'd noticed back at the club had returned. "It's a date," he said, and her stomach flipped.

They met and ate at Billown, watching the bats swarm out of their caves in thick clouds. The locals cheered, gossiped, talked, and shared recipes. Only two hours after they arrived, when there was no arguing that dusk had faded well into night, Fin gave his apologies.

"Work," he said, before Rain could protest.

"For that witch of a woman?" Rain crossed her arms in front of her chest, but Fin just laughed.

"If you only knew the half of it," he said, reaching out to touch her hair. She shivered. "Cold?"

"No." She thought back to that first night, remembering the door, far from the entrance. "Jonas heard you were a bouncer."

"Of sorts," Fin said neutrally, pulling his hand back and glancing over her shoulder, avoiding her eyes.

"For a back door no one uses?"

His look was sharp, as bright and dangerous as the studs in his ears. "You shouldn't have seen that."

"But…"

He reached out for her again, putting firm hands on her shoulders. "Rushen Abbey, Saturday afternoon?" He flashed her that carefree grin, but it no longer hid his worry so well.

"Saturday afternoon," she agreed.

They toured the island together, always during the day. They visited the Old House of Keys, the seat of government formed by the invading Norse, who had given the isle something akin to democracy and their first centralized government. Fin took her to several of the Norse sites in the north, showing her small collections of crosses that weren't large enough to make the heritage map. He'd obviously studied them, and he knew the people in the parishes well enough to find her experts. She took notes, finding that her independent study had changed from homework to a reason to travel with Fin. She even became accustomed to riding on the back of his motocross bike.

"Do you race?" Rain called over his shoulder one day, squeezing around his chest.

"No," he hollered back. "The big race here—the TT—stands for the Tourist Trophy." His voice was muffled through his helmet, but she could hear his amusement. "You could give it a go if you wanted to borrow my bike."

He took a turn faster than he needed to and Rain shrieked. That, apparently, was answer enough.

One night, at home, while she was typing up notes on her laptop, Jonas wandered in and perched on her bed. He watched her, never interrupting with words, just waiting for her to invite him to talk.

"Yes?" she said finally, not looking up from her keyboard.

"You really like him, don't you?"

She sighed, hit save, and swiveled around in her desk chair. "What is it, Jonas?"

"I don't think Brianna and Cole have bothered to notice how often you're gone these days," Jonas continued, ignoring her question, "but when a good looking guy like that keeps arriving on that bike of his, I'm aware of it." He smiled broadly to counter her glare. "Seriously, Rain, you never mope at me anymore. I'm beginning to miss you."

The blush crept up around her ears. "That's really sweet, Jonas."

"You miss confiding in me, too, right?"

Rain laughed, and realized that she actually *had* missed it. She started telling him about their travels and discovered that sharing her good dates was a lot more fun than moping about her non-existent ones.

"It's weird how many people he knows, and how much they respect him," Rain said after awhile. "Something about his family. Have you heard anything about the MacLeirrs?"

Jonas's eyes got big. "You are positively the worst mythology student ever."

Rain swiveled back and forth in her desk chair. "What is that supposed to mean?"

"What's Manannan's last name?" Jonas quizzed her.

She sniffed. "He's a god. He doesn't have a last name."

In response, Jonas settled into poetry stance, his eyes half-closed as he began to recite. "Manannan Beg Mac y Leirr/Little Manannan Son of the Sea,/Who blessed our island,/Bless us and our boat, going out well./Coming in better, with living and dead in our boat." His eyelids fluttered and he looked at her again. "It's a prayer, recited into the twentieth century by fisherman along the Isle."

"The whole thing about Manannan the god also being Manannan the necromancer, right." Rain stretched her arms out behind her, leaning the chair back. "So the MacLeirr family must be associated somehow."

Jonas stroked his chin. "Mmmm, Rain's dating a godling. Have you thought about sharing?"

"I can still kick you out of my room."

He feigned a hurt look and stood, placing a hand mournfully over his heart. "I forgive you, but only because I know you have been pierced by love's sweet sting." She grabbed piece of paper from her desk, crumpled it, and threatened to throw it at him, but he just grinned. "I have some poems I'd like you to look over, if you have time. Mostly responses to Manx hymns and such. They could use a mythologist's take."

She raised an eyebrow. "Because your poems are mythic?"

He sighed heavily and moved to the door. "There's no romance in your soul, Rain."

Jonas shut the door quickly enough to avoid the crumpled paper Rain had aimed for his head.

Maybe it was Jonas's association of Fin and the Celtic god of the sea that made Rain want to go back to the House of Manannan, which she considered the best of the formal museums on the Isle, or maybe it was that she hadn't been there since just after she'd arrived months before. In either case, she suggested it to Fin as they were leaving the Braaid, an archaeological site of two Norse longhouses next to an Iron Age roundhouse near the village of the same name. Their hands were intertwined, so she felt it instantly when he stiffened.

"No."

She looked up at his face, frozen and stiff, no longer hiding behind his lazy smile. Her fingers tightened around his, small hand around his long one, like she could protect him from whatever had him—*frightened,* she realized.

"It's okay," she said quietly. "What about Peel Castle?" She stopped, swinging around in front of him and grabbing his other hand. "We could look for the ghost."

His lips quirked, but he didn't smile. "It's a big black dog," he said. "Do you really want to look for the ghost of a dog that's bigger than you are?"

"It's supposed to *protect* people, not harm them," she chided. "And besides, I'd have you to protect me."

He pulled away, looking back over his shoulder at the ruins. "I might not be as much help there as you'd think," he said.

Rain put her hand on his elbow, hiding behind the leather jacket, and he didn't pull away. "It doesn't matter to me where we go." *As long as I'm with you.*

He turned toward her, running his long fingers through her hair, a touch that Rain had begun to suspect was the closest he would come to kissing her. She looked up at him, wondering when her feelings for him had stopped being pretend.

"Have you been out to the Calf?" She shook her head, feeling the tendrils loosen as she moved away from his hand. "Then that's where we'll go. Meet me at the harbor in Port St. Erin Tuesday morning."

The harbor was just a short walk from her house, so she nodded, again feeling the pull of her hair against his fingers. He pulled her closer then, kissing her forehead, so softly his lips might have been feathers. Fin let her go, backing away with his face still as closed as it had been when she'd suggested the museum.

"Bring warm clothes," he said, and she nodded.

On Tuesday, she waited at the harbor, watching boats leave and come back with families and picnickers, out to enjoy the wildlife so carefully preserved on the island just south of the Isle of Man's own shores. At noon, she took out the sandwich she had packed for herself. At two, she took out the one she had packed for Fin. She waited. He never came.

It took only three days of moping before Jonas dragged the story out of her. He sat her down on the sofa with mugs of their favorite teas—Earl Grey for Jonas and raspberry leaf for Rain—and convinced her to tell him everything. He paced as he listened, sipping only occasionally.

"Bastard," Jonas said when she finished.

"I just don't get it," Rain said.

"Men are idiots," Jonas said with a shrug. He pulled her up off of their sofa and looked her up and down. "Come on. We're going to get you all dolled up—"

"Jonas—" Rain protested.

"—and once you're looking incredibly hot, we're going out."

Rain sighed. "Do I have to?"

He put his hand in the middle of her back and guided her to her room. "Hot," he repeated, shutting the door behind her.

Rain changed, and little by little, she found herself feeling better. It was almost as though by changing her appearance, she changed herself. Eventually, she believed that she felt like going out, because her reflection obviously did. She pinned up her hair, letting two brown tresses fall just in front of her ears. Combined with the low dip of her blouse, the effect lengthened her neck, which she always thought made her look taller. She slid on a pair of heels, ones she usually left behind when she was going dancing because her ankles would be unforgiving at the end of the night.

Jonas had already changed and was waiting outside her door.

"That was fast," Rain said.

"I can only improve so much on nature," Jonas answered, holding out her jacket. She slid her arms into the sleeves and rolled the coat up onto her shoulders. "You cleaned up alright yourself."

"Hot?" she asked.

"Smokin'. Almost as good as me."

The taxi was waiting for them, and not long after Port St. Erin disappeared into the dark fog behind them, the lights of Douglas loomed ahead, diffused by the moisture in the air. As the cab navigated the streets, Rain grabbed Jonas's wrist and squeezed.

"Tell me we're not going there."

Jonas patted her hand with the one she didn't hold in a vice-grip. "You want to know," he said. "And the mystery will just keep bothering you if you don't find out."

She pursed her lips before responding. "You're so incredibly mean."

He peeled her fingers from his arm. "That's just one of the many reasons you enjoy my company."

Carter's looked the same as it had the month before, though the decorations in the windows had changed. They now sported lanterns that looked like large turnips. Painted on the windows in bright red were the words "Hop-tu-Naa."

"Halloween?" Rain guessed.

"Don't let the locals hear you say that," Jonas said wryly. "Hop-tu-Naa's the old New Year. There's singing, rather than trick or treating. Still costumes though. I learned one of the songs if you'd like me to recite."

"Not sing?" Rain poked Jonas in the shoulder. "If it's a *song—*"

"The world will be blessed for my having kept silent," he said, and opened the door.

Rain held her head high as she walked in, as though she and Jonas owned this place, as though they were the hottest people to come through the doors. She scanned the room, looking to compare their dress, intentionally *not* looking for Fin. "Top ten percent," she murmured to Jonas, who raised both eyebrows at her disapprovingly. "You're in the top one, but I'm dragging you down a little."

"I'll forgive you this once." He reached for her jacket and she slid out of it, letting him deliver both of their coats to the coat room. The music pulsed through the floor, just as bad as she remembered, but the familiar throbbing in her ribcage felt better than the sore heart she'd been nursing. Jonas returned, took her hand, and led her out to the dance floor.

"What are you doing?"

Jonas found a spot under the lights, near enough to the speakers that her whole body quivered. "Dancing, moron," he said. "Start looking for likely candidates so I don't have to spend my whole evening out here."

She smirked, squeezing his hand in thanks, and looked over his shoulder. She wondered what she would do if she saw Fin. The hurt of being left waiting for hours fought against logical excuses she'd made for him over the past several days. He didn't have a phone number for her because they'd always made plans in person. He could have gotten sick. Maybe he actually did feel bad. *And what if he doesn't?* she wondered. She pursed her lips, studiously avoiding letting Jonas see her face. *That's it,* she decided. *He gets one chance to apologize, and maybe I'll accept it. Then we remedy the lack of contact info.*

But when she saw him, her whole body froze. He was leaning against the wall next to the door she wasn't supposed to have seen, looking at her. But it wasn't his gaze that held her—it was how sick he looked; so pale his skin glowed almost as much as his hair in the dim lights, so thin he looked like a ghost. He wasn't wearing his jacket, like he had been every other time she'd seen him, and she wondered if he'd been losing weight since the first time they met.

"You can do this," Jonas murmured, taking her stillness for fear. But she wasn't afraid of talking to him. She was afraid of whatever it was that made him look like that.

Rain only moved because Jonas nudged her in the right direction, muttering how bad it made him look to be dancing with a mannequin. He made his way to the bar and she stumbled back toward the door Fin was supposed to guard. His eyes never left her as she walked toward him, stayed on her when she stopped just a few feet away. She reached for him with one arm and he cringed back into the wall. Her hand dropped to her side.

"What happened to you?" she whispered.

"I'm sorry, Rain," he said, his voice scratchy and rough. "I never should have—"

"Don't." The tears that pricked her eyes surprised her. "Tell me what's happening."

"Rain—"

"Tell me."

The club might have been silent for all Rain could tell, waiting for whatever words might come.

He leaned off the wall, looking unsteady on his feet, tipped her chin up, and kissed her, fully. But despite the heat of it, it tasted sad, salty. *Like goodbye.*

She pulled away. "Fin, whatever it is—"

"You have to leave," he said, and there was an edge of panic to his voice. "She can't see you here, Rain, or she'll think I've dragged you into the whole thing—"

"What whole—"

"Go!"

He pushed her away, roughly enough that in the heels, she only barely kept her balance. Fin leaned back against the wall, eyes closed, head tipped back, and lights sparkling off of his piercings. Rain stumbled backward, then turned and hurried toward the bar, looking over her shoulder every few steps.

The door behind Fin opened, and the red-headed woman stepped out, dressed to kill. Her hand wrapped around Fin's arm, nails grazing him until dark spots popped up on his white skin. Rain made it to the bar, nearly sobbing, and turned back, torn between getting away and wanting to help Fin, to stop the woman from hurting him. The woman yanked Fin down to her own height. Dark streaks ran down his arm and his face was pinched with pain and terror.

"Rain."

Rain buried herself in Jonas's arms, letting the sob come out this time. "We have to call the police," she begged.

"Put on your jacket," he said, holding it out for her.

"She's hurting him!"

Jonas gritted his teeth and forced one of her arms into sleeve, then whirled her around and shoved her other arm into the second. At once, the lights shifted, and when she looked at Fin and the red-haired woman, she saw bright glowing forms around them, the woman's much larger than Fin's. Rain looked away from them and out onto the dance floor, where others—maybe one in ten—had the same glow: a brilliant light surrounding their bodies that was so beautiful it was almost painful.

"The police won't be able to do anything," Jonas said quietly. "We've got to go."

He pulled her away and caught her as she stumbled on the too-tall heels. She kicked out of them, leaned over to pick them up, and then let Jonas help her outside. The concrete of the sidewalk was cold beneath her feet, but Jonas kept her walking three blocks until they got to a pub where three young people were exiting a cab. Almost before the last of them got out, Jonas was shoving her inside.

"In a hurry?" the driver asked.

"No," Jonas lied.

"Where to?"

"Surrey," Jonas supplied. "Port St. Erin."

The driver pulled back out into the street. "Turning in early," he said casually. "Your jackets seem to be inside out. Did you know?"

Rain looked down and saw that it was true. Jonas, ever perfect in his fashion, was wearing his jacket inside out, and he'd put hers on the same way.

"How clumsy," Jonas said, squeezing Rain's knee. Despite the driver's attempts at small talk, which Jonas would have normally engaged with flair, the conversation remained awkward and stilted all the way home.

Jonas refused to explain until she had changed clothes. Rain pulled on her most comfortable jeans and a hooded sweatshirt with her college logo. Then she went into the bathroom and washed her face, surprised that there were tear streaks along her cheeks. The water helped her to stop shivering, and when she finished, she felt almost pulled together.

Jonas was pacing in their living room, still wearing his inside-out jacket.

"I hate it when I'm right," he said to the floor, then scowled up at her. "And you really are the worst mythologist ever."

Rain slumped onto the couch, trying not to think of the blood she'd seen on Fin's arm or the glow around his body. "Fine. I'm stupid. Tell me what I'm supposed to know."

Jonas ran his hand through his hair, and she realized he was shaking. "All right. God, I wish I smoked. I could use a cigarette." He took a deep breath, and when he let it go, he seemed to have pulled himself together. "I didn't think it would do *that*, by the way, but I had this hunch, have since you said Fin's last name." Rain bit her lip, trying to keep herself from interrupting. "Turning the jacket—or frock or whatever—inside out is an old trick. It used to be used to see past fairy glamour."

She blinked at him, trying to make the words make sense. "I don't understand."

He sat down next to her on the couch, hard. "Rain, tell me what happens to the Tuatha de Danaan when the Milesians come."

"The Tuatha de Danaan, who had been like kings and gods of Ireland, lost the war to the new invaders, like the Fomorians had lost to them when they came," Rain recited. "The Milesians won all of Ireland, but the Tuatha de Danaan stayed, living in sort of a shadow Ireland, behind illusions."

Jonas wrung his hands. "They were forced underground, and they came to live in hills, so that they were called the Sidhe, the hill folk," Jonas said.

Rain frowned. "Those are fairy tales."

Jonas snorted. "Rain, what do you think happens to myths when they stop being religion?" He picked at the seam of his jacket, still on the wrong side. "And beyond that, what do you do when old folk tales completely change how you see the world?"

She looked at his inside-out jacket and thought of the glow that filled the night club, surrounding only a handful of the dancers, surrounding Fin and the woman who controlled him. "So you think it's true."

"Truth is for philosophers," Jonas said curtly. "I think that we have to look at the information we've got, figure out how to interpret it, and decide what to do from there. Option number one is we can forget all about this and never speak on it again."

Rain thought of the blood on Fin's arm and shook her head. "I can't."

"I knew that was too much to hope for." Jonas leaned back on the couch, drumming his fingers on his knee. "God, I can't focus. Remind me how the story of Manannan goes."

"What does that—?"

Jonas bit his lip, and she noticed that the knee he was drumming was bouncing. "Humor me. I'm in no condition to go over it in my own head."

"Fine." She pinched the bridge of her nose, breathing in and out, trying to focus. "In the Irish legends, he's the sea god, husband to a giant, father of Llyr, who later took over as the sea himself. Roughly." She rubbed her eyes, then pulled her knees up to her chest and hugged them. "On the Isle, he's the first ruler of the island, the *son* of Leirr—I looked it up after you called me an idiot last time. He was a wizard, some say a necromancer, and he would wrap the island in fog any time the invaders came. He only asked for a tithe or tax of rushes, once a year, from the people of Mann to keep them safe." She leaned her chin against her knee and looked at Jonas. "I'm not sure where we're going with this."

He was still bouncing or shivering—it was hard to tell. "Imagine just for a moment that when the Milesians came, not all the Tuatha de Danaan stayed." She started to interrupt, but he put his hand on her shoulder, leaning closer, and she could feel his jitters. "What if Manannan came here instead, with all the power he'd had before, and took the Isle of Man and made it his home? He would never have to hide the way the rest of the Tuatha de Danaan did."

"He could have had a family," Rain murmured, finally seeing where Jonas was going. "Children." She blanched. "When Fin's boss first grabbed him, the night we met, she called him an above-grounder."

"Because the MacLeirrs were never hill-folk," Jonas said, coming to the same conclusion she'd just made.

"So those others in the club—" Rain faltered. "They're *fairies?*"

"Minus the little green coats and leather hats," Jonas answered, and he stopped shaking. "I think I've just completely run out of energy."

Rain leaned back against the couch and Jonas mimicked her posture. They sat in silence, letting it all wash over them.

"Tomorrow is Hop-tu-Naa," Jonas said quietly. "The new year. It used to be a harvest ritual. And even you, the worst mythologist in the world, should be able to figure out what that must mean."

She didn't have the energy to be frightened any more. "You think he's going to be a sacrifice. You think they've made him the year-king, the one who has to die in thanks for the crops, to make sure that the land stays fertile for next season." Jonas nodded. "How are we supposed to stop that?"

Jonas's fingers drummed against his knee. "I don't know." He looked down at his hand, as if just realizing that his fingers were moving. "I don't even know where the ritual would take place. It doesn't seem like—." He cut off and then groaned. "Unless they're doing it in their own realm."

Rain thought of the guarded door in Carter's. "We'll never get through that door, not if that bitch is guarding it."

"Cronk Moar," Jonas said.

"The hill fort?" Rain asked incredulously. "It was a Norse fortress, and it might have a barrows, but it's never been properly excavated—"

"Don't you listen to anyone around here?" Jonas asked tersely. "Everyone in Port St. Erin says it's a fairy hill."

If Rain had slept better, she might have been able to convince herself the entire evening had been a dream. As it was, her night was less than restful, and she thought she could still feel, lingering on her lips, the kiss that Fin meant as farewell.

She swung out of bed, still in the jeans and sweatshirt she'd put on the night before. She'd been too tired to change. With a yawn, she stretched her arms above her head and looked out her window. The mist made it difficult to tell what time it was, but she suspected from what light shown through that it was past noon.

"Cronk Moar was a timber fort," she told herself. "Maybe a castle at the top of the hill, small trench dug around it for protection. Built around 11 A.D., if the people who did the excavation back in 1900 guessed right." She put her hands on the windowsill and looked out at the foggy morning, though even on a clear day, there were hills and houses in the way of the ruin.

"Fairies," she said, as though it were a curse. But Fin had glowed, right along with the rest of them. Not just his hair or his piercings or pale skin; he himself had glowed like a lantern. "Tuatha de Danaan. People of Dana. Danaans." That was somehow better. They'd been a people—fantastic though they were—that had ultimately been conquered in a war. "I wouldn't hold it against him if he were any other ethnicity," she said, knowing very well she was rationalizing to take the terror away. "Right. So, I just have to tell the queen of the Danaans that she can't sacrifice him. No problem."

"I'm glad you're so confident," Jonas said from her doorway. He looked rumpled, but at least had new clothes on. His jacket, however, was still inside out. "How did you sleep?"

She looked at his hair, usually perfectly in place. "About as well as you did, by the look of it."

"Then we'll both be exceptionally well rested for our stake out tonight," he said dryly. "Come on. I made sandwiches."

They hiked up to Cronk Moar, seeing the hill rise up from its flat surroundings well before were close. "It used to be a marsh," Jonas said, looking up from the book he'd brought along. "And fairies weren't supposed to chase you through water, so if you were able to stay in wet land until you got to a church, you were safe."

Rain looked down at the field beneath them—moist ground, certainly, but not marshy. "Great. What are you reading?"

He showed her the cover. *Manx Fairy Tales.* "Brilliant," she muttered.

"It's got a charm to say against the fairies," he offered.

Rain sighed. "Keep it ready."

Trees and brambles grew in the ditch that surrounded Cronk Moar and kept Rain from climbing the hill to see the ruins at the top, which she always assumed were overgrown. The shrubs were prickly—hard to walk through and worse to fall on. But there was no place to hide on the flat area beyond the trench, so she led Jonas down into it and behind a tree.

"Watch for the prickers," she warned, pulling her rain coat out of her pack and spreading it on the ground.

Sitting still, surrounded by damp air after a night with little or no sleep made it difficult to stay awake. Rain daydreamed, only really aware of her surroundings when she noticed how stiff her legs were. They ate sandwiches in the afternoon, then again when the sun began to set, and they shared a canteen of water between the two of them.

"Turn your shirt inside out," Jonas said as dusk fell around them.

Rain pulled her raincoat off the ground and shoved her arms through the sleeves the wrong way. The dirt she'd been trying to avoid sitting in now rubbed against her sweatshirt, and she tried to think of it as something other than a bad omen.

Dusk deepened into night, and Rain fought against the cramps in her legs. They could hear singing from Port St. Erin, presumably the celebrants of Hop-tu-Naa. But Rain thought she heard a harp as well, then flutes, all the time moving closer, even though there were no houses nearby. Rain looked at the hill beside them, seeing the light coming from the other side. She grabbed Jonas's arm and pulled him forward, both of them moving as quietly as they could through the underbrush until they saw the door. There in the hill, plain as the door on a house, was an open doorway. Light poured out of it, the same kind of glow they'd seen at Carter's.

Rain started forward, but Jonas pulled at her coat. "Don't eat anything," he said quietly.

She nodded and stepped inside.

It looked like the inside of Carter's, only brighter. She imagined that if she had ever been to the club during the day, with all the lights on, it would have looked like this. The dance floor was full of people, all of them glowing fiercely, some of whom she'd seen before. The place was just as crowded as the night club, and people sat around private tables, lounged in couches, and lined the bar. Despite the fact that she and Jonas were not dressed like they belonged there, no one seemed to pay them any mind. They danced, not to thump-thump music, but to harp and flute and drum.

As Rain started to head toward the mysterious door where she knew she would find Fin, it opened. The crowd parted as a brown horse pushed through the door, the rider on its back was the red-haired woman, fierce and terrible, her features as cold as stone. Rain pushed her way through the crowd as the second horse left the door, this one black, bearing a male rider she'd never seen before, but who glowed as brightly as the woman. And then, on a white horse, came Fin.

Rain burst through the crowd and grabbed Fin's leg. The white horse reared, and Fin tumbled from its back into Rain's arms. They both collapsed in a heap, and Rain held onto Fin's arm fiercely, as though he might disappear if she released him.

A scream from ahead of them stopped the music, and the club was suddenly silent. The red-haired woman dropped off her horse as Rain and Fin scrambled for their feet. Fin trembled and Rain held him tighter, wrapping her arm around his waist.

"I knew it!" the red-haired woman shrieked. "You had this planned all along." She reached her clawed hand out toward Fin, but Rain pulled him back. The woman whirled on her instead. "What did he tell you? That he was a human kept by fairies, trapped in their lands? That you could save him and be his bride?" She laughed, deep and terrible. "Those are the old stories, older than the world, but still people believe."

"He told me nothing," Rain said, surprised at how steady her voice sounded. "I object to this sacrifice."

There were gasps in the crowd, and the red-haired woman smirked. "You object?" she asked incredulously. "And who are you to stop us from breaking the veil?"

"You can't have him," Rain said firmly.

The smirk fell from the woman's face, and suddenly her expression was hideous, distorted in rage. "See if you can hold him."

"You shouldn't have come," Fin croaked, his voice worse than it had been the night before. He jerked in a spasm, and she looped her other arm around him. He was so much bigger than she was.

"I couldn't let you die," she whispered into his chest.

His knees buckled, and she held him from collapsing. "Then don't let go," he gasped.

His body jerked again, tight, and the glow that surrounded him shifted into flames. Rain shrieked, and then realized that there was no pain; the flames didn't burn.

"Take her jacket!" the red-haired woman shrieked.

Rain felt someone grab her collar and Fin's body quaked, jerking hard against her arms. He groaned in pain.

"Peace of God and Peace of Man!" Jonas's voice rang out.

The hands dropped away from her, and Jonas's voice continued over the crowd, but she couldn't hear the words over the bellows of pain from Fin. As she held onto him, Fin's eyes burst open wide, and his body shuddered and began to shift. His waist shrunk in her arms and his face narrowed; he thrashed back and forth, hissing like a snake. She locked her wrists, bracing against his pulls.

Then his eyes widened again, and he looked at her in terror. "No!" he shouted, shadows drifting across his irises, as though he was seeing something else. "I won't go! I won't be tricked! Let go of me!" He pushed against her shoulders, struggling to get free.

"Fin, it's me!" she shouted.

His hand tightened on her shoulder, pushing her away. Her fingers slipped on her wrist and she cried out. He pushed against her and she bit down on her lip hard, blinking back tears as she felt her teeth bite through, as the trickle of blood dripped down her chin.

And then Fin stopped struggling and the red-haired woman screamed.

"On every hole admitting moonlight!" Jonas called out.

"The blood is paid," intoned the man on the black horse. "The sacrifice given."

"I will not be trapped here!" the woman screamed, the brilliance surrounding her shifting from the fiery red of her hair to a hot white.

Fin threw his arms around Rain as the burst of energy seared over them, charging the air with static shocks that burst all along her body.

"On the four corners of the house!"

Fin yanked her forward, his arm around her shoulders, her arms both still locked around his waist. Rain saw Jonas in the crowd as he backed through it, brandishing his book of fairy tales like a ward, reading the charm from the page.

"On the place of my rest!"

They were almost through the crowd, Jonas scrambling backward, still looking at where they'd left the horses behind. Fin turned the door handle into the darkness of the field around Cronk Moar and he and Rain tumbled into the trench.

"And peace of God on myself," Jonas said, dropping to the ground behind them. He scrambled up the side of the trench and looked back down. "Get up! The ground isn't wet, remember?"

But Fin was murmuring in Manx, and the fog surrounded them—thick, cold, and almost suffocating for just a moment before the clouds above burst open in a shower of rain.

"Come on," said Fin, reaching for Rain's hand. She sobbed as she let go, her arms burning from exertion. He pulled her arm over his shoulder and lifted her into his arms. She was too exhausted to protest. Instead, Rain looked at Jonas, who was alternately staring up at the downpour then at the puddles forming around his feet.

"Fin, this is Jonas, my roommate," she said. "He's a poet."

"Nice to meet you," said Fin.

"Yes, well," Jonas stuttered. "Next time maybe we can do this without the sacrifice."

Fin adjusted Rain in his arms and started walking across the field. "I'd like that."

Jonas had to double his steps to keep up, which made Rain feel just slightly better about her own height. "Rain," Jonas said after a few moments. "You're glowing."

"It's the sparkle of success," Rain said tiredly. "Or the fact that I'm soaking through my coat."

"No," he said slowly, "I mean you're *glowing.*"

Rain looked up at Fin and saw the same haze around him she'd seen in the club and then in the hill. She held up one of her own hands to the sky, and against the rain, she had the same glow, dimmer, but there.

Rain leaned into Fin's shoulder. "Huh," she said.

The house on Surrey was a welcome place to dry off, though no one had any clothes that would come close to fitting Fin, so he ended up in an oversized sweatshirt and a skirt of Cole's (notably, not a skirt of Brianna's, but the wardrobe choice didn't seem a surprise to anyone but Rain). Cole and Brianna wandered off to bed, their usually unsociable selves, and Jonas, Rain, and Fin sprawled in the living room. Fin took up most of the couch and Rain curled up next to him. Jonas sat at the table, drinking a mug of Earl Gray.

"They've been trying to get out for a long time," Fin said finally, his voice sounding almost normal after the storm. "They thought if they had one of us—one of the Danaan—as the sacrifice, it might break the bindings of the old treaty. So here I was. She laid a geas—a magical obligation—on me, and that was it. I couldn't get out of it."

"But you are now," Rain said, hoping that it didn't sound like a question.

"Yes, thanks," Fin answered, pulling her into his body. He nodded at Jonas. "That was a foolish thing you both did, and dangerous, and I'm grateful."

"Yes, well, I'm a poet, so that's my excuse for foolishness," said Jonas. "And that one must just like you a lot."

"Mmmm," murmured Rain, not bothering to deny it.

"But speaking of Rain," Jonas said, "why does she glow now?"

"Residual effect of being in the mound?" Fin said hopefully.

"Jonas doesn't glow," Rain pointed out.

Jonas looked irritated. "You don't know." He ran his hand through his still damp hair. "What good is it to be—whatever you are—if you don't know the answers?"

"Part of the fun is finding out," Fin said, his carefree tone not hiding a single thing. Rain yawned in his arms. "I don't suppose I could kit out here tonight? It's a bit of a hike home to Douglas, and I don't really fancy taking the shortcut through Cronk Moar."

Rain pulled his arm more tightly around her. "Stay as long as you like," she offered through a yawn.

Jonas stood and threw a blanket over them, then shook his head, grumbling about fairy hills and house guests as he went off to his room.

"Fin?"

"Yes?"

Rain snuggled back into him. "Don't let go."

He squeezed her tightly, and then let up, leaving his arm draped around her. She laced her fingers in his, and when she woke up the next morning, they were still intertwined.

— THE LOOPHOLE —
A Story of Elsewhere
by L. Penelope

Rhenna stood at the back of the darkened alleyway, hands on her knees, retching onto the cracked asphalt. The aftertaste of human flesh coated her tongue. Laid out on the ground beside her, arms splayed out as if in flight, a corpse looked up, sightless.

She vomited again, expelling only bile from her empty stomach. This never got any easier. Soon, nothing came out but her breath.

With nimble fingers tipped in dark purple nails, she plucked the pouch hanging from a leather cord around the corpse's neck and placed it around her own. The pouch was nearly empty now.

The feel of tight clothing squeezing her skin was strange. Her skin was strange. She wasn't sure she liked this body. But she'd get used to it like she had all the others.

She wobbled on stiletto heels, taking each step slowly until she got her footing. These legs were long; they looked nice in the shoes, that much was true, though her toes were pinched.

Rhenna cracked her back and straightened her skirt, tugging down the too-short material, then, with more confidence, placed one foot in front of the other and exited the alley.

The night was cold, and this body hadn't been wearing a coat. It was a little matter, but she would have appreciated being warm. This city was much farther north than she'd have preferred. Brisk winds blowing in off the lake made it so residents stayed strangers, just people who passed one another with hands stuffed into pockets and heads down. Not a smile or friendly face to be seen. Though a face too friendly at this hour of the night usually meant something bad. Rhenna could deal with bad, but she'd rather not. Not with this new body to break in. Another time, maybe.

And there was a reason she stayed in this frigid town as opposed to moving somewhere warmer and more hospitable. Just one, really.

She decided to walk, though it was nearly twenty blocks to The Loophole, the bar where that one reason could be found. While she appreciated being around her kind—those cursed to be exiled forever from Elsewhere—tonight she was tired enough to go for just a drink or two, and then home to let this body rest.

As she crossed the distance, her steps grew quicker, more sure. Would he recognize her in this form? He usually did—scratch that, he always did. His kind were one of the few to see the spirit beneath the flesh, to always recognize her no matter what skin she wore. That was the main reason she kept going back.

Maintaining friendships through the years had been nearly impossible. She hated having to reintroduce herself to the same people. To prove that she was still the same Rhenna, no matter what she looked like on the outside. It was draining and made the homesickness swell.

For years, she'd traveled—a nomad created by circumstance. This was a part of exile that she hadn't expected. Not just being unable to go home, but unable to create a new one in this peculiar, human world. A sigh escaped her as she closed in on the nondescript building.

There was no sign advertising The Loophole—if you belonged there, you could feel the powerful wards protecting the clientele and keeping the place hidden from mundane eyes. But there were rules once you were inside. Only a few, but they were inviolate. No fighting, no soliciting, and no angering the fairy. The first two because it would ruin the vibe, and the last because no one wanted an angry fairy. Not if they wanted to stay alive and under the radar of the Enigmas—the powerful protectors of Elsewhere.

The wooden door slammed behind her, and Rhenna was enveloped in the dimly lit space. She wondered how a human would react if one could make it past the wards to gain entry.

Here, creatures of all kinds gathered, from an aswang, shifting from dog to human to munch on a plate of French fries before shifting back, to a zashiki-warashi, who looked disturbingly like a six-year-old child with a terrible haircut, downing a shot of tequila. Spirit beings hovered, a fire elemental lit up the corner booth, and a dryad and a spriggan played a card game on the ground.

Rhenna exhaled, comforted by the familiarity, and made her way to the bar, choosing a seat at the end. She glanced at her reflection in the mirror. A heart shaped face, medium brown skin, and brown eyes edging towards hazel stared back at her. Heavy eyeliner gave the face a tired quality. Going forward, she'd just stick to mascara.

A broad chest blocked her vision. She tilted her head up to take in the bartender. Tall, lean, arms corded with muscle visible beneath the rolled-up sleeves of his flannel shirt. Half a dozen leather bracelets graced his wrist.

"Blaise," she said, giving in to the smile that pulled at her lips.

He squinted at her. "Rhenna. New look?"

She shrugged and placed her palms on the bar top.

"The usual?" he asked.

He'd trimmed his beard. It looked nice. A safe step away from mountain man territory, where he'd been headed. She wanted to tell him so, but instead replied, "Yeah, the usual."

He moved away to make her drink, and she once again faced her reflection. Sad eyes, she decided. A figure settled on the stool next to her. She looked over and did a double take.

While the rules of The Loophole stated no fighting, they didn't prohibit weapons, and her new neighbor had taken this to heart. Two scabbards crossed his back, revealing the handles of dual swords above his wide shoulders. Judging by the vaguely revolting vibrations coming from them, their blades were forged of demonstrife, one of the few substances able to kill a demon.

The man was young and widely built. Based on that and his choice of weaponry, she judged him to be an Omen—half-human, half-demon, trained by the covens to protect them from Elsewhere's more violent residents, when they dared crossover to the human world.

Rhenna looked away. The Omen seemed a bit keyed up, probably demonborn. The humanborn ones she'd come across tended to be more mellow. That is, when they weren't trying to wipe her off the face of the earth. But she hadn't crossed paths with a member of any covens, and this *was* The Loophole, so she decided to forget about the kid.

Blaise came up with her drink and gave the Omen a glare, noting his weaponry but not saying anything. The bartender merely raised an eyebrow, awaiting a drink order.

The Omen clasped his hands together on the bar top as if he were at a business meeting. "Are you the fairy?" he asked.

Blaise's other brow rose to meet the first one. Where was this kid from, blurting out a question like that? So rude.

Blaise crossed his arms, and Rhenna took a sip of her drink. This might get interesting.

The aggrieved motion of the bartender caused more than one head to turn. Blaise wasn't the most effusive fairy she'd ever met—and she'd only met a handful since they were very rare in the human world—but she figured it would take quite a lot to anger him. If he didn't have a strong grip on his emotions, this building probably wouldn't be standing. But every single creature in the bar had a vested interest in him keeping his temper.

"Who wants to know?" Blaise shot back.

The Omen sized up the fairy, thumb tapping nervously, hands still clasped. "My name is Wilhelm—Wil. I was told you might be able to help me. I need a talisman."

Blaise raised a hand out to stop him, then pointed to the large sign in block letters taped to the mirror. NO FIGHTING. NO SOLICITATION.

Blaise glared icily at Wil for one long moment before stalking away.

"First time here?" Rhenna asked.

Wil swiveled in his seat, noticing her at last. Inexperience wafted from him like body odor. This might even be his first mission.

"It's that obvious?" he asked. If he were human, he would be in the military, straight backed and solemn.

"Kinda," she said, sipping her fruity drink. The little umbrella was missing, but she wasn't about to tell Blaise that. "Never ask anyone what they are. It's considered impolite."

Wil unclasped his hands and grimaced. "So, I offended him? There's no way he'll—"

"Nope." She popped her 'p' and set the empty drink down. "Another!" she shouted down the bar. Blaise nodded as he placed a freshly pulled beer in front of a gremlin.

"Did someone tell you to come here for a talisman?" she asked Wil.

"No. They just said this bar is fairy-run. Thought it was worth a shot."

"Fairies are hard to come by. So you can understand that if he started doing talismans for everyone who wanted one, he'd never get anything else done, right?"

"Do they really work?" His round eyes seemed skeptical.

Rhenna snorted. A baby, this one was. Was he even old enough to wield those swords on his back?

"You're asking me if a fairy-kissed talisman actually protects its bearer from harm? If you don't believe it, why'd you come down here?"

He pursed his lips and looked off. "My Prior told me to come."

"Was the head of your coven perhaps trying to haze you?"

She watched the thought cross his mind and he frowned, considering. "He's usually not the playful kind."

"Were you, I don't know, annoying him, maybe? Being too..." She waved a hand in his direction, "...earnest?"

His face fell. Poor thing. She could see it playing out now. A newly trained Omen, ready to do his duty and protect his coven. A Prior a bit annoyed by the headstrong, overgrown warrior eager to test his skills. But with no experience, only hunger.

"Don't feel bad, newbie," Rhenna said, patting his overgrown arm. "Everybody has to start somewhere."

Blaise dropped off her fresh fruity beverage, and she smiled brightly in response. The bartender's eyes widened a fraction, but he just grunted then returned to the other end of the bar. She spun around on her seat, taking in the view.

"Might as well enjoy it while you're here. A little slice of Elsewhere in the human world." She sighed, unable to keep the wistfulness out of it.

Wil's close perusal was heavy as a touch, taking her in. Wondering what she was, but after her admonishment earlier, likely too chagrined to ask. Others in the place were more obvious. She could almost feel the gears spinning in his head as he noticed the goblin, the gremlin, the shifters, and wights.

He tensed, and a hand went to the dagger at his belt. Rhenna grabbed his wrist before he could pull it loose.

"Is that a demon?" he asked through clenched teeth.

The demon in question, a female named Mazhira, sat in the corner laughing her ass off at something a centaur said. She showed off her rows of razor sharp, filed teeth. The tips of pointed ears just peeked out of her dark green hair.

"Yes, there are plenty of demons here. But those weapons won't be necessary. Didn't you read the signs?" Every wall held a large placard with the rules written in English, French, and half a dozen tongues found only in Elsewhere.

Wil remained rigid for a long moment and then finally relaxed, dropping his hand to his leg. Rhenna released her grip on him. The Twenty-two Enigmas only knew what would happen if this tender-footed child started a brawl in The Loophole.

"Besides, she's a Grim demon," Rhenna said. "The treaty between them and the human covens still stands."

He worriedly scanned the room. "Are Shade demons allowed in here?"

"Yes," she said slowly. Wil's jaw ticked. "And they follow the rules as well."

"Demons don't follow rules," he muttered under his breath.

Rhenna sighed and pulled another sip of her drink. "So prejudiced."

He turned to her, affronted. *"Prejudiced?* Against demons?"

"Yes, *Omen.* Are you or are you not half demon? If I'm not mistaken, your mother was a demon."

He backed up. "How did you know?"

"The demonborn have a certain... rigidity about them that humanborn Omens lack. At any rate, I should hope you would take the time to get to know some of us before forming opinions about a whole species."

His jaw unhinged, and he looked at her with even more scrutiny. She shot him a *what-are-you-going-to-do-now?* expression, and his shoulders relaxed a bit. "I suppose you're right. It's just that I was trained—"

"You were trained to fight demons who want to fight you. Does anyone in this bar look like they want to fight?"

Just then the pouch at Rhenna's neck began to vibrate. She closed a hand over it to still the movement. A firework of pain exploded behind her eyes followed by wave of dizziness. She swayed, holding a hand to her head.

"Are you all right?" she dimly heard Wil ask. "Hey! She might need some water or something."

The cocktail glass was plucked from her grip, and strong hands spun her around on her stool.

"Here, drink this." A straw reached her lips, and Rhenna sipped. The cool water eased her parched throat, and the dizziness faded.

When she opened her eyes, Blaise was gazing at her, concern creasing his brow. She could feel Wil at her back, nervous energy sparking.

"I'm all right. I'm fine. Just..." She took a deep breath. "Still acclimating."

Blaise nodded, understanding, and moved away, but Wil sat down next to her, frowning. "Acclimating? Did you just arrive?"

"From Elsewhere? Oh no, I've been here for years. Just..." she cleared her throat. Her pouch had come out from beneath her shirt and she tucked it back in, then pushed up her sleeves to get more air.

Wil tilted his head. "What's that?"

She looked down at a tattoo on her arm.

"'So it goes,'" he said, reading. "What does that mean?"

Rhenna stared at her arm, wondering what other tattoos this body bore. People rarely had just one, not at this age. She shrugged and drank the rest of her water.

"You don't know what your own tattoo means?"

"New body," she said, smiling.

Wil froze beside her. Rhenna felt her headache deepen. It had been quite a while since she'd rejected a body, but she had a strong suspicion that was happening.

What could cause such a thing? She vaguely remembered her youth and the endless warnings her *oma* had given, ones she hadn't needed in her many years of life. She'd had one rejection when she was first kicked out of Elsewhere, but since then everything had been smooth.

She had no desire to repeat those terrifying days. If this was a rejection, she had to get back out there and find a new body. She might have enough breath left for another change. Maybe.

She stood, wobbling on the stupid heels. Wil shot a hand out to steady her, but she brushed him away. Instead she closed her eyes and breathed deeply, trying to force this body to catch hold and not spurn her. Hoping for enough time.

"I know it's rude, but," Wil began in a low voice, "what *are* you?"

Slowly, she straightened to her full height. The rolling in her belly was a bad sign. There would be no more time. She sighed and caught Blaise's eye. Nodded with her head for him to come over.

"Feeling better?" he asked, taking in Wil's cautious demeanor.

"Need to settle up. Gotta go."

His brows rose, but he moved over to the register to pull up her bill. Rhenna fished some cash out of her purse.

Blaise returned, frowning. "You don't look so hot."

She shrugged. "Don't feel so hot either. Seems like my last meal isn't agreeing with me." She gave a wan smile and took another breath.

That simple act was getting harder. She needed to go, now.

What were the chances of her finding a suitable body in the time she had, with the breath she had left? Virtually none. How could this be happening to her? She should have fed again before coming here. She'd gotten overconfident.

As she stumbled towards the exit, she realized she had an unwanted shadow. Spinning around to face her young stalker made the dizziness return. "What are you doing?"

"Making sure you get out of here safely," Wil said.

Rhenna sighed. "So chivalrous. But I don't need it. I assure you that I can take care of myself. Everyone in here can, one way or another."

He looked down. "I know, it's just that..."

"What?" her voice came out exasperated. A hot pain was burrowing its way through her insides.

"I don't know what you are."

So, it was less her safety he was concerned about and more the safety of the public at large. Laughter bubbled up through the stabbing in her middle. It hurt, but she couldn't help it—the look on poor Wil's face was comical.

Tears streamed from her eyes. She clenched her sides and then bent over, gasping for breath. Her heel slipped and her palms hit the ground as she tried to steady herself. This time, the arm that helped her up was Blaise's. She gripped him like a lifeline. But the furrow on his brow wasn't good.

"Sorry," she said. "Thank you."

He blinked, his severe face growing more so.

"Uh oh," she whispered. "You don't look happy."

"I'm not happy," he gritted out. "What exactly do you need?"

"A dead girl would be nice. 5'4 to 5'8, under 180 pounds. Body mass makes a difference, especially since I'm short of breath." She tried to pat her pouch, but her hand missed.

From somewhere nearby she heard Wil suck in a breath.

"Figure it out yet?" she asked, as her vision swam.

"Holy Enigmas," Wil swore. "You're a Boo Hag."

And then she passed out.

Maintaining consciousness in a body that was rejecting your essence was hard. But though the flesh she wore lay motionless on the ground, Rhenna was still aware. Aware enough to be mildly offended at being called a Boo Hag.

If she could have controlled her mouth and vocal chords, she would have informed the young padawan that her kind preferred the term Breath Witch. But she could do nothing more than perceive the new body she'd so carefully chosen being lifted into Blaise's arms. Wil held the door as Blaise hustled her outside into the biting cold. Her essence didn't feel the temperature, but she sensed the breaths of the two males puff as they walked.

"So, she's… she's…" Wil stammered, cheeks turning red.

Blaise's expression was tight. He wasn't straining under the weight of Rhenna's body, the body she now felt so protective of, but he didn't seem to be in a talkative mood.

Rhenna wished she could ease the tension evident on his forehead. A line had formed there, right down the middle. He was certainly the frowniest fairy she'd ever met.

"She eats the dead and wears their bodies," Wil finally got out.

"Not exactly," Blaise said, turning onto a busier street. It was late enough that those around didn't look twice at a man carrying an unconscious woman down the street.

"She steals the breath of the dead," he said. Rhenna bristled. *Steal* was a strong term. The dead didn't really need what she took anyway. "It's how she survives. And every so often, when she needs a new body, she'll taste their flesh in order to wear their skin. She doesn't eat the dead, she just needs a bite."

And that's the part she hated the most. People tasted awful.

"How can the dead have breath?" Wil asked.

"Newly dead. Heart stopped, unrecoverable but with a final wisp of life still trapped in their lungs."

"The one that comes out with the death rattle?" Wil asked.

Blaise shrugged.

"What happened to her?"

"Sometimes the bodies are rejected, the way that organ donations go wrong."

Wil thought about that. "So, we have to find another dead girl for her to take? How are we going to do that?"

"We're not," Blaise answered. Wil looked as confused as Rhenna felt. She wished she could talk to him. He did seem to know quite a bit about her kind, but he must not know everything. This body was trying its damnedest to push out her essence, and she was holding on by a thread.

If the body succeeded, Rhenna would be set adrift without any tethers. No body meant no teeth, no way to consume flesh. No way to steal breath. She would be a wandering essence that would either die of starvation or, perhaps impossibly, find a portal to Elsewhere, where her original skin was kept. But if she was discovered back home, she might as well be dead.

Blaise stopped in front of a brownstone and shifted Rhenna's body to pull a set of keys from his pocket. Was this Blaise's house? The windows were all dark. It was as nondescript as the bar, but nice, on a quiet street.

He got the door open and they all spilled inside. Lights turned on of their own volition, sparked, no doubt, by the fairy's magic. Classic, high quality furnishings of dark wood and heavy embroidery greeted them. This did not appear to be the home of a bartender, though it did fit the aesthetic of a centuries-old fairy. The Omen stopped short. "This is your home?"

Blaise ignored him, setting Rhenna on a plush antique couch and sitting beside her, brushing hair off her face. She thought she sensed some emotion play across his face, but in her current state she couldn't be sure.

"How can you help her?" Wil asked.

"Sit there," Blaise instructed, pointing to the armchair next to the couch. "Drag it over."

Wil obeyed obediently, dragging the heavy chair so his knees touched the sofa near Rhenna's head.

Blaise kept rubbing her forehead, stroking it carefully. From Rhenna's perspective, his face was blank, but she thought she noticed a spark behind his eyes.

"You came to the bar because of what you heard that fairies can do, right?"

Wil tore his gaze from Rhenna to peer at Blaise. "Yes."

"And what, exactly, do you think that is?"

"Your... your joy emits a protective energy. A happy fairy can protect anything they kiss."

Blaise nodded. "And an unhappy fairy?"

Wil paled. "Is a ticking time bomb. A destructive force beyond even demonstrife."

"Hence the rules of The Loophole."

Wil nodded, but even through the haze of her perception, Rhenna could tell he didn't quite understand. He'd never seen the aftermath of fairy fury. Never walked through a mile-long crater created after one gave into their grief or rage.

"Rhenna here has never known how important she is to me."

In her disembodied state, Rhenna froze, straining to perceive Blaise more clearly.

"And if she dies..."

Wil straightened, his eyes growing large. "You'll be unhappy?"

"Very."

The Omen blinked several times. "What can I do?"

"She needs the breath of the dead."

Confusion crossed Wil's guileless face. Blaise moved with a speed faster than anything Rhenna had seen as he grasped one of the demonstrife daggers at Wil's belt and stabbed him through the chest.

Rhenna was shocked. Appalled. She couldn't even... But the look on Blaise's face was fierce. If what he said was true and he really cared about her, then if she didn't take Wil's breath, Blaise could destroy a large part of the city.

Her essence wavered, shuddering, hating this choice. She'd never killed. Wouldn't condone it. Didn't want to be responsible for something like this. But with Blaise's emotions foremost in her mind, she reached out towards Wil's gasping mouth.

The pouch tied around the neck of her body shook and jittered. Some part of her awareness sensed Blaise untying it, letting the remaining breath free. She'd thought it would be a snack for later, but now she needed all the fuel she could get. The breath of the dying kept her fed and only every hundred times or so did she need to take a new body by consuming its flesh.

She couldn't use Wil—he was far too large, and she never liked being a male. But he was an Omen and his dying breath very powerful. Worth about a dozen human breaths. That along with the other one released from her pouch gave her the strength to reconnect with her new body.

Though it would likely reject her again. All Blaise had done was buy her a few minutes. And at what cost?

She coughed and sputtered as her essence took hold of muscle and skin and bone again. The breaths flowed through her, sealing her together making her joints and tendons work. She sat up on the couch and blinked her eyes open.

Blaise peered at her, gaze intense. He took her head in his hands and kissed her. His lips were warm, strong. If she hadn't been so upset with him she might have enjoyed it. But instead she pushed him away.

He didn't appear hurt by her rejection, instead his eyes were bright. He was... happy.

She had to tread carefully. "Blaise... I...." She glanced at Wil's body slumped over in the chair.

Blaise came toward her; she shrank back against the couch. He couldn't be a monster, could he?

He firmed his lips and looked at Wil. Then he removed one of the leather bracelets from his arm, the one that made him look like a surfer dude, and blew on it before tying it to Wil's wrist.

His gaze moved back to her, warm and pleased. Patient. She held herself as far away as she could.

The sound of sputtered breaths drew her focus back to Wil. He sat up and looked down in horror at the knife sticking out of his chest.

"Here, let me," Blaise said, and before either of them could do anything else, he slid the knife out cleanly, like you would when testing to see if a cake is done.

There was no blood or gore. The demonstrife weapon was clean. Blaise handed it back to Wil, handle first. The young man took it with shaking hands. Then he noticed the bracelet on his wrist.

"I have to apologize to you, Wil. I'm sorry I had to kill you."

Wil looked at him, then at Rhenna staring wide-eyed, then back again. "O-okay."

Feeling came back into Rhenna's body. Her lips still tingled from where Blaise had kissed her, and the signs of rejection she had been feeling in her body went away. The sensation dissolved like dew in the morning sunlight.

She touched her mouth. "What did you do?"

"It's not a fairy's kiss that provides protection, though some of my ancestors did take full advantage of those who believed that." His lips quirked. "It's our breath."

Wil held up his bracelet, in awe of the rare talisman he now wore. "If I take this off will I...?"

"Will you die again? No." Blaise shook his head. "Your life is your own again. I just had to borrow it for a bit."

Wil hunched his shoulders, looking younger than his years. "You could have asked," he mumbled.

Blaise either didn't hear or pretended not to. He turned to Rhenna and reached for her, but paused before grazing her hands, giving her the choice whether to grab onto him.

It only took a moment for her to decide. She gripped his hands in her own and squeezed. "And did you give me your breath as well?"

A slow smile lifted Blaise's lips, curving them up, opening them to reveal perfect, white teeth. She'd never seen him smile before. He was like a light shining through the room. She could understand why he didn't smile more often; it was blinding. The joy and happiness shooting from him was a magical thing.

"Yes," he said. "Yes, I did."

She pulled him closer and wrapped his arms around her.

"What about when I have to change bodies?" she asked.

"Good thing I can see the real you inside there." He looked into her eyes, and Rhenna knew he was seeing her for real. The true Rhenna, regardless of what skin she wore.

He leaned toward her and kissed her again. Taking her breath away, but giving her his in return.

THE LAST HOME
— OF MASTER TRANQUIL CLOUD —
by Minsoo Kang

E ver since I was a child, I was taught by the elders of my family to revere Master Tranquil Cloud as the greatest among all the illustrious ancestors of our noble clan. While he is a well-known historical figure, a high official of the royal court, and a famed scholar who was celebrated for his brilliance and integrity, I found him to be a rather mysterious figure when I came to research his life as an adult. Despite the plethora of information on him in the historical records, I found it difficult to comprehend someone who lived in an utterly different cultural context than my own. I was further beguiled by two central mysteries of his life that have never been solved. The first is the nature of the unusual addendum to his most celebrated writing, and the second, the strange circumstance of his death.

Master Tranquil Cloud lived during a particularly patriarchal time of the country's history, one in which women were shut out of positions of power, marginalized in social life, and rendered invisible in its records. For that reason, the final addendum to his great work of judicial philosophy, *Treatise on the Moral Training of Righteous Judges*, is such a surprising text as it passionately advocates for women's legal rights. Of particular interest is his detailing of seventeen typical ways in which women are treated unfairly by the courts, with their testimonies ignored, treated with undue skepticism, or even vilified as feminine lies. It ends with an earnest plea to judges, urging them to be aware of their prejudice against women, which could lead to miscarriage of justice. He asks them to consider how they would like their mothers, sisters, and daughters to be treated by the courts, and use that as the basis of their moral guidance. Given the unusual nature of the writing that provides significant insight into the social status of women in the period, the addendum has been published on its own in a number of anthologies of traditional texts under the modern title of "In Defense of Women Before the Law."

Some scholars have expressed skepticism about the level of understanding and empathy toward women demonstrated by Tranquil

Cloud who was a member of a traditional family of noble lineage. A few have even suggested that the addendum is an early modern forgery, pointing to the fact that no extant manuscript of the text that is older than a century and a half has survived. But other scholars have shown that the style of the writing is consistent with Tranquil Cloud's other works, and they have unearthed a few contemporary references to the addendum. One feminist historian has speculated that the true author may have been a woman in Tranquil Cloud's household who successfully replicated his style and surreptitiously included it in his collected writings. A recent best-selling novel details such a scenario, featuring a fictional illegitimate daughter of Tranquil Cloud who was secretly educated by him, despite legal prohibition against the teaching of letters to women. After watching her mother, a concubine of commoner status, suffer through a case of egregious injustice, she composes the addendum and places it in among her dying father's works.

Despite the universal acclaim Master Tranquil Cloud garnered as an upright statesman, as well as the foremost legal philosopher of his time, his death is also clouded in mystery as it is unknown exactly when and how he passed. While the members of our lineage clan still pay particular respect to him on the days marked for the veneration of ancestors, they can only do so before a monumental tablet, as it is unknown where he was buried. What can be ascertained is that in his sixty-fifth year, when he held the position of state councilor of the left, he was exiled by the king for his vociferous defense of the queen dowager, who was being prosecuted for treason. He was sent to a remote village in the far northern province of Sturdy Hills where he disappeared some years later.

A fantastic tale that purports to explain his final fate can be found in a number of informal works of anecdotal history and regional folktales written as entertainment for better-educated commoners, though it is known that noblemen also read them as guilty pleasures. It can in no way be regarded as a reliable historical account of Master Tranquil Cloud's last years, as the story features supernatural elements. The addendum on the legal rights of women is not mentioned in it, but it points to what could be construed as an explanation of how he came to write it—that an uncanny encounter with spirits may have inspired him to do so.

When Master Tranquil Cloud reached his sixtieth year, he found himself in such a content time of his life that he could not possibly have imagined the calamities that would befall him in the years that followed. After lauded tenures as the minister of punishments, the director of the Office of Forbidden Affairs, and the governor of the province of Resplendent Fields, he was due to ascend to the highest level of officialdom in the State Council. His reputation as a great scholar had already been established with the publication of *Treatise on the Moral Training of Righteous Judges*, which was universally regarded as the greatest work of judicial philosophy produced in the land. In it, he argued against the old legalist philosophers who advocated the use of stringent laws, strict enforcement, and harsh punishments as tools of social and political stability and control. Tranquil Cloud asserted that no matter how necessary the laws were, they were liable to be perverted and misused if they were practiced by judges lacking proper morals. A country with few laws but with many good judges can be a just place, he reasoned, whereas one with many laws but few good judges will inevitably degenerate into inequity. The bulk of the book details a program of ethical education for the proper moral cultivation of judges, including the practice of benevolence for all those concerned in a legal case.

Given his high achievements as both a statesman and a scholar, he imagined an easy course through the rest of his life. But then, just as his time as governor was coming to an end, misfortune fell upon him like a series of lightning bolts from a suddenly erupting storm. His beloved son, an official at the Ministry of Military Affairs who was serving as an inspector in the northern border, was killed in a barbarian raid. Not long after, his daughter died in childbirth, her baby son surviving for only a month before joining her in oblivion. His wife then fell ill and suffered terribly as an invalid for years before finally passing.

Even as he had to face such personal tragedies, his position in the government became precarious. After he returned to the capital from the province of Resplendent Fields and took up his new position as the state councilor of the left, a major crisis erupted in the royal court. The king discovered the scandalous and unseemly circumstances under which his mother had been deprived of her position as queen and eventually executed when he was still a little boy, which sent him on a path of frenzied vengeance. He arrested all the old officials who had been in the government during the time of his mother's downfall and executed or exiled those he held responsible for her demise.

He ordered the death of all three surviving former concubines of his father as well. Then he went after the queen dowager who had replaced his mother as the royal consort. Many of those who were persecuted had indeed been involved in the execution of the king's mother for various political and personal reasons, but it was generally known that the queen dowager was innocent. She came from a minor lineage clan that had only a few junior-level officials in the government at the time of her marriage, and she had been chosen rather hurriedly to become the new queen so that the whole sordid affair could be forgotten. Yet the king meant to get rid of the woman who had taken his mother's place beside his father.

Because of his preoccupation with avenging his mother, the monarch was neglecting his duties of the state so that all the important works in the kingdom was at a standstill. Many officials, consequently, thought that sacrificing the life of the guiltless dowager queen was an acceptable price to pay to finally allay the king's wrath. But there were others, including Tranquil Cloud, who felt that the bloodletting had gone on long enough and claimed too many innocent lives already. In the crucial moment before the king was set to announce the prosecution of the queen dowager, Tranquil Cloud led the formal remonstrance against the course.

For ten days, he and many other officials sat before the throne room, begging the king to spare the life of the queen dowager. It ended with their mass arrest, which was followed by a trial for disloyalty to the monarch. Before Tranquil Cloud was deprived of his position and sent away in exile, he learned in prison that his long-suffering wife had passed away.

The journey to the remote corner of the Province of Sturdy Hills was long and arduous, but Tranquil Cloud's fortune brightened a little when he finally arrived. The local magistrate was a great admirer of *Treatise on the Moral Training of Righteous Judges* and also sympathetic to the circumstances under which Tranquil Cloud ended up in exile. So the magistrate provided Tranquil Cloud with a modest but comfortable home on the outskirts of the village and even assigned his head servant, a large jolly fellow who was called Bull Dung, to see to his needs. And so Tranquil Cloud settled down to lead a quiet life of mourning for his family and meditating on the unfathomable vicissitudes of life.

One mystery that puzzled and distressed him was the disappearance of a girl named Butterfly who was one of three servants he had been allowed to take with him in exile. She was young, not yet twenty, and had been an orphan street beggar until his wife had taken pity on her and brought her into their household. A diligent and modest girl, she had always appeared content to be in Tranquil Cloud's service, so he could not understand why she had run away. When he told Bull Dung that she was missing, the man offered to look for her but returned a few days later without having found any trace of her. It was yet another loss for Tranquil Cloud, who had been fond of her, but his sadness was soon eclipsed by the great grief that overwhelmed him when he was visited by the admiring magistrate, who informed him that the queen dowager had been executed by the order of the king.

About a year into Tranquil Cloud's exile, the magistrate came for his regular visit to pay his respects. He was accompanied by Bull Dung, who carried the magistrate's gifts of food and liquor on a wood-framed carrier. In the course of the leisurely afternoon conversation between Tranquil Cloud and the magistrate, the latter revealed that he was investigating an utterly confounding case of bloody murder. Five days before, the entire family of the richest merchant in town had been found dead in their sleeping chambers with their bodies mutilated. The merchant, his mother, his wife, and two sons had their bodies ripped open and their vital organs cut out in the middle of the night. The strange thing was, there had been no less than twelve household servants, but none of them had heard anything. They were arrested and interrogated for three days, and their rooms were thoroughly searched, but there was nothing that implicated them in the horrific crime. To add to the mystery, the magistrate's soldiers discovered a grave in an obscure corner of the backyard, which they dug up and found the body of a young girl. From the clothing on the corpse, the servants identified her as one of their own who had gone missing a few months before. As she had been deeply unhappy at the household, they had all assumed that she had run away. The body was too decomposed to yield any clue as to how she had died.

At the end of the day, as Tranquil Cloud walked the magistrate out the house gate, he noticed Bull Dung leaning against a nearby tree, apparently deep asleep. After they bade farewell, the magistrate walked over to his servant and woke him up.

"What is the matter with you?" the magistrate asked. "You seem tired all the time these days. Every time I turn around, you fall asleep somewhere. Are you ill?"

"No, my lord," Bull Dung said in a listless voice as he slowly got to his feet.

Tranquil Cloud watched them leave, feeling anxious with the presentiment that something terrible was about to occur. He mulled over the horrific story of the murder of the merchant and his family, the dead servant girl, and his own servant girl Butterfly who had gone missing. He shook off his unsettling thoughts, but that night he dreamt of an elderly servant woman who had taken care of him in his early childhood. The servant's mother had been a shaman, so she knew many stories of ghosts, goblins, and monsters. Despite the fact that most of them were scary tales, he was thrilled to hear them and always asked for more. Now, all the terrifying creatures returned to him in his dream and tormented him until the morning.

A few months later, Bull Dung returned with more food and other gifts from the magistrate. When Tranquil Cloud saw him, he was shocked to see that the once hefty servant was reduced to an emaciated state, with his eyes sunken and his skin pale. As he was panting desperately from the effort of carrying the gifts, Tranquil Cloud had him sit down at the edge of the veranda and had some water brought to him.

"You look worse than when I saw you last. Have you gone to a doctor?"

"My lord, the magistrate, sent me to one, respected sir. But he could find no cause for my condition. Since I have no appetite, he advised that I continue to work so that I would grow hungry from it."

"To no avail, I take it."

"No, respected sir."

"Have you been doing anything differently recently? Some new food or drink you've been taking?"

To Tranquil Cloud's surprise, Bull Dung's sickly face blushed with embarrassment.

"No, respected sir. Not that I can think of."

Tranquil Cloud had spent enough time interrogating people at the Ministry of Punishments and the Office of Forbidden Affairs to know when someone was lying. So he found it odd that Bull Dung was obviously hiding something that he apparently knew to be making his health deteriorate. It was apparently better for him to keep getting sicker than to reveal the cause of his illness. But the servant was not a prisoner brought before Tranquil Cloud to be examined, so he did not to press him further.

Bull Dung got some rest, and then he set out to leave. When he walked out the house gate, some vague intuition made Tranquil Cloud follow him. On the road, he saw that Bull Dung was not heading back to the magistrate's house in the village but going in the opposite direction, toward a nearby forest. Tranquil Cloud hesitated for a moment before setting off after him.

A few spans away from the house, Bull Dung suddenly left the road and entered in among the thickly standing trees. Tranquil Cloud went in as well, keeping his distance without losing sight of the servant. After a while, when he realized that Bull Dung was not alone, he quickly hid behind a tree. He peeked carefully around the trunk to see that the man was talking to a young woman in a white dress whose beauty, even at that distance, made her luminous. As he watched on, the woman stepped up to Bull Dung, took off his clothes, and pulled him to the ground. She then disrobed herself, revealing immaculate skin of pure white, and straddled Bull Dung. After she moved vigorously on top of him for a time, she got up, dressed again, and walked away.

When she was gone, Tranquil Cloud walked cautiously over to Bull Dung and found him dead with his eyes wide open with a look of horror on his face. The expression sent a chill down his spine. He looked around and saw that darkness was descending with the onset of dusk, so he started running back to the road. But the terror from what he had witnessed disoriented his mind, and he lost all sense of direction. As night fell, he found himself completely lost among the dark trees.

After wandering through the woods for an accountable period of time, he came across Bull Dung's body again, having apparently walked in a circle. When he approached the corpse, he was horrified to see three foxes feeding on its vital organs.

"It is all right, my lord," a quiet, gentle voice came next to him, startling him greatly despite its reassuring tone. "That will not happen to you. You are safe."

Tranquil Cloud turned and found another fox looking up at him.

"Do you know who I am, my lord?" the fox asked.

"I know what you are," Tranquil Cloud replied, on the verge of fearful panic.

"What am I, my lord?"

"You are a fox demon. You and the others."

"What do you know about us?"

"You appear before men in isolated places," he said, remembering the stories the old servant woman had told him during his childhood, "you tempt them into lying with you, then you take away their vital strength until they become weak and obedient. When they are at the end of their strength, you finish them off and eat their organs."

"Why do we do that?"

"Because you are hungry, and because you are evil."

"Are human beings evil because they hunger for the meat of cows and pheasants?"

"What will you do to me?"

"You will be not be harmed, my lord."

"Why do you call me that?"

"Because I have served you for a long time."

"What?"

"Do you not see who I am?"

Tranquil Cloud stared at the fox until the animal transformed itself into a young girl.

"Butterfly? Is that you?" he asked in astonishment.

"Yes, my lord."

"How... you ran away and became a fox demon?"

"I did not run away, my lord."

"What happened to you then?"

"When we first came to this village, Bull Dung befriended me. One day, I was on my way to the village market when I ran into him. He promised to show me a short cut through the forest. There, he raped me, killed me, and buried my body here. But my sorrow and rage over how I died turned me into a fox spirit so I could avenge myself. I met other fox spirits who had been women and girls who died under such circumstances. We came together, and we helped one another."

Tranquil Cloud jumped with fright when he realized that three other women were standing near him. One was elderly, another young, and the third a mere child. He could see that they were the foxes who had been eating Bull Dung's organs because their lips and chins were covered with blood.

"That is Cricket," Butterfly said, indicating the young woman, who bowed respectfully to Tranquil Cloud. "She was also a servant, at the house of the richest merchant in the village. He and his family abused her terribly, the merchant, his mother, his wife, and his sons. One day, they beat her so badly that she died. So they buried her body and pretended that she had run away. She was also transformed into a fox spirit, so that she could take revenge against the family."

Butterfly pointed to the elderly woman, who also bowed to Tranquil Cloud. "That's the blacksmith's widow. After her husband died, his brother wanted to take her property, so he accused her of having killed the blacksmith with poison. He bribed the judge who ordered her execution."

Butterfly turned to the last of the fox spirits. "And that's Spring Blossom." The little girl bowed to Tranquil Cloud. "Her father wanted a son as he already had three daughters. When Spring Blossom was born, he did not want to raise another girl, so he took her to a river and drowned her."

Tranquil Cloud looked at each of the women, feeling his fear replaced by pity for their terrible end.

Butterfly addressed Master Tranquil Cloud again. "Yes, we sometimes lure men into isolated places and sap their vital strength before eating their organs. We also sneak into houses and eat the people there without making a noise. That much of what you've been told about us is true. What's not true is that we are evil. We do not do such things out of hunger or desire to cause harm for no good reason. In this world where we do not have a voice, where we cannot attain justice for the evilest crimes committed against us, Heaven has seen fit to grant us a way of redressing the wrong done to us. We do not kill innocent people. We only harm those who harmed us. Those who have vilified us as evil, they judge us only for our actions without knowing the reasons behind them. But you, my lord, I know that you can understand our position, being such an eminent scholar of justice."

"If that is so, then why... why have you shown yourself to me? What have I done that I deserve the same fate as Bull Dung?"

"You do not, my lord," Butterfly said in a reassuring tone. "As I told you, you are safe. We have brought you here for a completely different reason."

"What is it?"

"Please come with us, my lord. I promise you once again that no harm will come to you."

Tranquil Cloud hesitated for a long time, but he ultimately decided to trust Butterfly's word. Besides, he reasoned, if they meant to kill him and eat his organs, there was no reason why they could not do so then and there.

"Very well," he told Butterfly.

They walked in silence through the dark forest for a long time until they came across a clearing with a great flat rock in the middle. When they got near, a gate appeared on the rock's surface, which opened to let them in. Beyond the gate, Tranquil Cloud found himself in a beauteous land of abundant fields of green and yellow grass, freshly flowing water, and willow trees with their slender branches dancing gracefully in a gentle wind. There were also clean and well-kept houses here and there, from which women of all ages came out to greet them.

In the middle of the wondrous place, there was a magnificent mansion with lofty pillars holding up a roof with bright red tiles. As Tranquil Cloud and the crowd of women approached the place, a screen door slid open and an elderly woman in a shimmering white dress emerged.

"Your Majesty!" Tranquil Cloud said out loud as he beheld the sight of the executed queen dowager. He immediately prostrated himself before her.

"Master Tranquil Cloud, please get up," the queen dowager said. "It is I who should be prostrating myself before you, for all that you did to try to save my life. I know that you could not even see your wife in her last days or mourn her properly because of your actions."

"Your Majesty! How I grieve over what befell you!"

"It was a sorrowful end for me indeed, but raise your head and see that I am well now. Heaven has seen fit to turn me into a fox spirit. Even as we speak, the fate of the man who has done me wrong is being sealed. For what he did to me, to you, and to so many righteous officials who sought to dissuade him from his unjust course, he will come to no good end."

"But why have you brought me here, Your Majesty?" Tranquil Cloud said with tears streaming down his face. "I feel nothing but guilt at how I failed you."

"It was not within your power to save me, so trouble yourself no longer. Come, stand before me, I beseech you."

Tranquil Cloud got to his feet but kept his head bowed in a respectful manner.

"I have remained in this world not just to avenge myself," the dowager queen said, "but also to reward those who sacrificed themselves on my behalf. In a few years, the current king will be gone, and a new king will summon you back to the capital. But you no longer desire to return to officialdom. I know this because my transformation into a fox spirit gave me the power to see into the souls of living people. You have secured your reputation as a brilliant scholar, a revered statesman, and a courageous official who stood up for justice when it was dangerous to do so. You have also lost all those you loved in this world. What you want now is to rest, to find some measure of peace in the remaining years of your life. For the service you have rendered me, that is exactly what I offer. Stay here with us, in this secret world of fox spirits, where you will lead a comfortable and tranquil life. If you decide to go back, I will not stop you. But I know that your soul is so very tired, and you want nothing more than to be at peace at last."

"Stay with us, Master Tranquil Cloud," all the fox spirits chanted in unison, their heads bowing in respect. "Let this be your final home."

The story ends in this way without revealing Tranquil Cloud's decision.

What is known in the historical records is that six years after Tranquil Cloud's exile began, the king was dethroned in a palace coup. The new monarch exonerated Tranquil Cloud and summoned him back to the capital. When the royal messengers arrived in the village, they could find no trace of him as, according to the testimony of the local villagers, he had disappeared some years back. The only thing of significance they found in his abandoned house was his last writings, which included the addendum in defense of women.

— YOUR TWO BETTER HALVES —
A Dream, with Fairies, in Spanglish
by Carlos Hernandez

Welcome! As you read this story, you will occasionally be asked to record a letter. Do so using the table below! (Suggestion: make a tiny mark, so you can read the story again and record your choices many times!)

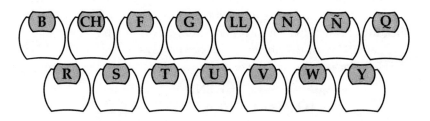

Don't read this story straight through! As you read, you'll be asked to make decisions. Jump forwards or backwards in the story to the letter or punctuation mark that corresponds to you choice.

Also, sometimes you won't have a choice, and the story will tell you where to go. Like now. To start dreaming in Spanglish, *go to ¡*.

— ¡ —

You are in Fairyland. ¡Llegaste después de todo! ¡You made it!
"Here" is a field. You stand inside a circle of boulder-sized mushrooms. It's a beautiful, blue, green-smelling day, clouds like dumplings, breeze rushing by like the blood of the world.

You're not alone in the circle. Quite the contrary: you're surrounded by fairies. Scores of them. They're just now deciding amongst themselves whether they should eat you.

¿How will you stop them?

If you brandish your mighty magical sword, *go to F*.
If you try to explain everything calmly and rationally, *go to X*.
If you grab the nearest wineskin and start drinking, *go to CH*.

– A –

Big mistake. The fey swarm you, baring their mismatched, impossible teeth. Some of their teeth are like bouquets of needles as they pierce you, fine, straight lines of pure pain, and some are like blunt knives that, yes, can cut, but only after a great deal of sawing.

Your screaming and begging matters not to them. When one fey has eaten its fill of your flesh, it makes way for three other fairies, who dine with equal gusto. It's only a matter of time until the last mouthful of your marrow has been sucked out of your bones. What's left of your skeleton lies scattered over the sward like a vase irrevocably shattered.

You are dead.

¿So what, exactly, was your big mistake? *You read this section.* There is no fair choice that leads to section **A**. That means you cheated, you cheating cheater. Your punishment is to be eaten alive.

¿Okay? ¿Got all the cheating out of your system? Excellent. Now, start the story again, and make an honest choice at the beginning.

THE END
TO START A NEW STORY, *go to* ¡.

– B –

¡RECORD THE LETTER B!

You love your cloak so. It is Bibliocapa, The Library Cloak, and it can take you anywhere. Every word that's ever been written is as easy to look up as making a wish. Every book that's ever been written lies waiting inside, begging for you to break its spine.

It saved your life. While your parents tried to trap you in an oubliette of words, to demean so thoroughly, you would become blind to truth and life and even yourself, you stole Bibliocapa out of the family treasure chest. They never noticed, for they hated reading. The Library Cloak was wholly repugnant to them.

But not to you. Whenever you put on Bibliocapa, you were transported, far from your parents. You became a bodiless watcher of other peoples' lives, a spectating specter who traveled to cities that exist and cities that don't.

All the while, your understanding of the human pageant grew. You have tasted foreign foods without tasting them; you have been governed by physical laws that do not apply to this world; you've had every kind of sex, thanks to Bibliocapa. *Every* kind of sex.

To be frank, however, Bibliocapa is part of the reason you feel confused. It is so easy to disappear within it. It is so easy to become an eye, just an eye and nothing else, absorbing any light that strikes your retina. ¿Wherefore an ego? ¿What good a point of view when the vistas are endless? ¿Why bother with an "I," when there is so much of everything else beyond the self?

IF YOU RECORDED THE LETTER F, READ THE BONUS TEXT IN THE BOX!

And the answer, of course, is that you'll wink into unexistence, just like la dragón Fuegadura once she pooped out that sword. The life in your eye will die without an I

In short, you're not sure if you will continue to exist if you lose Bibliocapa. You're keeping the cloak.

You strip off your dress and drop your sword beside it. You pull your cloak around you, but you leave the hood down defiantly, and look from fairy to fairy. The grass beneath your bare feet writhes like a bucket filled with fey who are half shredded paper and half earthworms. The wind smells like the blood of the world.

"¡A new fey is born!" say the fey, reverential, yet jocund.

"¿Where?" you ask.

But it is happening right in front of you. ¡The new fey is half your former sword and half your former pretty dress!

Now a unified, if violently hewn-together, whole being, the newborn fey hovers in front of you. Its posture brims with menace.

"¡Pelea! ¡Bronca! ¡Lucha!" yell the fey. "¡Fight!"

The newborn fey launches itself at you.

If you use your cloak to defend yourself, *go to* **G.**

If you refuse to fight your former pretty dress and former sword, *go to* **O.**

— C —

You have no history of swallowing swords, no training, no practice. You have no idea what will happen if you stick Quitanombre down your throat. On the one hand, this is a very bad idea.

On the other hand, fuck it. Que se vaya el mundo al infierno.

You brandish Quitanombre and, just as your name leaves your body, you slide the blade all the way down your esophagus. The sword goes down surprisingly easily: but as you proved when you swallowed your parents to get to Fairyland,

IF YOU RECORDED THE LETTER S, READ THE BONUS TEXT IN THE BOX!

as well as the size-13-men's-oxfords-shoebox-cum-diaorama,

you can gulp down great big objects when you have a mind to.

"¡No!" yells the Queen of the Fey. But she is powerless to stop you. When you swallow Quitanombre up to the hilt, you not only forget your name, but erase the Queen's name from *her* mind as well.

"¿Who am I?" says the Queen of the Fey, using your mouth. There's presently a huge hilt sticking out of it, so your voice is somewhat muffled.

"¡You are the handmaid to the Queen of the Fey!" yell all the fey at once. "¡You are sworn to obey the Queen of the Fey!"

"¿And who is the Queen of the Fey?" asks the fey formerly known as the Queen of the Fey.

"¡She is!" say the fey, using whatever body parts they have to point at you.

If you go along with their lie, *go to* **R**.
If you'd rather make up your own lie, *go to* **Y**.

— CH —

¡RECORD THE LETTER CH!

A fey folk is half of one thing yoked haphazardly with half of another thing. For instance, a fey may be half watermelon, and half advertising campaign that looked good during the presentation but somewhat missed the mark in execution. Or it might be half the best cursive L you've ever seen, and half male hagfish, lost and lonely without its enormous, monstrous better half. Or maybe it's half a coil of rope that hopes someday to be a lasso, and half the biome at the bottom of the sea that forms from the carcass of a dead whale. You get the picture.

When you went to grab a wineskin, therefore, you actually drank from the body of a fey who was, and remains, half wineskin and half a never-ending fireworks show.

"The name's Jesús," says the half-wineskin, half fireworks-show fey.

"I'm Rita," you say. "¿Was that a faux pas, to drink of your body?"

"No. But we are married now."

"Oh. I ... didn't mean to do that."

Jesús shrugs, as best a half wineskin and half fireworks show can shrug. "I don't make the rules. And the rule is, if you drink from a fey's body, you marry them."

"¿Even if by accident?"

"¡In Fairyland, the only way to get married is by accident!"

You phrase your next question especially delicately. "¿Is... is it okay with you? ¿To be married?"

"¡¿Okay?! ¡It's wonderful!"

¡Ah, what a relief! "¡Great! Then I think it's wonderful too."

"¡But soft, dear spouse! Tell me about yourself, my, um... ¿shall I call you wife? ¿Or husband?"

"Husband-wife, thank you. Well. I just ate my parents."

"¿Whilst standing in a circle of mushrooms?"

"Yes, exactly."

The fireworks speed up and grow more impressive. "You are a formidable husband-wife. Most humans lack the courage to eat their parents. That explains how you got here."

¡This Jesús is all right! "I'm done with the human world," you reply. "But tell me something about yourself my, um... ¿husband-wife?"

"Please refer to me as 'the old battle-ax,' husband-wife. Before I was half wineskin and half fireworks show, I was half one can of PBR crushed against a hipster's forehead, and half the word 'foudroyant' on the lips of the second-place finisher of a spelling bee. Irony and loss: not a good combination for a happy life. But fey can remake themselves, so I did. It's still as hard as changing your mind, which is as hard as changing the world, but it's not as hard as being a human like you, where every single idea needs a body of its own. How heavy and cumbersome, all that embodiment. I don't know how you do it, husband-wife."

"I don't either, my old battle-ax. That's why I'm here. To know me."

"I will help you any way I can, dearest husband-wife." Jesús sounds well and truly smitten. And that inclines you toward smitten-ness yourself.

You look around at the fey surrounding you. "¿So, my dear old battle-ax, are the fey still planning on eating me?"

Both the half-wineskin and the half-fireworks-show parts of Jesús inflate indignantly. "¿Eat you? ¿My husband-wife? ¡Just let them try! ¡I will defend you unto the last drop of wine in my skin!"

Go to I.

— D —

"Henceforth," say the fey, in a stentorian chorus of voices, "you shall be known, for all time, and in all places, by the name we give you now, that shall knit itself downward into your being and re-ligametize your bones. That name is: Rita."

¿But what is this? ¡You remember now! "¡That already is my name!" you say gleefully, quickly sheathing Quitanombre so you don't forget it again. "¡Thank you for reminding me!"

"Coño," the fey folk say dolefully. "Of all the lousy luck."

Go to I.

— E —

You undress out of your dress and fling La Ogrificadora into the sky. It doesn't fall, but rather grows and grows, until it becomes Fairyland's new sky. A red-with-white-polka dots sky.

"Weird flex, Rita," says the Queen of the Fey via your mouth, "but okay."

"¿My new fey form?" you prompt her.

"Ah, yes. There's just one more thing to consider."

If you recorded the letter CH and married Jesús, *go to N.*
If you didn't record CH and are still single, *go to T.*

— F —

¡RECORD THE LETTER F!

Your sword, named Quitanombre, the "Name-Remover," was created when the dragón Fuegadura, with a mighty snore, accidentally snorted up the blade from the hoard on which she slept. There in her belly, it was forged anew, annealed by magic dragón-fire. The eldritch runes running the length of its blade, which once recorded the history of the world, sublimated away.

Seven days later, Fuegadura finally passed the sword. The screams of la pobre dragón echoed throughout the countryside. So intense was her pain that she forgot her name, and that she was a dragón, and even that she was alive. And everyone knows that the second you forget to Cartesianly believe in your own existence, you disappear. Fuegadura vanished with a pop.

¡The people cheered! ¡They were finally free of the dragón! And then, being people, they murdered each other, fighting over her hoard, until very few remained. Someone of your lineage must have numbered among the survivors, since you have the sword now: but that ancestor's name is lost to history, which isn't surprising, since they stole a sword that erases names.

You've never drawn the sword, since you're fond of your name (the one thing your parents got right). But, as they say, desperate times. You brandish Quitanombre now and, careful to remind yourself that even without a name, you still believe in your own existence, say, "¡Back off, fey folk, or I shall slay you with my magic sword!"

"¿And who are you to threaten us?" ask the fey.

"I have no idea," you reply.

¡The fey-folk—¡surprise!—love this! They cavort, caper, carouse, creep, combust, canter, cantan canciones, and, all the while, carefully, Cartesianly confirm their own qualia.

Each fey is half one kind of thing and half another kind of thing unceremoniously thrust together. There is the fey that is half butter churn and half capybara; the fey that is half the melancholy of a misspent youth and half last-gen iPhone; the fey that is half quockerwodger and half a tornado of DaVinci notes; the fey that is half patchouli and half flock of flying mustaches, etc. They dance all around you with whatever parts they have. It's a joyous, if messy, cotillion.

"¿May we name you?" they ask. "¡If you let us name you, we won't eat you!"

If you let them, *go to* **D**.
If you don't, *go to* **J**.

– G –

¡RECORD THE LETTER G!

The newborn fey's attack is eager, but clumsy. It was only just born, after all, and the sword has never had to wield itself. Plus, your pretty dress has never had to move on its own. You spare a pitying smile for the poor thing's stumbling, preposterous salvo.

But it *is* trying to kill you. With matadorial elegance, you envelop the newborn fey in your cloak, and Bibliocapa swallows it and teleports it away, and now it's part of someone else's story.

You flip the cloak off your arms and enjoy the spears of cool wind striking your body. "I don't think I know me any better," you say, "but winning a battle makes me *feel* more like me."

"Knowing's overrated," the fey respond. "Feeling like yourself is all that matters. ¡That's how we roll, and look how happy we are!"

"Feeling's not good enough. I also need to know."

The fey metaphorically and, where anatomically possible, physically shake their heads. "Fine. You'll have to meet the Queen of the Fey, then. Only she can help you."

"Okay. ¿Where is she?"

The fey grow reverential. Religion fills their voices. "She is all around us."

You look around. "¿Is she invisible?"

The fey consider this. "Practically. She's microscopic."

"Okay. Anyone have a microscope?"

"Nope," say all the fey at once.

"So. Then. ¿How do I meet her?"

All the fey with fingers hold up one finger to ask you for a moment. All the fey with noses scrunch their noses and, if they have hands, rub them. But it doesn't stop all the fey that surround you, the scores and scores of them, from sneezing on you, all at the same time.

You're caught in a germy cloud of contagion. Virulent vapor sparkles in the sunlight all around you. It is the most infectious of rainbows.

"¡Gah!" you yell, trying not to breathe. "¿Why did you do that? ¡That's disgusting!"

"We would appreciate," say the fey, a little haughtily, "if you would not speak of our Queen that way. You said you wanted to meet her. Since the Queen of the Fey is half ragweed pollen and have rhinovirus, the only way to meet her is to contract her. Now, we are unified by the permanent sickness that is a monarchy. ¡Long live the Queen!"

Go, sniffling and snuffling, to **H.**

You cough. Your nose flows. Your aching body makes you moan.

You have clearly contracted a cold. Or maybe it's your allergies acting up. Given that Queen is both allergen and virus, ¿porque no los dos?

"¿Why did you make such an... unpleasant fairy your sovereign queen?" you ask, having a seat in the grass. The urge to curl up and sleep is growing more and more irresistible.

"She is the most powerful among us," say the fey, not without regret. A dozen fairies rush to help you to your feet. "¡Don't fall asleep! ¡She'll kill you if you succumb to her!"

"A few minutes ago you were ready to eat me. ¿Now you're trying to save me?"

Those fey who have both a left foot and a hallux screw their big toes into the ground bashfully. "Well, you're almost one of us now."

You sniffle. "¿Almost?"

"Well, you're half

IF YOU RECORDED THE LETTER Q, READ THE BONUS TEXT IN THE BOX!

> sword of forgetfulness,

IF YOU RECORDED THE LETTER B, READ THE BONUS TEXT IN THE BOX!

> library cloak,

IF YOU RECORDED THE LETTER W, READ THE BONUS TEXT IN THE BOX!

> pretty polkadot dress,

but you're still half-Rita. You have to fey-ify the other half you came in with to make you fully fey."

"That is, Rita," says a voice that isn't your voice, yet coming out of your mouth, "if you still wish to become a fey."

You touch your face. "¿Who said that?" you ask.

"I am the Queen of the Fey," your mouth says, though, again, it is not you who speaks. "I am in you, and I have in part joined with you. But only in part. You still cling to your mortal half, and all the limits therein. ¿Will you shed it now and join us?"

"I didn't eat my parents for nothing," you say, between coughs and throat-clearings.

"Excellent," the Queen of the Fey says in your voice. "Then let us begin the final transformation."

If you recorded the letter Q and kept your sword, Quitanombre, *go to* **L**.
If you recorded the letter B and kept your cloak, Bibliocapa, *go to* **P**.
If you recorded the letter W and kept your polkadot dress, La Ogrificadora, *go to* **Z**.

— I —

"So," say the fey, who, though they still surround you, aren't looking nearly teethy and hungry. "¿What brings you here?"

"I'm tired of not knowing who I am," you reply. "Eating my parents only removed pain. Which is nice, don't get me wrong. But it didn't teach me anything about myself."

"Oh," the fey, who, in perfect choreography, pshaw you. "Removing pain is the most important part. Now you can think clearly. The rest is easy."

"¿It is? ¿Then tell me: who am I?"

"You are two things violently cloven together."

You blink.

"Tell us your halves," the fey add, "and you'll know the whole."

"Well," you start, unsure. "I am a human woman named Rita."

"Good, that's one half. ¿What's the other?"

"I don't know."

"¡She's half Rita, half sword!" says one factions of the fey.

"¡She's half Rita, half cloak!" says a second faction.

"¡She's half Rita, half pretty dress!" says a third.

IF YOU RECORDED THE LETTER CH, READ THE BONUS TEXT IN THE BOX!

"¡She's my better half!" adds Jesús. All the fairies in fairyland take a moment to heartily congratulate Jesús and you on your marriage.

The fey fall silent. After a while and a great deal of thought, they finally say, as one: "Too many halves. That's why you're confused. Get rid of two things."

If you keep only your sword, *go to* **Q**.
If you keep only your cloak, *go to* **B**.
If you keep only your pretty dress, *go to* **W**.

— J —

"I've got a better idea," you say. "¿Why don't you help me remember my real name?"

"It's pretty dangerous, that," say the fey, in unison. "It's one thing if you just tell us your name. Then it's just a word, just sounds lined up in a certain order. We don't know everything that the name's invested in, all the history you've shoved into it, and probably we'll never get to. But to *derive* a name. Well. We'll have to know all about you. And then. Well. Then you're *known*. ¿You sure you want us, the fey folk, to know you that well?"

If you say "Yes," *go to* **X**.
If you say, "On second thought, you give me a name," *go to* **D**.

— K —

"I will wear my cloak forever," you say.

And once you make that statement, you assume your true fey form: in less than a second you become half the most complete library in the universe and half the joyous, cozy feeling of being alone inside the universe's most complete library.

Your body disappears. The cloak that is you now hovers above the ground of its own accord. Omniscience courses through your entire being. Omniscience, curiously, tastes like warm apple cider.

"¡Tell us a story!" the fey say to you, as one.

You have no mouth and no voice, but you can make your feelings known. You spread your cloak-self open and fill Fairyland with the feeling of this question: "¿What kind of story would you like to hear?"

"¡One where fairies eat humans!"

You know just the thing. A book that has never been is born within your eternal folds of knowledge, and your cloak-self spread and grows to become pages so large that every fey in Fairyland can read them, even if they lack eyes.

"Once upon a time," the story begins, "there was a girl named Rita."

THE END
TO START A NEW STORY, *go to* **¡**.

— L —

"You kept Quitanombre," you begin, but it is the Queen speaking through you again. "That means you favor discarding your history over keeping it. You will defend yourself before you forgive others. You like to bring a sword to a knife-fight."

"Sounds about right," you agree.

She sighs. "The fact is, you'd rather surf history than study it. The future, in your mind, is a lotto-ball mixing drum: any guess you make about the future is probably going to be wrong, ¿so why bother? Lotto is a sucker's game, and so's the future. ¿Am I right?"

"You're not wrong," you reply, a little less pleased with yourself. She's right about you. *Too* right about you.

The Queen, accustomed to being too right, nods. "You are too tied to the present. You're scarred by the past and scared of the future. You need a new start."

"¿How?"

"Make a present of your sword to me, and I will give you a form that will heal your emotional damage and let you contemplate the future without fear."

If you would rather swallow your sword than give it to the Queen, *go to C.*

If you give your sword to the queen, *go to Ñ.*

— LL —

¡RECORD THE LETTER LL!

"You are so generous," says the newborn fey, now named Rita, like you.

"I don't own Ritaness," you reply, sheepish and pleased.

"But look, Rita. I don't want to get in your way. I can make it easy for both of us."

And with that, the newborn fey named Rita grows, just the way the dress La Ogrificadora gave you the power to quadruple in size and eat your parents.

Only new Rita doesn't stop growing. She grows and grows and grows. Pretty dress and cloak fill the sky. Soon, they *become* the sky—the firmament is now that lovely crimson color that drew you to the pretty dress in the first place, and the polka dots have become the new stars. The cloak exerts its influence, too—it organizes the polka dots into constellations from all over time and space and imagination, drawn from the stories housed in every library that ever was. Light and myth and wonder rain over you and all fey.

"¡Thank you so much!" say the fey. "You've given us the gift of astronomy *and* astrology. ¿How can we repay you?"

"Take me to your queen," you say.

"Of course," they say.

And then, as one, they sneeze on you.

Imagine a foggy morning. Water vapor hangs in the air, swirls all around you. Each tiny water droplet wears a crown of rainbows bestowed upon it by rays of sunlight. That is exactly what the current mucosal fog in which you suddenly find yourself looks like.

"¡Gross!" you yell. "¿Why did you all sneeze on me?"

"You asked us to take you to our queen," the fairies reply, a little shocked at your rudeness. "And the Queen of the Fairies is half ragweed pollen and half rhinovirus. So, well, now that you're infected by her, there is literally no way we can take you any closer to her. So you're welcome."

Go to H.

— M —

"Being Rita," you begin, slowly turning in circles to address the fey, "has been kind of a bummer so far. On the other hand, becoming a force of the universe, without awareness or desire, sounds like Nirvana. I'm gonna do that."

"So be it," says the Queen of the Fey, through you.

In an instant, La Ogrificadora makes you bigger than the mushroom circle, bigger than Fairyland, bigger than the planet, the solar system, the galaxy. You stop being able to know how long all this is taking, as space and time combine within you and you become both at once: spacetime. You exceed the size of your supercluster, several of them, all of them, you fill the universe, you can't tell the difference between you and the universe. Matter dark and light, all energy known and unknown, all of everything *combined* takes up less room than you.

But then, you stop taking up room. You stop being an object of your own and start to act as a medium for other objects. You stop rubbing up *against* things and instead move *through* them. You bind, or break the bonds, of subatomic particles. New combinations of matter emerge through you. You excrete new physical laws into being.

Thanks to you, quantum physics grows slightly stranger—¡and it was already demasiado extraño!

Someday, perhaps, some genius will figure out the laws of you, the exact, weird role you play in the order of things. But that won't happen for a long, long time, if ever. For now, enjoy the silent, subtle power over all matter that you now mindlessly exert.

THE END
TO START A NEW STORY, *go to* ¡.

— N —

¡RECORD THE LETTER N!

"Beloved husband-wife," says Jesús, your half-wineskin, half-fireworks show spouse (aka "the old battleax"), "since we are married, we have the option of joining our bodies together."

"¿Like conjoined twins?" you ask.

"Very much like conjoined twins, yes. But with a difference: the half you choose to bond with will double in size."

"¿What do you mean?"

Jesús takes a deep breath, the prelude to the drunken soliloquy that follows: "You can, husband-wife, partake of either my wineskin half or my eternal-fireworks half, and it will become a *whole* thing, which is what happens mathematically when two halves are combined. ¡Double the booze! ¡Or double the fireworks! That's whole will be where we connect, the seat of our union. We'll still keep one half of ourselves distinct from the other, however—the object of a union isn't destruction of the self, after all, but enhancement. So if being double the wine or double the fireworks than any one fey can be sounds appealing to you, well, I would welcome such a connection with you."

"It's tempting," you say.

To decide whether to combine bodies with Jesús, *go to* !.

— Ñ —

¡RECORD THE LETTER Ñ!

"I give you my sword," you say to the Queen, unsheathing Quitanombre and laying the blade on your palm as you clutch the hilt. You kneel and bow your head, even as your name disappears from your mind, and hold out the sword as far as your arms can stretch.

"Cool," says the Queen. "Now, since We are a microscopic being and don't really have a use for the sword, We are going to make you Our Keeper of the Sword, Our Exciser of Appellations, Our Name-Slayer: Rita who Wields the Magical Sword Quitanombre."

Ah. Yes. Rita. That's your name.

The Queen of the Fey pauses thoughtfully before continuing. "But now that the sword is mine, now that you must *wield* Quitanombre instead of *being* one-half Quitanombre, you're back to being a fully-mortal Rita. You'll need two separate halves calamitously jammed together to be immortal. ¿What two shapes shall you take?"

"¿What are my choices?"

Your big smile comes from the Queen of the Fey's desire to smile. "Your choices are your opportunities. Here are the shapes that are available to you."

To take on your final fey form, *go to !.*

— O —

You close your eyes and brace for impact. Thanks to Bibliocapa, you know what it feels like to die from a sword to the gut.

But at least you'll be able to speak as you die. You quickly begin to compose your final soliloquy.

You feel your pretty dress wrestling you. It has launched itself at your head; when you open your eyes, you can't see much, since the dress covers your face. It wriggles itself down your torso and straightens itself onto your body. The sword's sheath has belted itself around your waist. Once you untuck your cloak from the back of your dress, it's as if you'd never removed anything from your person.

"Oh, great," say the fey, metaphorically and, where physically possible, throwing up their hands. "¡Now we have to start all over again!"

Go to I.

— P —

"Survival for you, Rita," the Queen of the Fey begins, using your own mouth to speak ever-so gently to you, "has required you to abscond from your life. You fled not only your parents—and great gibbering gibbons, ¿¡who wouldn't run those awful people?!—but your own self. To feel less pain, you set your mind free of your body and let others' lives supersede your own in your mind. The reason you are lost is because you had to lose yourself in books, just to survive."

"It's all true," you agree. "¿But now you're saying that I don't need books anymore?"

"Yes. You may choose to enjoy books now as often as you'd like to, but they aren't a requirement for your continued existence."

"So I could take off the cloak, and—" but oh. Big mistake. As you begin to unfasten the cloak's clasp, you faint for 2.3 seconds. You wake on the ground, with a halo of fey-heads looking down at you.

"Bibliocapa," says the Queen of the Fey, "has become, literally, half of who you are. Removing the cloak will require a little bodily violence, which may kill you. Imagine a turtle trying to rip off its own shell."

Sitting up, you ask, "¿Why would I even try, then?"

"If you live, you can choose two new halves with which to form your final, immortal fey being."

"¿What will happen to me if I keep Bibliocapa on?"

The Queen rolls your eyes heavenward, pondering. "You will be trapped forever by your cloak. It will be as if you are confined within the most complete and most constantly-updated library in the world, forever. Which, when you think about it, would be some people's idea of heaven. ¿Is it yours?"

If you want to be trapped in the folds of Bibliocapa forever, *go to* **K**.
If you want to risk taking off Bibliocapa and try to get a new fey body, *go to* **V**.

— Q —

¡RECORD THE LETTER Q!

You love your pretty dress and your cloak (La Ogrificadora and Bibliocapa, respectively). Their magical powers have saved your life more than once. But when it comes to handling the unknown, nothing's better than a magic sword that makes you forget who you are.

IF YOU RECORDED THE LETTER F, READ THE BONUS TEXT IN THE BOX!

> After all, Quitanombre saved you from getting eaten by the fey by erasing your name at just the right moment.

You unclasp the fastening of your cloak; it crumples at your heels. It's harder to get your pretty dress off: you unbelt the sheathed sword, reach behind you and, with difficulty, unzip the dress, and then, pulling your arms free of the straps, let it pool around your feet. You step out of it and, because you came to Fairyland unshod (as is tradition) and because underwear is for losers, you are now naked: except of course for the sword and sheath that you belt back onto your hip.

There's no baggage about being naked here. It's nice. The wind is a most solicitous dance partner, even as you stand still. You feel better.

"¿What now?" you ask.

"¡A new fey is born!" proclaim the fey.

And a new fey is born: right at your feet. The pretty dress and cloak assemble themselves into a half floating-pretty-dress, half floating-cloak fairy.

"¡Hey Rita!" says the newborn fey. "¡Love you, girl! You've always been good to us."

"¡Hello!" you say, a little breathless. "¿What's your name?"

"I get to choose one. I was thinking of," and it spreads its "hands"— it has no hands, but it feels like it spread its hands—like a Hollywood producer sharing his vision, "'Rita.'"

"¿Rita? My name's Rita."

"¡Yeah! We'll be like sisters, except we'll have the same name, which is actually very unusual for sisters. ¿What do you think?"

If you say, "¡Sure! ¡We can both be Ritas!" *go to* **LL.**

If you say, "¿Won't it be confusing if we're both named Rita?" *go to* **U.**

— R —

¡RECORD THE LETTER R!

"Yes," you say out loud. "Yes. We are the Queen of the Fey. And thou art my handmaid."

"Excellent, my liege," says the fey formerly known at the Queen of the Fey. "¿What is your Most Excellency's bidding?"

"Half of my fey self is Quitanombre, the sword in our mouth. But I require an immortal second half."

"Of course, my liege. Your choices are your opportunities. Here are all the fey halves from which you may choose your immortal shape.

To choose your final fey form, *go to* **!.**

¡RECORD THE LETTER S!

As the biologists among you know, a superfluity of eyes that a creature uses as a means of transportation benefits from producing copious amounts of slime. Paseculo's slime, lumpy as overstewed stew, pours into your open mouth before Paseculo itself does, and continues to fall down your throat as Paseculo squeezes its whole diorama-body into your head.

It's a good six minutes of incremental progress until Paseculo has passed all the way inside you. And it's another 30 minutes before it exits. As per its name, it doesn't exit the way it came in. Let's pull the veil on its egress and just be glad you decided to wear your pretty red-with-white-polkadot dress today since, all things considered, it has allowed for some preservation of modesty.

"¡Wait till you see!" says Paseculo brightly to all the fey and lastly, with keen eyes and many, to you.

Its diorama has changed. It's no longer an operating theater. It's your life.

Well, as much as can fit in a shoebox. The diorama depicts the moment just before you came to Fairyland. You're standing in a circle of mushrooms in a state park in New Jersey, a sword belted to your back. You're with your parents. You are much larger than they are; you're dangling them over your tremendously open mouth. Your papi's glasses, through a clever use of fishing line, are already halfway down your open mouth. Your mami may have already died of fear before you've eaten her, judging by the x's that are her eyes.

"By the way, your papi says hello," Pasculo tells you. "He says he understands now why you ate him and your mami. They're sorry they're so closed-minded and intolerant. They said you can be whoever you want to be. No more fights, no more threats. So, he's wondering if you will por favor shit him out now."

"Nope," you answer.

"That's what he said you say. He said, 'If I were Rita, I wouldn't shit me out either. I'd burn me in stomach acid for all eternity, too.'"

"Rita," say all of the fey folk, their voices united in admiration.

"So," you ask, "¿are you going to eat me now?"

"¿Estas loca? We only eat people who don't eat people. ¡You're practically one of us now!"

Go to I.

– T –

¡RECORD THE LETTER T!

"Since you are not married," says the Queen of the Fey, "you have the option to become the Queen of the Fey. ¿Would you like to be the Queen of the Fey?"

You frown with thought. "¿What are the benefits?"

"Well," says the Queen of the Fey, "Everybody has to do what you say. And you get to be half plague or disease or pathogen or whatever, if you choose. It's pretty fun."

"¿But what will happen to you?"

"Oh," says the Queen of the Fey, putting your hands behind your back and making you stroll contemplatively, all the fey watching closely. "We'll become just another fey, yours to command." The Queen of the Fey tries to put a brae face on your face, but fails and instead uses your face to weep.

"So maybe I shouldn't be queen, then," you say. "If it means that much to you."

"¡Don't toy with my emotions!" emotes the Queen of the Fey. "¡Of course you're going to be Queen! ¿Who wouldn't?"

"Maybe I would and maybe I wouldn't. I haven't decided yet."

To decide, *go to !*.

– U –

¡RECORD THE LETTER U!

"I am trying to figure out who I am," you say to the newborn fey whom you will not allow to share your name. "It's hard enough if I'm the only Rita. If you're named Rita, too, I'll only get more confused. You understand, ¿don't you?"

"All too well," says the newborn fey. And then it dies.

Specifically, it falls to two separate pieces. It used to be half pretty-dress and half cloak, but now a pretty dress and a cloak lay on the ground, each unto itself, each unalive. Even the magic which with they were once imbued is gone.

"¡No!" you yell. "¡I didn't want that!"

"You made it forget its name," say all the fey.

"¡I did not! It asked me if 'Rita' *should* be its name. It hadn't actually chosen its name yet."

Insofar as their various bodies allow, the fey tsk-tsk you. "Don't insult our intelligence, please. In the asking was the choosing. You know that. And then you took that choice away. You're a lot like your parents, you know."

"¡No, I don't know that! I am here to find out what I am like. I have no idea who I am like and who I am not like."

Disappointed, the fey say, "We should have eaten you when we had the chance. Oh well. Let's go see the Queen of the Fey. If anybody can help you find yourself, she can."

Then they sneeze on you.

All of them. All at once. Even the fey who don't have noses, or the fey who only have half noses, spontaneously generate complete noses, so that they can sneeze on you. A scintillating mucosal cloud envelopes you.

Trying not to vomit, you yell, "¡Disgusting! ¿Why did you do that?"

"Because," they respond, "the Queen of the Fey is half ragweed pollen and half rhinovirus. And now you've caught her. ¡All hail the Queen!"

Go to **H.**

— V —

¡RECORD THE LETTER V!

Removing Bibliocapa from your person is exactly like flaying off the skin of your back and buttocks and the back of your legs down to the calves, where the hem of the cloak reaches.

You scream. That scream, and the pain that causes it, is the entirety of what remains of your mind.

"¡Quickly!" says the Queen of the Fey. "¡Before you die, flay off the front of you, too!"

Somehow you are able to hear these words, and somehow you know them to be true. You grab two fistfuls of your skin, and rend.

Not only does your skin comes off, however. *You* come off. Literally you flay your entire body off your body, and, as your flesh and bones and nervous and lymphatic systems vanish in the air like the perfume cast from an atomizer, all your pain vanishes.

All that is left of you is your coloratura soprano's voice improvising a song called "Rita."

"¡Keep singing!" says the Queen of the Fey. Her voice, however, isn't coming from you anymore, but from all of her fey subjects, all at once. "And while you sing, choose the halves that will make you an immortal fairy. Remember, your choices are your opportunities."

To take your final fey form, *go to* !.

— W —

¡RECORD THE LETTER W!

Your sword, Quitanombre, is the best eraser ever. ¿How many times have you disintegrated the impediments in your life simply by unnaming them? Your cloak, Bibliocapa, is the sword's opposite: within that fabric's folds is every book in every library, every utterance ever penned or chiseled or typed, the entire history of words that someone somewhere thought to preserve. Each treasure is immeasurably valuable, both objectively and to you personally.

And yet you choose to keep, above all other things, your red-with-white-polkadot dress. Why?

Because a body is merely the body you inherit: the result of your mutation-riddled genes mixed with the misfortunes of your life, recorded in scars and bone calluses and body parts gone missing. A dress, however, is that part of the body you choose. You choose red. You choose polka dots. To give those up would be to flay yourself.

Plus, let's not forget the dress is magic. It has the power to let you grow to four times your size. It is called La Ogrificadora, and whenever anyone has tried to diminish you, it has made you a giantess. And in this world, large things smash small things. Large things, like ogrified daughters, eat small things, like small parents.

Fairies, contrary to popular belief, aren't always smaller than humans. Some of them surrounding you are quite immense, like the half-isthmus, half-tropical-depression fairy; or the half enough-kudzu-to-cover-the-American-South, half every-spider-ever-rolled-into-a-ball-of-spiders fairy. Better than the might of the sword, better than the wisdom of the ages, is to remove your foes' ability to harm you, to remove the *scope* of harm from their purview. So you unfasten the cloak's fastening and you unbelt your sword from your hip. And then you grow huge.

Huger than usual. You don't stop growing huge. Hugeness becomes you, and you become hugeness. Wider and lengthier and taller and denser you grow, extending, soon, past the confines of the sky. Everything on Fairyland and Earth becomes as imperceptible as amoebas to the naked eye. If the fairies fled from your sudden immensity, or if they stayed to watch you exceed their field of vision, gawking and dumbstruck, you can't tell. Your head has pierced the exosphere. Don't worry about suffocating; your dress is breathing for the two of you. You're free to look around and enjoy the tumbling ballet of all the Earth's space junk swirling past you.

Until you sneeze.

Space junk scatters, breaking orbit and launching past the sway of Earth's gravity and out into the greater solar system. You're shrinking suddenly, faster than freefall, rushing down through thermosphere and mesosphere, stratosphere and troposphere until, once more, you are a Rita-sized Rita.

Apparently the fey had not run off in fear, but had stuck around to see you grow and ungrow, since they're all here now, watching you straighten your dress and rub your nose with a finger.

"I sneezed," you say.

"¡Ah, good!" they reply. "¡You've met the Queen of the Fairies, then!"

"¿Why does a sneeze mean I have met the Queen of the Fairies?"

"Because the Queen of the Fairies," say the fey in hieratic unison, "is half ragweed pollen and half rhinovirus."

Go to **H.**

— X —

"Go ahead," say the fey. "We're listening."

"Well, so, okay," you begin. "I, um, am a friend. And I mean no harm. I come from—"

"Nope, not working," say the scores of fey, all at once. Your bones hear them better than your ears do. "We can't understand you."

"¿What do you mean? I understand you just fine."

"Oh, well, yes, we understand you, but we don't *understand* understand you, ¿comprendes? We have to get inside you our way, ¿entiendes?"

"No."

Not all of the fey folk have eyes. Since each fey is half one thing violently smashed together with another thing—half manatee and half déjà vu, half assemblage of dinosaur bones that don't add up to a dinosaur and half Robert's Rules of Order, half white lie and half I Can't Believe It's Not Butter, etc.—some have two eyes, some have one eye, some have no eyes, and some have a superfluity of eyes. But every fey in the mushroom circle rolls whatever eyes they have at you.

"Paseculo," say all the fey folk except one of the fey folk, whom the rest of the fey folk seem to be addressing, "show her what we mean."

Paseculo is a fey who is half superfluity of eyes, and half shoe-box diorama of a surgical theater. She approaches you, climbs your cloak, rolls over your cheek on "wheels" of eyeballs, and says, "Okay, if you please, open your mouth, and I'll get myself inside and dig out all the truth we need."

"¿You want to crawl inside my mouth to dig out truth?" you ask.

"I don't really crawl," says Paseculo. "I rather trundle upon these many eyes of mine. But, yes, in general, that's the thing. Open wide, now. My shoebox-self used to carry men's size 13 oxfords."

If you open your mouth and swallow Paseculo, *go to S.*
If you brandish your mighty sword to fend him and the rest of the fey off, *go to F.*

— Y —

¡RECORD THE LETTER Y!

"They're just kidding," you say. You have to talk around Quitanombre, which remains shoved down your throat. "You know the fey. A tricksy folk, they are." And then, thinking fast, you add, "The fey don't have rulers."

"¿We don't?" ask the astonished fairies, including the half-virus, half-allergen fey formerly known as the Queen of the Fey.

"Nope," you say, growing in confidence. "¿Why would immortal beings need a ruler? No parents to put limits on your sense of self, no bureaucracies to force you to behave in soul-crushing, monstrous ways. Everyone here is free. Freer than any human could ever be."

"¿We are?" ask all the fairies.

"You are. That's why you're so nice to humans. You pity them. You want them to be as happy as you."

"¿We do?"

"You do."

"Well," says the fey formerly known as the Queen of the Fey, "you're human. That means we should be nice to you at least. ¿What can we do for you?"

"Make me fey."

You smile, for the fey formerly known as the Queen of the Fey smiles through you. "Your choices are your opportunities. Choose your new self."

To choose your final fey form, *go to !.*

"More body, more problems," says the Queen of the Fey, sadly and patronizingly, by manipulating your mouth. "That dress is a curse in disguise. Keep it on, and you'll never stop growing. You'll grow so big you won't recognize yourself anymore. You'll stop being you."

"¿What do you mean?" you ask.

"Let me put it this way. ¿Is gravity happy?"

You pause to think before replying. "It's not happy or sad or anything, I guess. It just influences everything, but it doesn't care one way or the other."

The Queen, agreeing with you, makes your head nod. "Keep this dress on, and you'll be like gravity. You'll become kin to electromagnetism. The strong force and the weak force will be your siblings. Except you won't love them like siblings or hate them like siblings or be a family or be anything because you'll just grow and grow and grow until you have no mind and you have no desires and you have no personality and you become Rita: a universal force that has some small effect on matter, but who gives zero fucks about anything because really you won't be a 'who' anymore."

"¿But what happens to me if I take off La Ogrificadora?"

"Well, right now it's serving as half your fey body, so we'll have to get you fitted for a new fey form: two brand new halves Frankensteinianly sutured together. Meanwhile, your dress will begin its journey to become a cosmic force without you."

"So, either mindless Nirvana or tabula rasa."

The Queen of the Fey shrugs. "Looks like. The choice is yours."

If you want a tabula rasa new you, *go to E.*

If you want mindless Nirvana, *go to M.*

– ! –

¡WELCOME TO THE END OF THE STORY!

¡The fey are happy to welcome you into their midst! All you need to do is choose what form you will take. Select *two* letters from the ones you recorded to pick the two halves of your new fairy self. ¡Choose wisely!

A: ¡You did not record the letter A! Coño, compañero, stop trying to cheat.

CH: You are half Carlos Hernandez, the author of this story. You now have a great deal more body hair. ¡Enjoy!

F: You are half misericord, which in this case is *not* a dagger used for mercy-killings, but rather the kneeler that preserves one's patellas at church. ¡Sweet relief!

G: You are half finish line. Racers of all kinds—runners, cyclists, jockeys, drivers, hares and tortoises—come careering top-speed past you. You spend your life bestowing trophies, taking victory photos, and stretching yet another yellow tape across yourself that is destined to be broken by the next winner.

LL: You are half twelve signs of a brand-new zodiac. You have to create them. ¡Have fun!

N: ¡You married Jesús! That means you may conjoin your body with one half of the old battleax, causing the half-wineskin to become a whole wineskin, or else the half eternal-fireworks show to become a complete, eternal fireworks show. Either way, you two are destined to be the life of any party you attend. ¡A toast to the newlyweds!

Ñ: You are half war-cry. Your guttural howl strike fear into enemies and hearten your comrades in arms. ¡Scream your war-cry now!

Q: You are half the blueprints for clockwork before the first functional prototype was ever completed. You will carry with you the brio of invention and discovery all the days of your immortal life. But you lose the ability to tell time, which, you will discover, is actually yet another benefit.

R: ¡You are half three flying heralding trumpets that play a royal fanfare wherever you go, announcing to all of Fairyland that they are in the presence of royalty!

S: You are half sturdy tree, from which hangs a tire swing. The fey love to take turns playing on you. You're a source of winsome, childlike joy. Ah.

T: ¡You can become the Queen of the Fey! Half of you must be some kind of plague, disease, allergen, virus, pathogen, poison, or parasite. ¡But as Queen, you may choose which one, Your Majesty! Write it in here:

U: You are half woodchipper. The fey have a *lot* of secrets they want to get rid of. You're going to have a lot of friends in Fairyland.

V: You are half the feeling left behind after someone tells a joke that's more philosophical than funny. You evoke smaller smiles, but they're sincere, and not without their own joys.

W: You are half planetarium, with exhibits changing every month. Your shows feature the voice talents of beloved actor and reading advocate LeVar Burton. ¡Light refreshments follow every performance!

Y: You are half the concept of egalitarianism. You are useful, yet unexpectedly problematic. But you certainly mean well.

Whatever halves you used to assemble your whole, now you know who you are. ¡Go forth and live your best life!

— TAKE ONLY PHOTOS —
by Shanna Swendson

T he first thing I noticed when I staggered through my living room in search of coffee was that my Christmas tree was all lit up. That was odd. I hadn't plugged it in the night before because I'd been out late at the office holiday party, and I'd gone straight to bed as soon as I got home. I'd only had a couple of glasses of wine, so I hadn't been drunk enough to have memory gaps, and I'm not nearly sentimental enough to come home from an office party so full of good cheer that I have to bask in the glow of the Christmas lights before going to bed.

On the other hand, I live alone, and the lights weren't on a timer, so I was the only one who could have done it. I must have plugged in the tree without thinking.

Once the coffeemaker was doing its job, I went to unplug the tree. It wasn't plugged in. And the lights weren't really on, now that I looked at the tree again from another angle. I must have just seen the bulbs reflecting the light. Shaking my head, I made a beeline to the coffee pot and poured a cup. I was sure it would make sense as soon as I woke up completely.

The morning went back to normal as I ate breakfast and got dressed, until I went to find the shoes I remembered stepping out of on my way from the front door to my bedroom, at the same time as I dropped my purse and laptop case. They weren't where I thought I'd left them. My purse was hooked over the arm of the sofa, and the laptop bag rested against the sofa, below the purse. The shoes were nowhere in sight.

I checked the closet, in case my generally tidy nature had overruled my exhaustion, but they weren't in there. I was on the verge of settling for a different pair of shoes when I thought to check where the purse and laptop bag were. Sure enough, the shoes were just under the sofa, as though someone had kicked them there to get them out of the way. I supposed I was so obsessive that even when I tried to be sloppy, I just couldn't stop myself from being neat. I didn't have time to think about it too much because I had to get to work, and by the time I reached the office, I had other things to worry about, like avoiding my coworkers.

The receptionist was on the phone when I entered, which allowed me to get away with a smile and nod as I passed through the lobby. The hallway was empty, so it looked like the coast was clear and I'd be able to reach my office without having to chat about the party. That was the problem with work social events: they made everyone think we were all friends.

I was almost to my office when Beth popped into the hallway from her office. "Hey, Meg!" she said.

I tried not to wince visibly. She was the worst possible person to run into when I didn't want to chat because she was the closest thing to a work friend I had. Not that we were really friends, but I managed to tolerate her because she was as detail-oriented as I was and didn't try to socialize too much. "Hey," I said, not breaking stride and hoping she got the message.

She didn't. "Did you have fun last night?"

"Yeah, it was great, but it's back to the grind today."

She didn't push the point beyond that, which was why I actually almost kind of liked her. Most of my coworkers would have kept trying to talk. With a great sigh of relief, I entered my office, set up my computer, and got to work on all those columns of lovely, lovely numbers. Numbers made sense in a way that people didn't. There were so many jokes about how boring accounting was, but I loved it. I found great joy in putting everything in order.

Once I fell into my zen-like flow, the hours flew, and soon it was the end of the day. I'd even managed to forget about the morning's weirdness, and when I came home, everything was just the way I'd left it.

I couldn't say the same thing the next morning. The Christmas tree was lit up. I'd left my purse and laptop in their usual spot, staged on the path from the bedroom to the front door, but they were back by the sofa again. I thought the coffee table seemed to be closer to the sofa, and on closer inspection I found that there were dents in the carpet to back up that impression. My chest tightened with fear, and I glanced around for something I could use as a weapon. Someone had been in my house during the night while I slept. All my valuables were where they belonged, so maybe the intruder was still inside, lurking, waiting for me to leave so he could walk out with all my things.

I took a golf club from the bag in my hall closet and crept through the house, checking under the furniture, behind curtains, and in closets. I didn't find anyone. I was reluctant to leave the house, though. I knew I wouldn't be able to concentrate on work while wondering who was in my house, so I called in sick, faking a cough and raspy voice, and said I'd work from home.

If someone was lurking, waiting for me to leave, I hoped he now felt trapped. I situated myself on the sofa, the golf club across my knees, and waited. I didn't hear a sound, saw not the slightest hint of movement. The Christmas lights faded, and I couldn't bring myself to check whether the tree was plugged in. Eventually, I got out the laptop and did some work, since just sitting there on high alert was boring. By the end of the day, no burglar had fallen out of the closet or tried to creep past me.

That should have been a relief, but it wasn't. As horrible as it would have been to have an intruder in my house, at least it would have been an explanation. All I could think was that I must have moved things around without realizing it. Or there was the possibility of sleepwalking—I was getting up, tidying, rearranging furniture, and then going back to bed.

That evening, I very carefully set my shoes and a newspaper in the middle of the living room floor. One last glance before I headed to the bedroom confirmed that they were where I remembered putting them. I also verified that the Christmas tree was off. I hung a string of jingle bells from my bedroom doorknob, which surely would wake me if I was sleepwalking. I moved a chair to the path between the bed and the door, so I'd bump into it on my way out. Just to cover all my bases, I kept the golf club handy.

I woke early the next morning, before my alarm went off. The chair was where I'd left it and the door was still closed. With the golf club in hand, I rushed down the short hallway to the living room to see what had happened and barely stifled a scream.

The tree was lit, the newspaper was carefully folded and set on the sofa, and my shoes had been moved under the coffee table.

Someone had definitely been in my house during the night.

When I got to work and saw Beth heading into the break room, for once I didn't retreat to my office. I went straight into the break room after her. She was the only person I'd ever given a key to my house, so if someone was getting in without signs of a break-in, she had to be involved.

"You didn't give my key to anyone while you were looking after my place last summer, did you?" I asked, probably more forcefully than I should have.

She finished filling her mug without spilling a drop—a demonstration of calm I found highly suspicious. "No, why?"

"Things in my house are being moved around in the night. Not stolen, damaged, or anything like that. Just moved." I left out the part about the Christmas lights because it sounded way too weird. "I know some people have played pranks like that in the office, so I was wondering if someone's pranking me now." It sounded absurd when I said it out loud, but it was too late to take it back.

She leaned against the counter and took a sip of coffee. "No, I didn't give your key to anyone, and I gave it back to you when you got home from vacation. I didn't tell the rest of these idiots that I had it." She arched an eyebrow slightly. "Stuff's been moved around?"

"It's like they're clearing space on the living room floor."

"Your midnight visitors must be having a big dance party," she said with a laugh. "If they'd been cleaning, I'd say you had a brownie."

That wasn't what I'd expected her to say. "A brownie?"

"You know, like in fairy tales. The helpful little creatures who clean in the night. They're a kind of elf or fairy."

"I wish. You don't know how I'd go about getting some of those, do you?"

"You'd make a fortune if you could figure it out."

I knew she was joking, but still, when I got back to my desk, I did a quick internet search to see what I could find. There were stories about elves who made shoes during the night, brownies who cleaned unless they were insulted, and various kinds of household spirits, but nothing about just moving things around and making lights come on in spite of them not being connected to a power source. It also seemed like I was in the wrong part of the world to have these kinds of visitors. America appeared to be sorely lacking in invisible nighttime cleaning creatures.

Not that I was in any way worried about having elves, fairies, or anything like that in my house, because I am a functioning adult with a firm grasp on reality.

Even so, I couldn't resist testing the situation that evening. After all, ruling out a possible cause without any evidence was as bad as believing in something without evidence. The scientific method would help me get to the bottom of this, or at least rule out one possibility. I would set up conditions so obvious that I would be certain whether or not anything was changed during the night and see what happened.

Although it tormented my soul to do so, I cluttered the living room, strewing clothes, shoes, and papers not just on the floor but also on every horizontal surface. I left out bags of snacks and a couple of half-full glasses of wine. I took pictures of the whole thing with my phone so I'd know for certain how the morning compared to the night before. I double checked all the locks, including the interior deadbolt and door chain, made sure the Christmas tree was unplugged, and hung jingle bells on the front door.

The next morning, a space had been cleared on the living room floor, like someone had made a dance floor. Everything else was exactly how I'd left it, except the snack bags and wine glasses were empty. I wanted to scream, but I didn't let myself because I didn't think I could explain it to my neighbors. Instead, I clapped my hand over my mouth so I could make muffled noises behind it. I felt invaded, violated. Someone, or something, had been in my house. It was like finding mouse droppings in the kitchen and knowing that meant something unseemly was happening in my home when I wasn't looking. But what? "Okay, this is getting ridiculous," I said, maybe to myself, and maybe to whatever intruder I had. I knew it wasn't my imagination, but I had no idea what it was.

It was a Friday, so I decided to stay up that night and see what happened. I settled on the sofa with a pillow and blanket and marathoned episodes of *Star Trek*, something nice and logical. I must have fallen asleep at some point, because when I woke during the night, things were different. The Christmas lights were on and the floor had been cleared. I could have sworn I heard music, but it sounded distant, like perhaps my neighbors were throwing a party. I could see my furniture clearly, but when I looked at the middle of the room, everything became blurry, as though there was something there, but I couldn't bring it into focus. Or maybe it was a dream. As much as I'd thought about this problem, there was a pretty good chance it was seared into my subconscious. I'd be surprised if I *didn't* dream about mysterious visitors moving things around. In the morning, the floor was still clear, and the tree was still lit, but all was quiet. The tree lights faded when the sun came up.

That day, I went out and bought a security camera setup with night vision. I aimed all but one of the cameras at the middle of the living room, with the last camera pointing at the door, and then I arranged the living room with things on the floor and snacks on the coffee table. I was up at the crack of dawn on Sunday morning to watch the footage.

The video showed that there was *definitely* something in my house. They came across like hot spots on the video, vaguely human-shaped and small, but too bright and blurry for me to see features. I recoiled, jumping away from the computer as though the bright spots might come through the screen at me. What *were* those things? I felt dizzy and realized I was hyperventilating. I sat down, put my head between my knees, and took slow, deep breaths until the dizziness passed.

When I felt reasonably stable, I looked at the computer again, starting the video from the point where the bright spots appeared. They started out by clearing the floor, and then they danced. The more they danced, the brighter they grew, until the video was just one big bright spot.

I shook my head as if to clear it, but it didn't help. None of my rational explanations worked. The intruders definitely weren't human-sized, so it wasn't a burglar or someone from the office playing a prank. I didn't think mice would bother clearing the floor or dancing. There was no way to deny that there were small creatures that didn't show up well on camera dancing in my living room. If the rational explanations didn't apply, that meant I had to broaden the possibilities I was willing to consider.

So, aliens or ghosts? The images did look a lot like what was shown on ghost-hunting shows—not that I'd ever taken any of those seriously. But why would aliens or ghosts be having a party in my living room? Even *I* didn't think of my home as party central. Maybe elves, but this didn't match the behavior of any elves I'd read about. Then again, were fairy tales valid source material for this sort of thing? Was it absolutely insane to even consider that it might be elves?

I felt like my brain was giving me the "does not compute" signal. I was fairly certain I wasn't losing it, since I did have video evidence, but I needed a sanity check with another person. I didn't exactly want to tell anyone that I thought some kind of magical creatures were having nightly raves in my living room, but I'd already told Beth something was odd, and she was the one who'd mentioned elves, so I caught her in the hallway Monday at work. "Hey, you got a minute?" I said, trying to sound casual even though my pulse was pounding.

Her face lit up, like she was glad that I'd approached her. "Yeah. What's up?"

There was no way to say this casually. "You know that thing I mentioned about what was going on in my living room? Well, you've got to see this." I didn't wait for her to respond before I dragged her into my office. I pulled up the video that I'd uploaded to the internet and played it for her. I'd seen it before, so I watched her watching it. She frowned at first, then her eyes widened. She leaned forward, her mouth hanging open.

"What is that?" she asked.

"This is what my security cameras caught."

She leaned her hip on the edge of my desk. "This isn't a prank, is it? You're not setting me up?"

"I don't have that level of technical ability. Or imagination. I don't know what they are or where they came from, and I don't know why they picked my living room, of all places."

"Where do they go in the morning?"

"They just seem to fade away as they leave the dance floor. What are they? What do I do? How do I get rid of them?"

"Are they causing any damage or disrupting your life?"

"Well, no," I admitted. "All they do is clear their dance floor and eat or drink anything I leave out."

"Then why are you so worried about them?"

"Because there are creepy little things in my house!" I said, my voice going a bit shrill. Too late, I realized that the sound probably carried throughout the office.

"In some cultures, you might be considered lucky."

"I haven't exactly seen luck coming my way."

"Possibly because you're so stressed. Maybe you should try keeping the floor clear, and then you won't know they're there."

"But I'll know. I can't un-know what I've seen. I have to deal with this if I want to ever feel comfortable in my home again."

"Do you mind if I come over? Seeing it in person might help me think of something."

"You're an expert on elves?"

She looked away, and her cheeks flushed slightly. "I wouldn't say that I'm an expert, but we lived in England a few years when I was a kid—my dad was in the Air Force—and we lived in this really old house. I thought it was cool that our house was older than the United States. But strange things happened there. No matter how untidy I tried to be, my room was always clean in the morning. I had to start keeping things neat for myself or I'd lose anything I left lying around. The old lady who lived next door claimed that we had a brownie that had been with that house for centuries. I've been fascinated by that sort of thing ever since. And no, I never caught it, and I didn't do anything to send it away."

"Why couldn't I have got the thing that cleans your house for you in the night?"

"Like I said, it wasn't all that helpful, other than forcing me to clean for myself if I didn't want to lose all my stuff."

She came over that evening after work and surveyed my living room, her arms folded across her chest. "Are you sure it's not a brownie? Because this is pretty tidy."

I winced. "This is normal for me. I only noticed something was happening when I came in late and left my shoes out, and they moved them. And they turned the tree lights on—but without plugging them in. There's no telling how long this was going on before I noticed. Brownies aren't known to be party animals, are they?"

"No, that's a different class of creature. What we have here is something different." She wandered around the room, pausing occasionally to look closer at something, and I felt a bit awkward at her scrutiny of my home. We'd worked together for years, but our relationship hadn't extended beyond work. She was the one I hung out with at office parties, but we'd never done anything after hours one-on-one. Now she was in my home, looking at my photos and souvenirs from my travels. I wondered if she'd noticed that I didn't have pictures of people, only places.

Did that have something to do with my discomfort with my visitors? I didn't really do people. I interacted with people at work when I had to, and then I went home to my sanctuary. I seldom had guests. And now I had a party raging in my house behind my back every night. It was unsettling. I wondered what my visitors would do if I had a party—hide for the night, or join in? Frankly, the thought of having people in was more unsettling than the invisible intruders.

"Oh, this must be from your trip to Iceland this summer," she said, leaning over to look at the series of photos on the fireplace mantel.

"Yes," I replied. "I was camping."

"By yourself? Wow, you're really brave."

That wasn't something I was often accused of. "There were people around. I wasn't in the wilderness." Well, except that one time when the official campground had been too full for my taste and I'd set up my tent nearby.

"You know, Iceland has a very strong tradition of fairy-like creatures." She inhaled sharply, as though being struck by a sudden idea, then she frowned in thought as she continued moving around the room. Stopping by the end table next to the sofa, she picked up the rock sitting there and said, "Is there a story here, or is this art?"

"I got it in Iceland. It was on the edge of my campsite, and I thought it looked interesting—better than the kind of souvenir you get at a gift shop. I know, I probably shouldn't have taken it—take nothing but photos, leave nothing but footprints, and all that—but it was just a rock." I didn't want to say that the rock spoke to me because that sounded odd, but something about it had captivated me. Even now, I didn't think I could articulate why. It was sparkly and a funny shape, but not so strange or beautiful that it should have even caught my eye.

"Okay, I think I know what you have going on here." She got out her phone and pulled up a website. "See, this sounds similar," she said, showing me the screen. "There are people in Iceland who believe in fairies, or 'hidden folk,' even today. There was a big controversy over whether a road should be rerouted to avoid interfering with the rocks where some people thought fairies lived."

"You think I brought a fairy house home with me in a rock?"

"Maybe. These fairies are known for coming out at Christmas. Typically, it would be Christmas Eve, while the family's at church, but since you already have the decorations up, they might think it's Christmas."

"This is crazy!" I said, throwing up my hands.

"Look!" she showed me her phone again.

I took the phone from her and scrolled through the article. "They had machinery breakdowns?" I said, shuddering.

"They must not be too mad at you for moving their home if you haven't noticed anything breaking. They might even have made you want to take that rock so they could move. Let's stay up and see what happens."

"I tried that, and I didn't see anything."

"But did you believe in them then?"

"I'm not sure I believe in them now."

She wagged a finger at me. "Oh, you believe. It's the most logical explanation, really. It's the only thing that fits the evidence. And I believe, so even if you don't see anything, I will." She plopped down on the sofa, making herself at home.

It would have been far too awkward to try to get her to leave, so I asked, "So, uh, can I get you anything?" I wasn't sure what I had to offer her. The fairies had eaten all my snacks, and I so seldom had guests that I didn't keep party supplies on hand.

"We can just order a pizza." Which she proceeded to do.

I wasn't sure which was worse, tiny invisible invaders who only made their presence known while I slept, or a full-sized human making herself comfortable in my living room. Worse, a full-size human who wanted to make conversation that wasn't about work. She asked me about my travels, my family, my relationships, and told me all about hers. When the Christmas tree lit up at midnight, it came as a massive relief.

Now I could see them, little people wearing red and green outfits that looked like something out of the tourist brochures at historical sites, and they swarmed around my living room. I couldn't help but pull my feet up onto the sofa, the way I would if I'd seen mice. "Oh my, they're real!" I whispered.

Beth's eyes shone. "They are," she breathed.

I squeezed my eyes shut, then opened them again, hoping maybe they'd go away. They didn't. Elves were real. My brain gave me that "does not compute" message again, so I stared at the creatures until I had no choice but to accept that these things right out of a fairy tale were as real as I was. This entirely changed the way I saw the world. I'd always focused on concrete things, on science and reason. I'd never been all that keen on fairy tales. I'd questioned the existence of Santa Claus at a very early age and had never bought into the Easter Bunny or Tooth Fairy. My idea of a flight of fancy was imagining a future with spaceships that could travel between stars. Now I had to face the fact that tiny elves were far more realistic than faster-than-light travel.

"What else that's supposed to be imaginary is actually real?" I asked, my voice shaking. "Ghosts? Magic? Is there really a Santa Claus?"

Beth's smile was enigmatic. "Maybe. We do have to consider the possibility."

"Are all these magical things all around us, all the time?"

"There are tiny insects around us all the time that you don't see. How often do you think about dust mites?"

"More often than is probably healthy," I admitted.

"Still, you know they exist even if you can't see them. You may see pictures of them under a microscope, and maybe that makes you want to keep a cleaner house, but it doesn't change the world. It just changes your knowledge of the world. You've learned something."

That I could deal with. I'd learned something, which was good. I liked learning. And knowing this one new thing meant there were so many other things out there to learn. I could feel my mind expanding, my sense of the universe shifting as I adjusted my parameters.

But that didn't mean I wanted tiny elves in my house any more than I wanted dust mites. "What do I do about them? Should I just get rid of the rock?"

She glanced at her phone, where she'd been researching the folklore about the hidden folk of Iceland. "Well, they often move to new places on New Year's Eve."

"But that's weeks away!"

"I have an idea, but we should probably discuss it elsewhere because we don't know how much English they understand. Do you want to come over for dinner at my place tomorrow night? I don't think we want to talk about this sort of thing at work."

I reluctantly agreed, but this whole thing was starting to feel suspiciously social. Still, one dinner after work wasn't nearly as bad as an Icelandic elf infestation. I could get through this, and then I could get back to normal.

It looked like the fairies were going to party all night, so Beth went home, and I went to bed. I thought I wouldn't be able to get to sleep, knowing what was going on elsewhere in my house, but I drifted off right away and woke more refreshed than I would have expected after staying up so late.

If having someone in my house had felt odd, it was equally weird to visit someone when I only knew her from work. "I made soup," Beth said when she greeted me at the door. "I hope that's okay."

"Um, yeah, that's great," I said, fighting the urge to flee. I wondered if I should have brought something. It had been so long since I'd been to someone's home that I'd forgotten the protocol. As I followed Beth to the kitchen, I noted that her home was far quirkier than I'd have expected before a few days ago. It didn't at all fit the straitlaced persona she maintained at work. If I'd known she was the sort to go in for paintings of unicorns, I might not have made the connection I had with her. Now, though, it seemed her love of fantasy might be my saving grace—if it even was fantasy. What if she had a clearer and more realistic view of the world than I had? A few days ago, I might have dismissed her as an airhead, but maybe she was really just wise and open-minded. I felt something click in my brain as my view of the world shifted yet again. Maybe my view of reality, as logical as it seemed to be, hadn't ever been the most realistic one.

"What was the idea you had?" I asked while she stirred the soup. Only after I'd spoken did I remember that small talk was generally expected before diving into the main topic.

Beth didn't seem to mind. "I was thinking maybe we could trick them. If you took down your Christmas stuff, they might think it was time to move on. Supposedly, leaving a pathway of candles from your door will guide them away. If they leave on their own, then they might not take it out on you the way they might if you just evicted them."

"No fairy revenge sounds good to me."

"But we need to think about where to guide them to."

"Anywhere outside my house."

"But I was thinking, we may be able to kill two birds with one stone here. Is there anything near you that you wouldn't mind disrupting?"

"You mean like that road they were building in Iceland? Put the fairies there, and if they like the place, they won't let their home be destroyed?"

"Yeah. Is there something you don't want to have built?"

I thought about my neighborhood. There was a vacant lot nearby, and I'd noticed the zoning change signs on it. I liked it the way it was, almost like a park. I didn't want the office building they were proposing. "I have an idea. You think it would work?"

She shrugged. "It's worth a shot. We might as well have some fun with this. Worst-case scenario, you get rid of your invaders."

Actually, I thought that the worst-case scenario was that they wouldn't leave, but I figured we'd worry about plan B when the time came. We strategized over soup, and that turned into chatting, and before I knew it, I was carrying on a conversation—and liking it. Was this what friendships were like? It wasn't like what I'd experienced growing up, when I just got picked on for being good at math and sat alone in the cafeteria. I felt safe and warm. My face hurt from smiling so much, and I was in no rush to go home and be alone. When I did leave, I found myself looking forward to the next time we got together.

That Saturday, Beth came over to help me take down all my Christmas decorations. "Normally, people have tree-trimming parties, not tree-dismantling parties," she said with a laugh as we worked. We hid the decorations in my bedroom before setting up a line of luminarias on my front walk. Then all we could do was wait.

At midnight, the fairies emerged from their rock. They milled about, as though looking for the Christmas tree and other decorations. That was my cue to fling open the front door. They saw the candlelight outside and followed the line of lights. I ran ahead of them, setting out and lighting more candles to lead them down the block and across the street. Beth came after them, holding the rock. She settled the rock on the vacant lot, under a shrub that probably would be bulldozed when construction began.

The fairies moved around the lot, as though trying to figure it out. While they were occupied, Beth and I ran back to my house, snatching up the candles as we went, so they wouldn't be able to find their way back. "Do you think it worked?" I asked once we were inside.

"You'll find out in the morning," she replied. "And then we'll see what happens about that building."

"Maybe they'll make it a park, instead."

After Beth went home, I set out my shoes and a newspaper on the floor before I went to bed, and they were still there in the morning. The house was also untouched on Monday morning. When I got to work, I headed to Beth's office. "I think it worked," I said.

"Awesome! So, do you need help putting your decorations back up? I've got some friends who might be up for pitching in. We could make it a party."

My first instinct was to decline, but then I thought, why not? I'd had fun with Beth, so maybe more people would be even more fun. And then there were other things I wanted to explore. "Sounds great," I said. "And if you don't have plans for Christmas Eve, I was thinking about staying up and investigating Santa. You're welcome to join me. I'll make the cocoa."

— OLD TWELVEY NIGHT —
by Gwendolyn N. Nix

She had hands again.

A jolt of joy suffused through her, like the sudden spread of heat lightning, at the slow collapse of the earth. Pale roots twined between her fingers, and she ripped them away with a muted pop, clawing out of the tree's cradle and angling toward the surface. Mud filled her mouth, but she was kept breathless in different ways.

It happened the same way each time. *Exhilaration.* Sudden wakefulness compounded by the desire to rise.

It happened the same way each time. *Exaltation.* Wishes smoldered between her ribs. Please, this time—*this time*—she'd be fast enough.

Anticipation. The loam crust broke and a thin ice layer shattered. Wrenching out of the cold tomb of the soil, she blinked blindly against the white sunbeams of a late afternoon. She bit the apple-heart of her hope—*but it kept happening the same way each time*—and her hope curdled into browned pulp, and oh, she simply wanted to see a sky full of bird song.

Disappointment nearly crushed her. The quiet grove expanded before her, sleeping within the blanket season of frozen water, of *wend*. Winter. Pitch-dark trees reached toward the gray sky. Wind whistled through the wide spaces between the trees, stirring up crusty chunks of snow aged to tan from muck and sod. Beyond, slush covered the humped meadow in patchworks of brown and white.

The roots waving around the hole she'd just emerged from lunged, winding into a tight chain around her wrists, dragging her back into the radius of the winter-blackened tree. *Don't go past the root system,* they vibrated against her skin. *We're sorry we couldn't have brought you back faster. But don't go past the roots.*

Yet the apple tree spirit didn't cry or scream from frustration, because it wasn't happening the same way, and lingering at the tip of a spindly branch withered a bud. Hibernating and small, but lined with a stripe of green framed by a lace of frost.

—◦●◦—

Snow floated over the grove, the flakes soft like cotton, collecting in the barren arms of the boughs. The apple-spirit cooed to the green nub on her tree as it crumbled and hardened into a wrinkled shell over the following days. "I'm Datura," she whispered, her rosy lips spreading over broad white teeth. "I stole the word from a bunch of human children who threw rocks at my tree once. They said I only produced thorn-apples, that I should be cut down because I was nothing but a forsaken blasted *datura* flower." She paused, anxious for a response. Under her long feet, the fluff of new snowfall soaked up the sound, leaving a stillness to the air.

Datura reached up to stroke the blackened shell. Poor thing. It had held out for so long, yet it had fallen asleep, just like the apple tree she'd been sworn to, dormant like the field of apple trees surrounding her, all tended by their own spirits.

She thought of her own short life cycle and frowned. When the season turned again, she'd become the blackened husk to be dragged underground. She'd be cradled in her own sleep, encaged by roots that never saw the light, as the tree ate from her bones until winter came again. Awakened once more, sent to tend to the grounds of her tree and protect it from mischief-things—those unsworn creatures who liked to lurk and linger and whisper.

"You're the first alive thing I've seen," she told the bud. "The first green thing."

Oh, she saw other apple-spirits and humans and mischief-things, too, but nothing grown and anchored in the soil. Nothing of the treasured gold of red fruit, plucked and enjoyed. Of the white blossoms dusted with burnished pollen. She only saw the puny leftovers of autumns past, and as her fellow apple-spirits raked the earth around their trees until the dark rich health of it mingled around the roots, Datura daydreamed about green-colored days and warm summer nights. As her good fellow apple-spirits pulled the shrouds of old weeds clear and scraped the budding fuzz of fungus from the bark, Datura imagined what it would be like to arise under the spread of leaf-heavy branches, of the sweet taste of pulp spilling across her tongue, of soft gold dusks peppered with firefly light.

"The other apple-spirits don't like me much," she admitted to the bud as it detached at her gentle touch, tumbling into her palm. She bit her lip. All of her apples simply fell, never picked for pies or cider, if the wrinkled leftovers meant anything. "Between you and me, they say it's no surprise my apples have worms in them. And they're right."

Clean the rot out, they tsked at her, their noses wrinkled at the fruit putrefaction covering her tree stand. *Leave your dreams for your sleep. It's a dangerous thing, leaving such sweets to rot black. Might attract bugs. Might attract mischief.*

The cluster of children scampered throughout the copse under a purple sky with big whoops and cheers.

Datura scrambled to her apple tree, her hands wrapped around the hilt of the sword embedded in the trunk, prepared to hoist the blade from its sheath. *Was it time, already? Had Old Twelvey Night arrived so soon?*

Her heart thundered in her chest with the instinct to protect, but the sword was too big for her—she wasn't yet mature enough to hold it. Another holler caused her to whip around, waiting to see if the other apple-spirits would shuck their pastoral forms in favor of one fit for warriors.

No, they simply milled and toiled and puttered.

The roots encircling her wrists cooed against her skin, *Not yet, not yet. The cold does not have bite to it, the first omens have not shown. Be still. Be at peace, guardian.*

No mischief-things lurked and lingered and whispered, either. Datura stroked the root-chain, felt the answering thrum of the orchard against her skin. *We are still strong.*

The children galloped past her tree. Coins weighed down their palms, copper and silver flashing in the moonlight. Whiffs of tangy-sour fermentation floated on their breaths. Datura smiled in relief, and with a final caress of the sword's hilt, she bounded to the edge of her root-circle to watch the children. She knew where they were headed. Oh, how she wished she could go, too!

She drew in a deep breath and strained forward, as far as she could go. The tree's root system had always been a radiating ring that she could not cross. The roots around her wrists, worried smooth from her anxious touches, tensed as she tested their limits.

A human girl smacked her lips against a boy's, and then she brandished a penny in the air. "I wish to kiss you again!" She laughed and pushed her coin into the bark of the old wish tree.

The tall tree wasn't the oldest, but it had been chosen by the grove's visitors, who year after year, slotted their round metal into the bark and spoke their dreams to the cold air. The wish tree's spirit had given up on tending to apples or gardening, had taken to polishing the wishes instead, keeping them bright in the winter days.

"I want to make a wish," Datura called out, patting her mud-spattered clothes for money, wringing her garden-soiled hands. The humans couldn't hear her. They never could. "Can I borrow a coin?"

"I can lend you a coin."

Datura spun around, her eyes narrowed, and she crouched, ready to spring on the new voice cutting through the revelers' shouts. *Defend.* Just outside the radius of her roots, a hand shot straight out of the dirt and waved, the shine of a gold piece held between two fingers. Datura inched closer—the roots around her wrists strained to pull her back—and the long-fingered hand disappeared into its hole. Datura peered down into the opening and was met with a gap-toothed grin, yellow eyes burnished like the coin, a face sprinkled with rich earth. "Here you go," the creature said, flourishing the coin—ancient with the profile worn smooth—at her. "On the house."

Mischief-thing.

"I can't take that," Datura said softly and eased back into the safety of her ring. Caution warred with a striking, sudden need. The other apple-spirits always scoffed at her meandering conversation and wild wishes, waved their hands for her to *get on with it.*

The mischief-thing levered both hands out of the hole, wriggling herself up and out. She shook her head, sending dirt cascading from her short black hair. "There's no rule against accepting a gift," she said.

Datura shook her head, and watched the mischief-thing slide up to the edge of the tree's root system, perched as if at the edge of a precipice. Where Datura was apple-round, this mischief-thing was long-legged and reed-slender. "I'm not supposed to talk to things like you," Datura answered. "You're only here to cause chaos and ruin the orchard."

"Who says you can't talk to me?" The mischief-thing raised an eyebrow.

"That's not the point."

"Feels like a pretty big point to me."

"The orchard god," Datura sighed. "The Apple Tree Man."

"Oh, that old moaning thing?" The mischief-thing propped up on her knees and held her arms out stiffly, her face twisted into a parody of agony. "What's he gonna do, chase you out? This is just as much your home as it is his. You bloomed from your apple-tree seed, just like he did." She learned forward and peered at Datura's tree. "I like what you've done here. Smells sweet. Lots of interesting things. Not all desolate and cleared out like those other trees. Is that an old dandelion patch? It must be huge in the spring!"

"Stop causing trouble," Datura huffed, trying to ignore the idea of her, Datura, blooming like a tulip. Of a dandelion patch, thriving in her space.

"I'm not! I did the nice thing—I came with an offer of a wish."

"You're trying to poison the grove with your mischief."

"Not me, not old Tibb. I like the orchard. It's beautiful in the summer, lots of shade. I like to lay in the sun and listen to the crickets."

Datura paused, ran her fingers through the muddy ground. "You've seen it in the summer?"

"Spring, summer, fall, you name it, I've seen it."

"That's my wish," Datura said softly. "To see the orchard in the seasons. To see green life."

Tibb rolled the coin between her hands, flipped it until it turned over her knuckles. "Done," she said. "I'll make the wish for you." She scampered across the grove. slinking like a cat, and waved at Datura from the foot of the wish tree until Datura gifted her with a small smile. Tibb pushed the coin into the bark and Datura's smile transformed into something blinding and genuine as the wish tree's spirit chased old Tibb away. Tibb ran back to Datura, hands on her knees, thin ribs heaving, shooting her a look that pulled at Datura's heartstrings and plucked out the tune of *recklessness, wildness, foolhardy*.

And Datura's special sparkle of gold gleamed amongst the silver and copper, and it was something that hadn't happened in the same way, not once. Something that had never happened before.

The cold transformed into a bone-deep freeze that chilled even the clouds. Frost sparkled on Datura's skin like a layer of reflected diamond light. It hadn't snowed in days. The approach of Old Twelvey Night came closer with each turn of the moon and Datura had become foolish in her loneliness, had invited Tibb to rest under her tree. Tibb shivered beneath a blanket stolen from the new crowd of drunken humans, cider sloshing from their wooden cups to wet the roots. Flower masks covered their eyes, crowns slipped from their foreheads, and Datura studied them in marvel: the long romantic ferns, the delicate white blooms, small fragile purples buds like stars.

"They're still dead, you know," Tibb said, sliding closer and leaning her head on Datura's shoulder. "All pretty and colorful, sure, but those flower crowns might last a couple days at most. What a waste."

"Are you saying you won't want yours, then?" Datura asked. She broke the stems off black thistles, weaving their spiked tops among hollow grasses, tied them with wet and stringy brown leaves to make a crown of her own. She placed it on her head.

"Didn't say that," Tibb grumbled.

"Thought so," Datura finished and wove tan and beige stalks together, used white branches pockmarked with knots like eyes to craft a halo headpiece and wiggled it down on Tibb's head.

The troublesome creature grinned and batted her eyes. "All we need now is a drink and a song." Her smile faltered. "That means it's getting closer, doesn't it?"

"What's getting closer?" Datura asked, but she knew. They both knew. Her sharp sword still nestled at the foot of the apple tree, worn smooth and rusted from countless slayings on Old Twelvey Night, when the grove was weakest and the mischief-things the strongest. The night when she would shuck her apple-soft body and emerge as a defender of the orchard, her instinct baying to protect and drive out evil.

"The *waeshaeil.*"

Datura bit her lip, felt the sharp cut of Tibb's cheek nestled back against her shoulder, and tried to unknot the deep-sea net that pulled in dread like the catch of the day. Her hand snuck to hold Tibb's, and Tibb turned her palm, her fingers lingering on the chain of roots tight on Datura's wrists.

Datura wrapped her arms around Tibb with a thrill of disobedience and a blush hot on her cheeks. Tibb sank into her apple round curves—a crow huddled next to a well-fed sparrow—but the mischief-thing could never let things lie. "Will you fight for the grove?" she asked oddly, her head still down. "I've survived it before, you know. Been driven from my share of orchards."

"Then why linger here?" Datura asked as Tibb shivered. "Why not go somewhere warm? Somewhere safer?"

Tibb shrugged. "I like the taste of apples. The smell of cider. I like it here." Her eyes flickered to Datura.

Gold replaced the blacks in Datura's life, her days brimming full of the luster from Tibb's eyes, to the disc of the auric sun, to the wink of her buffed coin glimmering in the distance. She closed her eyes tight, and her mind threw up glimpses of a possible future: straight-up-and-down Tibb, her hand outspread to stop Datura's blade from driving her out for good, fear as a patina in her gold stare.

"Tell me what it's like in spring then, when the apple-spirits aren't here," Datura said, feeling the scrape of Tibb's crown brushing her face. "Maybe next resurrection cycle, I'll rise with enough time to see the fruit ripen."

"It's our blood that makes the trees grow apples," Tibb said, like a dog with a bone. "You apple-spirits rattle your swords and bash our brains in and chase us away and our blood soaks the earth. Without us, nothing would be here."

"But what about spring, Tibb?"

"Who cares about the spring? I want to know if you're going to stab me in the stomach. Maybe I should cut my loses now, get out while I still can."

"Maybe you should," Datura said, and fought the sting of tears. Her heart knew evil leeched from Tibb, but Tibb had promised not to poison the copse, swore up and down she'd never make Datura sick. Right now, the orchard was strong enough to withstand it. Already, other mischief things wandered the orchard, lured in like moths to a flame. Their sharp claws raked across bark, their fangs gnawed at the soil. A few times, the creatures had pointed and laughed at Datura when she pulled the stolen blanket over Tibb's shoulders as she dozed. It never failed to send chills down Datura's spine, make her hang her head and feel the fool.

And she promised her apple tree that this would be the last time. When Tibb woke, Datura would throw her out, would never give her shelter again—but then Tibb would tease with that smile, would tell her a story about dragonflies, and Datura couldn't break Tibb's spell. It happened the same way every time.

Will you fight me? she wanted to demand. *You ask if I will hurt you, but what will you do to me if I lay down my weapon? You'll make it so I can't see the spring ever, because you'll kill my tree, which will kill me.*

Datura's fate was to make the soil rich. It was her destiny to ensure a good harvest. There wasn't a choice. But she couldn't stop envisioning a summer morning, the two of them running through the tall grass, the scent of petrichor on the air, maybe just on the edge of autumn when the leaves had veins of orange and red, and it was something that she could never ever have because it always happened the same.

"Have you tasted an apple?" Tibb said, quiet and tired.

"You know I haven't," Datura said. "Look around you. The apples are all dead and full of worms or mold."

"Do you want to know what they taste like?"

Apple was one of the first words, Datura thought. You could call anything an apple that was gifted from the earth. Tomatoes and cucumbers and potatoes—they all were once apples. Datura grasped the peace offering. A story for shelter. "Tell me."

"It's crisp and good, but once you bite—even just a nibble—you have to eat the whole thing." Tibb sat up, propped up on her hand in the mud. She stared at Datura and Datura wanted to smile, to reach out and fix Tibb's crooked crown, to smooth the red mark of her shoulder pressed into Tibb's cheek, but it seemed important to Tibb that she listen.

"The fruit browns right away," Tibb continued. "It starts to go bad from the start. So you have to know, when you take a bite, that you have to eat the whole thing. You can't save it."

Datura's root-chains shuddered, as if to speak, but she shushed them. Her mouth opened, imagining what it would be to *crunch*, to know the meaning of *crisp*.

"I could bring you one," Tibb hedged. "Not from a grove here, but somewhere else. Somewhere down below. Someplace I came from. Past the roots."

"No," Datura said and shook her head, sending her own headdress falling. "I don't think that's a good idea."

"Coward," Tibb said fondly, and if Datura hadn't been looking for it, she would've missed the ghost of relief crossing Tibb's face.

The orchard trembled. Above, the moon shone as a silver coin. Datura closed her eyes against its light and placed a wish on it. Around her, the winter air of Old Twelvey Night panted for the *waeshaeil* to begin, eager for a different kind of metal: one of bloodshed and war, one of flashing guardian swords and slavering catastrophe. Tonight, Datura would fight. She would defend. And she would die.

The first omen of *waeshaeil* began: the apple god wandered the grove with wide steps that left a gentle thunder running under Datura's feet. He passed her spindly tree, and she looked up, up, up— he towered as tall as the sky, and she wondered if he heard the song of the sun, if he could glimpse a bit of blue beyond the night's cover of dark. The apple god never spoke to his apple-children, his orchard defenders, but Datura mouthed the old tale of genesis under her breath: that he'd been borne in the bag of a utopian-infatuated monk, that he carried bloodlines of tree-gods past when he'd been planted, inert within the small husk of his seed.

A scream followed by an aria of manic laughter. The second omen of *waeshaeil*. The small mischief-things overran the grounds, wild with the joy of destroying. Their shadows elongated from their bodies, a grotesque glimpse of what twisted and sought release underneath. *Waeshaeil* was a thing of evolution, progression, and soon those tiny mischief-things would become atrocious giants, given the chance. Now, they taunted the guardians. They climbed the apple-god's legs, chopping at his bark with weapons made of debris: slices of steel, branches whittled to stakes, plucked brown grass braided into whips.

Datura looked for Tibb.

She shooed other nasty mischief-things away that teased her and ran around the radius of her roots with grinding teeth. As her enemies transformed—scales emerging from flesh, sharp nails becoming talons—Datura responded in kind. The shift began slowly, but brought with it a welcome breath of familiarity. Roots slithered around her legs and became the foundation of her bones. Her weak hands broadened into ones with strength. She grew beyond the scope of her apple-tree, felt her thistle crown become a helmet of thorns, molding with her long curls to present her with a stiff headdress of battle glory.

The third omen arose with a gaggle of humans, a song of Old Twelvey Night boisterous on their lips, the greetings of *waeshaeil* echoing around them. Gunshots filled the air, followed by the sulphuric reek of gunpower being poured and mashed and lit with flint. Strong boys lifted the *waeshaeil* queen and she sliced her fingertips, let small beads of blood coat the rim of the large wooden cup that passed between their hands.

They would frolic and celebrate and pretend to chase away the evil. They would send up prayers for a good harvest. They would be blind to the true fight happening all around them.

Datura's eyes curved and widened, the realms of reality shifting while the humans played. She reached for her sword, eager for its heft, but found the sheath empty. Her ancient form stilled, the song to protect reaching a ringing conclusion. Her worthy blade—gone. *Stolen.*

"No," she breathed, her voice deep and rich, and she thought back to Tibb, absent Tibb, always so interested in her, curious to watch her sharpen the blade, getting closer and closer until Datura placed a wish on the moon for her: keep Tibb safe this night.

She spun, saw her fellow apple-guardians mighty and entrenched in war to keep the weak orchard safe, and she looked at her wrists. Her chains should have slipped to free her by now, but they'd become black and swollen, ooze sticky against her skin. "No," she said.

Her talons dug into her skin as she tried to peel back the blackened roots. An unknown scent rose from her flesh: a bad decay, one that promised desecration, not resurrection.

A screech of agony stopped her from gouging her wrist, and she saw a towering mischief-thing standing before the apple-god. Armored plates stacked across her shoulders and down her arms. A flashing grin revealed endless rows of fangs. A crown of woven hay lay on her head. Datura's sword was gripped in her hands.

"Tibb, no," Datura yelled, as Tibb swung the sword, wild with inexperience. The blade hacked into the apple-god's shoulder. The god bellowed—Datura should've listened to the rules of the grove, to the wisdom of her peers: mischief-things are good for nothing but hurt.

Datura yanked on her chains, but the decay had spread, seeping to the trunk of her tree and quickly making it blacken. Datura stifled a retch, feeling sick, feeling her insides churn as she fell to her knees. The decay weakened her, sapped her strength. Tibb wrenched the sword from the apple-god and readied to strike again.

"Tibb," she called out. Hoarseness ruined her alto voice. "Please."

The moonlight remained steadfast. Datura turned her eyes to it and wished Tibb had never betrayed her. She wished she'd had the sense to forget a far, unattainable future. She wished the ballooning hurt in her chest would pop under pressure. But she had no more coins to pay for these wants.

Once you bite—even just a nibble—you have to eat the whole thing.

And Datura had devoured the companionship Tibb offered, hadn't she? This was just the last few bites she had to swallow. The branches of her tree curled, as if the robust hardiness of the wood had atrophied. The other mischief-things circled her. Watching. Waiting.

As the decay crept deeper, she knew there would not be another awakening. This time, when the poison took her, it would be for keeps.

Tibb swung again, a clumsy attempt, and threw an uneasy glance at Datura. Datura gasped in pain as the root-circle began to dry up around her, her life bleeding out into a decomposition that couldn't be pruned.

The mischief-things crossed her threshold. The final bite loomed before her. Humans danced around her. Datura rose as best she could, ready to fight with what little strength remained. One of the mischief-things lunged, slashed her across the cheek, grabbed her throat. Datura scrambled for purchase, fighting back, all the while hoping her fellow apple-protectors would come to her rescue.

Why should they, though? Why protect a guardian who couldn't protect herself?

The pressure around her neck disappeared. The mischief thing was thrown from her and Datura gasped. Her hands clung to the dirt, her head hanging low, and she waited for the final blow of another creature, but it never came, it never came—

Squeals and shrieks echoed around her and she looked up, her eyes misty from the ooze, to see Tibb circling her like a panther, batting away the mischief-things, tightening her circle as the apple-guardians chased the other foes from the grove. Her thin face filled Datura's vision—the gold of her eyes molten with worry, with regret.

"Datura," she said, her voice wrenched, "I can show you the spring. I can show you the summer. I'm sorry for what I did, but you're the first bite, do you see? You're the first bite that kills the grove. I hate the grove. I had one once, and it threw me out. Cast me out."

The cry of denial shivered in Datura's spine and rose into her lungs, something too awful to think on. *It starts to go bad from the start. You can't save it.*

"But you can survive," Tibb said, her voice high with want, bright with the hope Datura used to tend and grow and croon over in her own heart. Tibb held out a pomegranate, another apple of blood-red origin. "Eat my apple and you can live. We can go down to the hot core of the world or to the tips of the sky full of thunder. We can be free of this orchard. It's poisoned now, but you don't have to rot with it. Once you bite, you can live."

Datura paused, her chest heaving, the pollution puddling in her mind. "I'm not supposed to," she wrenched out, falling back on old turns of phrases, old policies.

"This was from my grove," Tibb said, breaking the red skin to show the pockmarks of crimson seeds inside. Offered it, cradled in her palm. "I wanted to see the summer, too. I let the mischief-things plunder my trees, let them poison my life, and it's your turn now. See? The orchard already falls."

Datura looked around her, saw that the blood coating the roots came from the wounds of her fellow guardians. The apple-god toppled, his ancient soul bare before the hacking picks and daggers of the mischief-things. Datura had brought a blight to the copse with her wants and dreams and wishes. And she still felt like she hadn't seen anything, still ached that she hadn't *done* anything.

"The orchard's fate doesn't have to be yours," Tibb whispered, holding the temptation out with a steady hand. "Please, Datura. Choose this. Choose summer."

And Datura took the rind, placed her mouth along the ruby red seeds that looked like teeth in the white flaky pulp, and for the first time in her life, she tasted something that could be described as crisp.

— THE SEAL-WOMAN'S TALE —
A Tale of Arilland
by Alethea Kontis

Ah, humans. My guilty pleasure, my fatal flaw. They were always just so... fun.

My first affair with a human started out harmlessly enough. A young man—Nikos—came by to say that his love potion had not worked. They usually didn't. Love potion customers either found the confidence to step up and admit their feelings, or they admitted defeat. They rarely returned.

"Ah," I said, appearing to give his dilemma great thought. "This is a far more serious matter." I hoped my expression did not betray the joy I felt instead.

"I will do whatever it takes, Kyria. Ask me for anything. I will loot the Troll King's treasure room; I will carve out a piece of the moon. I need Damara in my life."

"You must understand," I told him. "The human heart is not mine to give. I can only persuade it."

But Nikos was relentless. His lust was like a drug that seeped through my thin skin. My heart leapt inside my tiny human-sized chest.

"If you cannot promise me forever, promise me one night," he pleaded. "Even one night with Damara would ease this ache that tortures me."

I doubted that. Humans were always bursting with one emotion or another. But a single night with his love... that, I could do.

I leaned in to him, lowering my voice as if the gods might overhear. "Bring me what you can of her. An eyelash. A nail clipping. A lock of her hair. A scrap of her clothing. A tear on a handkerchief. You get the idea."

"Yes, Kyria."

He rushed out the door, and I retrieved my little trunk.

He returned that night with a scarf full of items.

"Wait here," I bade. I went outside and lowered the bucket into the well, deep enough to bring back seawater. Into this I emptied the contents of the scarf. Then I opened my trunk, tore off a pinch of my true skin, and dropped it into the mixture. It did not take long to grow. The new skin had ample curves and long, dark hair and eyes as bottomless as the cenote. I slipped it on with incredible ease. Becoming Damara was almost as effortless as returning to seal form.

Nikos did not stop to ask how his love had suddenly come to this door, or why her homespun dress looked so familiar. He simply took her—me—into his arms and kissed her—me—with all that passion. It was decadent.

I gave that young man one deliciously carnal night with the woman he loved. In return, he gave me an exciting new world of possibilities.

I do not remember how many people I became after that, or how many human lovers I took. Each time was as thrilling as the time before, and come morning, no party was ever unsatisfied.

Until the last.

I should have recognized danger when it walked through my door. Despite the cenote's presence as a surefire escape route, I had not been raised to play safe. In truth I had not been raised at all—Love and Strife were my sires, not my parents.

That he had come bearing a scarf of tidbits without having previously solicited a love potion should have been the first warning sign. But he was tall, with cheeks and hands the color of flawless sealskin and kind, dark eyes that reflected the moonlight. Black hair surrounded that handsome face in a halo of twisted locks. His shoulders looked as strong as his lips looked soft.

And, unlike the rest of my custom, he was fey.

I would have sworn that I had seen nothing in the world as beautiful as that man. I knew what pleasures could be gained from the touch of thin, mortal skin. My soul was drawn to him like a wave to the shore. I could not wait to possess him for my own. And because of that, I did not ask certain very important questions. I did not even stop to think. At that moment, I wanted nothing more than to kiss the life right out of him.

He withdrew a small bag from his pocket and emptied the contents on my altar. Gold coins spilled out, displacing the rocks and shells and lines of salt drawn there. The troll king's stamp scowled up at me a dozen times over.

I should have asked a question then, but I did not care about the money. I wanted this man so badly, I would have done the spell for free.

"I must tell you what I tell them all," I said. "The human heart is not mine to give. I can only persuade it."

"She is a sorceress." He indicated the scarf full of ingredients. His deep voice echoed in my bones and my knees went weak. "Not entirely human. Will that be a problem?"

I would have this man *and* some magical ability? I could feel my human form flush from head to toe. "No problem," I said. "Wait here."

I went out back and drew up the bucket of seawater. I tossed in the bits of his lover and a pinch of my true skin. The wait for that new skin to grow almost killed me. In that time, I should have noticed the clouds that rolled in to cover the stars. The absence of sound as the animals silenced. The acrid smell, like marshland. The reflection of the moon in the bucket as it turned red. The universe gave me every sign, and I ignored them all.

I did not even bother to look at the skin before I stepped into it. I felt my face widen, my waist thicken. The skin of her—my—hands was now mottled, her—my—hair now coarse. Not that any of that mattered. I rushed back to my beautiful man without a care in the world. I hoped he would be as passionate as all the lovers who had come before. I could not wait to see his face. I could not wait to taste him.

But instead of delight, the sight of me made him scowl.

"What's wrong?" I asked in a voice that was not my own. "Am I not what you desired?"

"You are perfect." He lowered his eyes to the floor. "But you are not for me."

He opened my door, and two enormous men covered in leather armor swept in. Their stench filled the room. I fell to my knees, choking on the scent.

Trolls.

Each one took an arm and lifted me off the floor.

"Well done, Jason," grunted the one on the left.

"The king will be pleased," grunted the one on the right.

They dragged me outside and threw me into a cage on the back of a wagon pulled by a pair of massive aurochs. The wagon creaked beneath the weight of the trolls as they mounted. Jason, that gorgeous traitor, sat in the back beside my prison.

"What have you done?" I whispered.

His scowl deepened. He still did not look at me. "What I had to."

The wagon crossed the plain and rose into the mountains, up and up, farther and farther away from the sea. I grew tired and listless. My ears felt strange. The chill air crept through my homespun dress and into my bones. I had never been this far from the sea, from my home, from my seal skin. The loss was like a bottomless sinkhole in my soul.

The trolls' castle was an ugly beast of a thing. Dead bodies were lashed to the iron gates: some fresh corpses, some nothing but bone. The gates smelled worse than the trolls.

Is this what they did to foes? Friends? Not that it mattered. Any intelligent being was automatically an enemy of the troll kingdom. I noticed a half-rotted skull smiling at us as we passed by. I found it a fitting welcome.

The trolls carried me through a back door and up a tower to a small chamber. My new prison. They dumped me onto the floor beside a pile of red cloth and then left. Their stench lingered.

"Those are robes," said my beautiful jailor. "Put them on."

Even in the skin of a sorceress, I could work no magic in this weakened state. I managed to summon only enough energy to do as ordered. The robes were bulky and awkward, but I was grateful for their warmth. I did not rise from the floor.

"Can I get you anything?"

My home? My true skin? A ride back down the mountain? Freedom? But only one word escaped my parched lips. "Water."

He poured me a glass from a pitcher on the small table. Fresh, no salt. Desperate, I drank it anyway.

I still felt empty.

I half expected him to leave the room, but he did not. He lowered himself to one of the chairs beside the table and said nothing.

In time, I was able to lift myself up off the floor. Tapestries covered three walls; the fourth had a small window. Beneath this window was a large couch, or a small bed. I crawled onto it, turning myself so that I could stare at Jason. What had the universe had been thinking, creating someone so exquisite and cruel? If he truly was fey, what sort of magic did he possess? Could his magic *be* his beauty? Surely not. I, above anyone, knew how mutable a person's outward appearance could be.

I might have asked him, but I did not. Instead, I watched him not-watching me.

I was not surprised when the king, Atatroll, arrived. By then, I'd thought through my situation enough to put that much together. I had been captured for the king. But why me? Or, rather, why her? This body I wore would be useless in an armory, or in the mines. Did trolls even care about anything else? It couldn't be power—wearing a sorceress's skin didn't give me anything like her full abilities, or I would have escaped long before this.

I braced myself, sure that this encounter would not be pleasant.

He was large and smelly, as all trolls were, but his stench was no worse than the guards who'd brought me here. That part did surprise me a little. I'd assumed that a king of trolls would be bigger or stronger or smellier, somehow. This troll simply had eyes a little wider set than the others. His skin was a shade yellower. He wore layers of furs on top of his leathers. His necklaces were made of teeth and claws. What I could see of his own teeth were stained and pointed. A large golden hoop pierced one side of his giant hooked nose.

He reached out a meaty hand, grabbed my robes at the neck, and lifted me off the couch until my face was level with his. I forced myself to remain as limp and calm as I could manage. I would not gag. I would not scream. I would not beg. I would not cry.

He was all muscle and menace. The spelled skin I wore was thin and mortal. For the first time I wondered what death would be like. It might be preferable to whatever the troll king had in store. If only that window were wide enough—

He slapped me in the face with his free hand. My head snapped back, my cheek and jaw exploding with pain. There was blood on my—her—lips. The salty mineral taste was almost refreshing.

Somehow, I managed to stay silent. I knew I had no control over what happened next, so I merely stared into the troll king's eyes. They, too, were yellow, like bile, the pupils so large I could almost see myself—herself—in them.

The troll king gave a fetid huff, and then tossed me to the ground like a discarded rag doll. "She'll do." The nasally growl was addressed to Jason. "For now."

Jason bowed low to the troll king. "Yes, your highness."

The troll guards outside flanked the king at attention. They shut the door firmly behind their sovereign, leaving Jason inside the room with me.

"A-ha." My voice and my lip both cracked. My laugh was a low, raspy cackle.

"Something funny?"

"You are not so much my jailor as you are a fellow captive." Only half the words emerged from my dry throat, but Jason understood. He fetched my glass and refilled it with water. My pride did not want to take it from him. My desiccated body demanded otherwise.

"They killed my wife," he whispered. "They will kill my daughter if I do not help them." He sat down on the floor with me. After what had felt like ages, those soulful dark eyes finally met mine. Hers. "I'm sorry."

The spiteful laugh died inside me, not that I had the energy to continue it anyway. There were so many ways both of us could have avoided this mess. And yet, here we were. His apology didn't change anything. I was still glad to have it.

"Who am I?" I raised my robe-covered arms. "Whose body is this?"

"Gana. Atatroll's sorceress."

My recollection was hazy with lust, but I vaguely remembered something about a sorceress. Never let it be said that elementals were ever overly intelligent. "A sorceress? Surely not. Her nature should grant me some little power. Even in my weakened state."

Jason shook his head. "She works in blood magic."

I glanced around the small room. "No blood and no water." Not unless I stabbed my cellmate, at any rate, and even then I wouldn't know what to do with it. Blood magic was learned, not inherited. I wore this Gana's skin, not her history. I could not help but laugh again at the irony of it all. "You could not have chosen a more perfect prison."

"Water will help you to heal?"

I nodded.

"I will arrange for a bath to be brought here." He stood and walked to the door.

"Salt, too," I said after him. "If you can manage it."

He knocked on the door. The guards opened it a crack and spoke to him. I could not hear the exchange.

"What did you say?" I asked when the door had closed again.

"I reminded them that if you die, you will be of no use to the king."

"What use *am* I to the king in this state? Who is this Gana to him?" *Please don't say his lover,* I silently begged the universe.

"She is Atatroll's closest advisor," said Jason. "More importantly, the blood magic gives her power he will never possess. And no one should have more power than the king."

"I bet that drives him crazy."

"He hates her as much as he needs her," said Jason. "Maybe more."

I narrowed my eyes at him. "You're fey. Doesn't that make you more powerful than the king as well?"

"If only I had been smarter about it," he said, as if he'd plucked my previous thoughts right out of my head. "Wiser fey moved south when the trolls began to flex their muscles. But I was too proud of the life I had built here to leave it all behind. So instead of fleeing, I decided to find a way to keep my home. I became a seeker in the mines, and the king valued my service. I thought it would keep my family safe." He looked up at the small window. "I could not have been more wrong."

"Your magic is finding things," I deduced. Seekers found gems and ores and veins of gold in the mines. He had found me easily enough. Found my weaknesses as well.

"Yes."

"Then I suppose I am here to be... a whipping boy, of sorts. When the king gets frustrated with his sorceress, he cannot take his rage out on her. But he can take it out on me."

Jason hung his head. "Yes."

I gave him a moment to steep in his shame. "Are you sure you can't find a way out of here?"

"I haven't yet," he said to the floor.

Love and Strife help me, I reached out to take the hand of this man who had been my doom. "We will survive." Even with a foreign throat I sounded so sure of myself. I'd had years of practice consoling sad souls with worse lies. "But only if we work together. You must promise to never again betray me."

"I cannot make that promise if my daughter's life depends on it."

Gods bless his stunning, stalwart heart. The child was most likely already dead, but I wasn't about to tell him that. He'd dive headfirst out that window I'd been eyeing, and then where would we be? "What is her name?"

"Rashida." I could almost hear his heart break as he said the word.

"When you are about to betray me for her sake, say her name," I suggested.

"I can do that." He squeezed my hand. I tried not to enjoy it. "Can you ever forgive me?"

"Give me time," I said, though I was already nodding.

We did survive after that, though each day was worse than the next for a while. I would have lost count, had I bothered counting them at all from the start. The troll king did not come to me every night, but he visited often enough. Jason continued to walk the line between warden and fellow prisoner. Eventually, he even became my friend.

He tended my wounds between abuses in whatever way he could. Soaking in a salt bath worked the most wonders—the sorceress's skin healed faster when I was wearing it, but the pain halved when

I removed it. And so we maintained that delicate balance. Atatroll would beat his sorceress fiercely enough to relieve his rage but not fiercely enough for me to die, and then Jason and I would patch and soak her—and me—at whatever speed and pain level I could tolerate.

Removing the sorceress's skin was the most blissful part of those long, wretched days. I relished the ability to simply exist as beautiful, graceful *me* for some precious little while. Yes, there was still pain, and yes, I was still a thin-skinned mortal, but all the hair and lips and eyes and nose and fingers I wore were *mine*.

I remember Jason's reaction the first time I'd slipped out of Gana's skin—he had not laid eyes on my human form since the night he'd betrayed me. His face was a vision of pure remorse. I would have consoled him had I not been in such pain from a particularly brutal session with the king, so I let him console me. I let him vent his shame and apologies. I let him cry for me. For his daughter. For the displaced fey. For himself. His tears added more salt to my bathwater, and maybe a little magic as well.

More time passed. Seasons changed. Snow fell on the mountaintops outside our small window. I wondered about my home, my cenote, my seal body in the trunk beside the well. I hoped it was safe. I truly would die in this skin if it wasn't.

Rare days came that weren't so bad, and Gana's skin was able to heal by itself in the salt bath. On those days, Jason and I pretended we were strangers in another place, with far less horrible fates. We shared stories. We shared the small bed. Eventually, we found sweet solace in each other. We made our own magic.

He tasted as delicious as I'd imagined.

My days featured little else besides Jason, pain, and time, so I took the opportunity to do the thing I had neglected to do before: I listened. I did not ask questions—the king would have sliced me with a thousand cuts before giving me a direct answer—but I learned how to obtain information. Jason used his own fey gifts to subtly acquire intelligence elsewhere in the castle. Late at night, or while I soaked, paralyzed, in the bath, we shared our discoveries.

There is a saying among immortals: if one is patient enough, one can move mountains.

"The dungeons are filled to capacity. Humans and fey, though the fey keep using what magic they have to escape when they can. It's frustrating the trolls to no end." There was pride in his voice as he made his report. "But what's the point? What are the trolls doing with them all?"

I rested my head against the back of the tub. It had been a particularly physical day. One ear was half gone, one eye was swollen shut, and my arm might have been broken. My toes, my fingers, even my teeth hurt. "Mmm," I managed to say. I tried again, concentrating on forming whole words. "Mines? Food for winter?"

"The king already has more gold and gems than he could spend in seven lifetimes. If he hollows out any more of this mountain, it will fall down around his ears. As for food, Aurochs are much easier to corral and breed than humans or fey," he pointed out. "They also yield far more meat. And that's not counting all the other livestock possibilities. No… it must be something else. Something they need man power for."

"But troll power," I muttered.

"Yes. Trolls are definitely stronger than humans and fey put together. So what is it that we can do that they cannot?"

I drifted in and out of my pain, trying to think. "Love," I said finally.

"I would kiss you for that, if you weren't so miserable," was his response. As a consolation, I imagined the kiss behind my closed eyes. It was perfect.

"Art," I added, after our fantasy kiss had played itself over in my head a dozen times. Art required love, compassion, and a depth of emotion I was sure that trolls could never experience.

"Craftsmen," Jason said, after a moment. "Didn't you say last week that they'd rounded up a bunch of woodworking fey and an earth elemental at some point?"

"Mmm," I affirmed. It might have been last week, or last month. I had tried to stop myself from imagining how many families had been slaughtered to press those fey into service, or what horrible trap they'd set for the Green Man. The king had been particularly proud of his handiwork that day, whatever it was. I hoped all his terrible stories were hyperbole, but I knew they weren't. Jason and I were proof enough of that.

"They have to be building something. But what?"

I forced my split lips open once more. "War."

It was always war with trolls. War and money and power. Another battering ram, another sword, another plate in the armor. The trolls would not be happy until every corner of the world was under trollish rule. And even then, I suspected they'd turn on each other just to have something to do.

I'd also gathered tidbits about the sorceress—the real sorceress—but I couldn't summon the words to tell Jason. I wasn't sure what to say, anyway. I only knew that something big was brewing, a magic spell that Atatroll resented not being a part of, even though it was being made for him. It was all for him.

"Way out?" No matter how bad the pain, I always asked if his fey gifts had found us a way out. Not that it was something he'd ever forget. But I did love how the question made him smile.

"I might have a lead," he said. "There's a story going around about a certain fey… the trolls have captured her three times now. And every time she disappears again, the youngest and oldest and sickest of the prisoners seem to vanish right along with her."

I did not ask about his daughter. It had been a very long time since he'd mentioned her. I allowed him the dream of imagining that she'd escaped. Dreams like that were what kept us both breathing most days. Dreams and secrets.

I silently thanked the gods. If this fey was real, she'd come at the perfect time.

The next time I was delivered to the troll king's chambers for a session, I kept that rebellious fey in mind. I intended to see what I could discover about her. But the king had something else in mind.

"Tell me I am the greatest," he bellowed as I entered. The demand was no surprise; our visits usually began this way. I would lavish praise upon him, list a myriad of achievements, and cower in his shadow.

I chose to skip to the end of the pleasantries. "I tremble in your presence, your greatest majesty." He usually struck me at that point, and we went on from there.

"Of course you do." He motioned to a sitting area. "Have some tea."

It was an odd request, not that it was a request at all. Glancing down at the oversized pot and cups large enough for troll hands to manage, I was immediately on my guard. What fresh hell was this? I would have suspected poison, but no troll worth his salt would have carried out such a lazy, passive murder. Especially not a king. Kings were physical, loud, and as bloody as possible. I would know.

Dutifully, I sat.

"I changed the world today," he said as he settled down into the lavish sofa opposite me. "Henceforth I will be known as the greatest troll that ever lived."

"And the strongest and richest, to be sure," I added.

"Riches? You mean *garbage*," spat the king. "My men can harness the aurochs in gold and gems for all I care. I have no use for them anymore. I am beyond wealth."

Beyond wealth? My mind was racing. I forced my skin not to show it.

The only thing trolls valued more than gold, jewels, and iron was power. Had he found a way to subsume his sorceress's gifts? Taught himself blood magic? That was a chilling thought. Not only would he be a most dangerous beast, but he would also have no more need for me.

"Your brilliance is unmatched," I said.

"YES!" He slammed his cup down with such force that the table shook. "The Thaumater was *my* idea. You may have sacrificed a thousand human souls to your profane gods to make it work, but it would not exist without *me*." He slapped me in the face. "You remember that."

"Yes, your majesty."

"And whatever magics we manage to extract will come to me, do you hear? The power will be mine. Not yours. *MINE*."

Each sentence was punctuated with another slap. "Yes, your majesty."

"My trolls will march down from the mountain, and then I, King Atatroll, will conquer the world. Not you. *ME*."

Punches this time, then a sound kick. I answered each with "Yes, your majesty," until I lost the ability to speak at all. When that happened, I left Gana's skin to absorb the beating while my mind wandered. The trolls would be coming down the mountain to conquer the world. Atatroll would be leaving the castle. Which meant a significant change in my and Jason's situation. On top of that, the most direct route from the top of the mountain to the rest of the world was through town. My home and my true skin were no longer safe.

I hoped that fey was real, because we needed her. Now.

The king was in high spirits. The beating lasted for hours. The guards dragged my carcass back to the room where Jason had a salt bath waiting. It was several more hours until the water had healed me enough to speak.

"Escape." It was more of a moan than a word.

"I spoke to one of the scullery maids who gets food to the dungeons," he said. "The rogue fey woman isn't just a story. She's real, and she's here. I will find a way to contact her."

"Now," I said. There would be no escape if the trolls caught this woman. We could not risk her becoming one of the souls sacrificed by the sorceress. I could not wait until the trolls were on the move.

"What is it that you say to me?" Gods, his eyes were beautiful when he smiled. "Patience can move mountains."

"Skin," I said to him. It was time to play my hand.

Jason's smiling brow furrowed with worry for me, and I loved him all the more. I had not shed Gana's skin in months—I only ever risked it when the pain was too great. And though my pain was great now, I feared his was about to be worse.

I sunk beneath the surface of the bathwater, slipped out of Gana's skin, and stood. Well, I almost stood. Jason caught me when I began to falter. He helped me steady myself. He even smiled at my foolish show of bravado. And then he saw my rounded middle.

Every muscle in his body tensed. His brow furrowed. His face hardened. He said nothing.

"I'm sorry," I said, though I wasn't sure what I was apologizing for. It had taken both of us to create the being that now grew inside me. I suspected the universe had played a hand as well—I should not have been able to conceive in this manner. Immortals could not do this. But I had not worn the skin of an immortal for a very long time.

I know I felt some guilt for hiding my condition for so long, but I did not regret that. Had Jason known about the pregnancy, he would have done something, despite the fact that I was the one with the power to hide the babe and keep it safe. He would have found a way to stop me from visiting the troll king. I envisioned him physically putting himself between us. That scenario never ended well for anyone.

Truth be told, I was probably apologizing for myself. I was a poor substitute for the woman who had loved him and willingly shared his life. This child, if it lived, would in no way replace the one he had lost. Yes, the trolls had most likely murdered both of them before Jason ever met me, but I was the one here now. With him. Carrying his child.

He reached out a hand and his skin met mine. Tears slid down his cheeks. "Rashida. She's gone."

"You will see her again," I said softly. "You will see them both again. On the other side." There was that practiced surety again. Only, I hoped this lie were true. If I could not save my skin, I might be joining them there.

We held each other in silence for a while, until I involuntary shivered from the cold. Slowly, he helped me back down into the bath. I donned Gana's skin once more, to heal and hide. And then we made plans.

Jason had not heard of the Thaumater the troll king had mentioned, but he knew that Gana and the king were spending more and more time behind closed doors. The dungeons these days contained far fewer humans and far more fey. Whatever Atatroll's infernal device did, if it could facilitate a world ruled by trolls, it needed to be destroyed.

Jason located the rebel, Teneka, whose fey power was the ability to walk through walls. Together they arranged a wagon that would quickly deliver me to town and, hopefully, to safety. I begged Jason to come with me, though I had no idea how to hide him once I became a seal again. I would cross that bridge when I came to it.

But he would not be dissuaded. If the fate of the world rested on destroying this Thaumater, he trusted no one else to the task. After all, the troll king and his sorceress would surely have hidden such a powerful device. Jason was the only fey guaranteed to find it. Once he had it, he would use his gift to find a place deep in the mountain where he could destroy it.

I gasped when Teneka appeared through the locked door of our chamber. She was a petite thing—the halo of her hair was almost half as large as the rest of her—but I had no doubt of her strength. If this woman said she could drive a team of aurochs through the mountains undetected, I trusted her. Granted, it wasn't like I had a choice.

"It's time to go," she announced.

Jason and I pulled each other into as tight an embrace as my belly would allow. Dreamers until the end, we stubbornly refused to call it a goodbye.

"I fell in love with you the moment I laid eyes on you," I whispered in his ear. "I was doomed from the start."

"I found you a way out of this room," he whispered back.

Lord and Strife help me, I laughed, even as tears fell from my eyes.

"You," he said. "You were my way out."

"There was always the window," I suggested playfully.

I felt his lips smile against my cheek. "You were the better choice."

We kissed then, long and deep. The goodbye we did not say in words was said with that kiss. Then I stepped back into Gana's skin, hopefully for the last time.

Teneka gasped as I shifted into the sorceress. "Amazing."

"At this moment, I envy your power much more."

"Take my hands," she said, and then she pulled us through the door as if it were made of water. Once we got to the bottom of the tower,

Teneka and I took the left corridor. Jason took the right. I felt his hand slip from mine, but I did not look back.

There was no turning back for either of us now.

Teneka's arrival—and our escape—could not have come at a better time. The wagon was halfway down the mountain before the cramping in my belly began in earnest. It might have started sometime earlier, but I had borne so much pain for so long that I did not take notice until the child was almost upon me. My body took over, or the universe did; I was too far gone to care, and Teneka had her hands full driving the wagon. I shed Gana's foul skin—or it was shed for me?—and the babe burst from my loins in a rush of... something. Blood? Brine? I could not see, but I definitely smelled salt on the air. I gave birth twice, once to the child, and once to its seal skin. Until that moment, I was not sure what my child's nature would be. I cried out in joy. Immortal or otherwise, whatever elemental magic ran through his veins would make him far heartier than any fey or human babe. If any of us survived, it should be him.

Him.

I had a boy.

If only I'd had Jason as well.

I wrapped the babe in his seal skin and cradled him in my arms and wept. I might have been weeping since I left the castle. I didn't care anymore.

I was a mother for the length of a wagon ride. I memorized every beautiful inch of him. There were so many stories he would never know. Perhaps that was for the best. I told him to remember me, no matter how long his life was. But he would not have a life if I did not act swiftly.

I cried out again when the wagon came to a stop, this time in anguish. Teneka hopped down from her seat, and froze in utter shock. I could only imagine the mess of me in a pool of fluid and Gana, desperately clutching a newborn seal to my breast. I sobbed as if the world were ending. And maybe it was.

Reluctantly, I thrust the babe into Teneka's arms. "Water," I said forcefully, and then remembered she was not Jason. She did not know what I meant, because we had not spent months—years?—in each other's company. "Take him to the water."

"Come with us," she said as she cradled the seal-babe.

"I will die without my true skin," I told her. "I must fetch it from my house."

"Your house is the first place the trolls will look for you."

I knew that. "Which is why you must run to the water. It is his lifeblood. Find a ship, whatever ship you can, and go as far from here as you're able. If... anything happens, throw him into the sea." I did not want to imagine what "anything" might entail.

Thankfully, Teneka needed no translation. "Throw him into the sea," she repeated.

"He will thrive in the sea. It is his nature." I pushed her away from me, though it killed me to do so. "Go."

Teneka slowly backed down out of the wagon. "What shall I call him?"

Such a mundane thing really should have occurred to me on the wagon ride. "Use his father's name," I said.

"And what is your name?"

"What?" It had been so long since anyone asked me the question, I'd almost forgotten. They'd always called me Kyria in human form. Even Jason had called me Kyria. But that was never my name. "Malia," I told her. "May you both live long enough for him to know it."

"May you live long enough to find us again," she replied. "Gods bless you, Malia."

I watched her run with the babe, in the direction of the water, until I could not see her anymore. Gingerly, I slid myself out of the wagon. I was not sure if my legs would hold me, but they did. Slowly, one tenuous step at a time, I made it back to my home.

The trolls were waiting for me at the well, the same guards that had been with Jason when he captured me. The same guards that had waited outside that locked door for the length of my imprisonment. They held me until their king arrived.

Atatroll strolled through my courtyard as if it were his own. He walked right past the trunk at the base of the well. The trunk that held my true skin.

So close.

I needed to find a way to get him to throw me—and that trunk—down that well. That didn't seem so impossible. And yet...

So close.

"Hello, Kyria. My trolls tell me that this is your true form."

Your trolls know nothing. Smash that trunk and I'll show you my true form, I didn't say. The troll king deserved none of my words. He deserved nothing. He would get nothing.

"I bet you thought you were so clever turning my fey slave against me."

He was never you slave, I didn't say.

"He may have destroyed my Thaumater, but no matter. My sorceress will make me a new one. My true sorceress."

He said the words "my" and "me" with such ridiculous emphasis that it took me a moment to comprehend what he'd said. To realize that the sounds beyond my house were not the ceaseless waves but screaming. To smell smoke on the wind.

A thousand human souls—that's how many his foul sorceress had sacrificed. In order to make another one, she would have to kill enough humans to fill a small town.

My town.

"Gana told me about skin walkers like you," he said.

How had he admitted to my existence to her without severely wounding his pride? I hoped the experience had been terrible for him.

"She told me that there would be another skin, a true skin, and that if I destroyed it, it would destroy you."

I closed my eyes so that I could not look at the trunk. He found it anyway. I heard the iron bands spring away as he crushed it into splinters. I opened my eyes then. My true skin dangled from his fist.

He had to throw it down the well now. It was the only sensible place to discard it.

So close.

Atatroll stared at the skin until he realized what it was. "When we are done here," he said to his guards, "kill all the seals."

The troll guards grunted in agreement.

I bit back a laugh at the order. *The seals will be safe,* I didn't say. *They are in the sea, far beyond the reach of trolls. Like my son is in the sea,* I thought. I hoped.

"As for you…" He didn't finish the sentence.

He opened up his mouth and swallowed my skin whole instead.

I would have collapsed had the trolls not been holding me. My death, that thing I had never contemplated, was now a surety. Maybe not today and maybe not tomorrow, since Atatroll loved torture so much, but someday that end would arrive.

My obvious defeat put a spring in his step. "Come," he said. "Join me. When the new Thaumater is finished, you shall have the honor of being the first drained of power." He smiled at that, with his mouthful of yellow, pointed teeth. "And then, we will drain every fey we can find." He all but skipped back to the road.

The troll guards dragged my limp body behind him.

I had almost no power without my skin, and there were no fey that I knew of in town. How in the name of Love and Strife…

The sun hit my face as the troll guards stepped out the door, and that's when I saw them. Many ships, massive ships, larger than any I had seen before, large enough to each hold a complement of trolls. They glided through the streets of town on wheeled conveyances pulled by teams of aurochs.

This. This is what the woodworkers were for. This is why they had trapped a Green Man. This is how they would kill the seals. This is how they would capture the fey. This is how Atatroll would conquer the world.

I struggled, scrambling for anything I could use to kill the troll king, to kill myself. I managed to wrest a dagger from the belt of one of the guards.

"It's okay," said the king. "Let her go."

I ran at him, knife brandished, screaming for the fate of the world.

He was laughing when he struck me down.

I woke lashed to the mast of his ship, like the dead bodies on his castle gates. I could taste the sea on the air, but I could not drown myself in it. I thought there could be no truer torture. And then I heard the groan beside me.

I turned my head, tried to open my swollen eye, but there was no need. I knew it would be Jason there, tied next to me. He was not dead—of course he was not dead. Atatroll would desire Jason's power most of all. Once he had it, he would be able to find all the fey, everywhere.

I struggled against the bonds, hoping to move my hand enough to find his. I managed to link a few of his fingers into mine.

He said something, one word, but I could not hear him over the rush of wind in my ears. I slipped more of my fingers beneath his hand and squeezed. He turned his head to me, lips almost touching mine.

"Rashida."

I closed my eyes. He had figured out what the Thaumater was for. I had told him to say his daughter's name when he was about to betray me. He said it now, knowing that his power was about to betray the whole of fey kind. Rashida's soul may have been long gone from this world, but it was for her sake that I did what I did next. At least, that's what I told myself.

The man, this beautiful, tortured man, had chosen life with me instead of death by window. It had not been the better choice. But I had loved him, with whatever love my sires had deemed fit to put inside me. Love and Strife... all things being equal, if any force was going to save the world, it was Love.

And so I filled my heart with as much love and magic as I could muster and did what I had wanted to do since the moment we met.

I kissed the life right out of him.

I would have wept as I felt him go, but there was nothing left in me. I turned my face into the beautiful sea air and let the salt bless my lips. Death could have me now, come what may. Love and Strife would both take me to task for what I had done. I had taken a mortal life this day, but I had also brought one into the world. Perhaps the universe, at least, would be satisfied. Perhaps the gods would find my life payment enough for the chaos I had caused. And perhaps somewhere out there a young seal boy would live long enough to sing the song of his mother.

Perhaps.

— THE STORYTELLER —
by David Bowles

I t was Doña Florestela's birthday, and the entire family had gathered at the Big House, right in the middle of the greenest orchard in the Rio Grande Valley. No one could say for sure how old Florestela Monteverde de Kinski was—she had already seemed old, the grownups said, back when she had guided her daughters, daughters-in-law, and granddaughters across the border during the height of the confluence of the Mexican Revolution and the First World War, nearly two decades earlier. The deaths of her husband and youngest son at the hands of revolutionaries—as well as the loss of the family's beautiful, verdant estate—had etched themselves, her daughters affirmed, deeply into her flesh.

Fortunately, in the first decade of the new century, Florestela's two oldest sons had found work as machinists in the United States, to which country they had voluntary exiled themselves to escape the madness that was brewing in their native San Luis Potosí. Once news of their brother and father's deaths reached the men, they had sent for their mother, sisters, sister-in-law and nieces, as their status as US residents permitted them to do. The six women and four adolescents had then set out on a harrowing trek, across nearly a thousand miles of mountains, wilderness, and desert, across battlefields and broken towns, by train and on foot, till they met the Kinski-Monteverde brothers in Nuevo Laredo and crossed into their new homeland.

The stories of this amazing voyage had for years filled the minds and hearts of the great-grandchildren who now gathered around the stately magnolia tree that stood at the river's edge, the pride of the orchard, its miraculous flowers the envy of many magnates of Valley horticulture. Even John Shary would pay a visit to Doña Florestela from time to time, eager to take a bouquet of fragrant flowers back to his wife, who loved to festoon the Shary mansion with those unlikely blooms.

Now the old woman sat serenely in her rocking chair, looking out at several dozen grandchildren and great-grandchildren, her green eyes twinkling with lively humor, her magnolia-white hair glowing softly against the deep, wrinkled mahogany of her skin. The tug of the spring breeze against her flower-embroidered blouse and green skirt seemed the playful touch of her husband's hands, spectral yet insistent, calling her on. Though she felt her body's hold on her spirit slipping slowly, she clung to this life a little longer.

There was one last tale to tell.

"Would you like to hear a story?" Her voice wavered, like the flowing of a small brook over mossy stones.

"Yes!" the children shouted, scooting closer to the storyteller, their faces expectant. One of them, a girl of seven named Rosamaría, peered intently at her great-grandmother with eyes of the same forest green. *Will she tell us a story we already know? Perhaps she will whisper of the ancient gods, forest spirits, shape-shifters, and thousand-year curses. Or will she tell us family tales? Will she repeat the story of the Polish aristocrat, Joseph Kinski, and his escape to Spain? Or will she hearken back to her wedding day and the majestic balls she and José Antonio Kinski Fernández held to celebrate their many anniversaries? Will she narrate Madero's escape to San Antonio and the plan he came up with that would destroy the life and land of José Antonio? Will she tell us of Pancho Villa and how she convinced him to let the ten women continue their journey? Of the Spanish Flu and the granddaughter she lost to it?* The stories had braided inside Rosamaría, twining themselves integrally with the fibers of her soul. She would not hope for a new tale. To have the strings of her heart strummed with her great-grandmother's voice one more time was quite enough.

The storyteller's eyes fell upon Rosamaría then, and the old woman smiled at the love and awe that shone like beacons from the little one's face. Her own spirit fluttered in mute anticipation, for it knew the spell that bound it to this world was fading fast.

In a hushed and raspy voice, she intoned the glamour: "Once upon a time…"

The breeze stilled, and the children shivered at the familiar magic.

"…the son of an exiled courtier found himself betrayed by the woman he loved. Heartbroken, the young man fled Spain and came to Mexico, where he acquired a huge tract of land and a marvelous mansion. He frequented balls and parties of the most magnificent aristocrats of that country, and many a girl's hand was offered to him in marriage.

"None of them, of course, could compare with the lady who had betrayed him. Their beauty was drab in his eyes; their conversation, insipid and trite. So the young man, despondent, took to wandering his vast property for days, unable to forget, unable to move on.

"Finally, in the lushest, densest part of high hills that were shrouded in mist, the young man discovered a magnolia tree upon which a thousand golden butterflies flitted like divine sparks. The tree was impossibly beautiful, its bark smooth and flawless, its leaves broad and perfectly shaped, its flowers worthy to be woven into a garland for the gods. And in its gentle swaying, its nearly balletic response to the mountain wind, the wanderer seemed to perceive an awareness, a vegetable mind of amazing kindness.

"The young man dropped to his knees and regarded the tree, unable to speak, overcome by emotions that he could not name. In all his travels a more suitable being to be his wife had never met his eye. He knelt there, unmoving, for days, his entire soul yearning, reaching, striving to shrive the bonds of mortality and touch the fey intelligence he sensed within those festooned limbs.

"And as he lost touch with the world willingly, caring only for a single whisper from the object of his love, he sensed a sort of tearing in the air about him. Instinctively he poured every ounce of his love and awe into that gap, trembling to the root of his being with the effort. With a sound like the soughing of the wind in a million boughs, the tree was transformed into a breathing lady fair, with hair as white as magnolia flowers; deep, dark forest-green eyes; and lovely golden-brown limbs.

"The young man took her into his arms, then, and they both understood their destinies lay intertwined forever."

Doña Florestela's breath grew short as she stopped her tale, happily-ever-afters dancing in her great-grandchildren's heads. But the effort of telling the tale had drained her of vitality, and the old woman slumped with enervated surrender. The grown-ups shooed the children softly aside, gently taking the matriarch by her arms and leading her back to the Big House, where they laid her in her bed for the very last time.

Late that evening, she passed away without another word. The children wept when they learned she had gone, and their parents could find no comforting words to ease their loss. Florestela's passing had left them equally bereft. Compared to her absence, the freeze of '25 and hurricane of '33, both of which had pushed the family close to an oblivion from which they were only now recovering, seemed paltry setbacks. Without their matriarch, the Monteverde clan's very warp and woof seemed likely to unravel.

But Rosamaría did not shed a tear. Something was rising in her, a joyous urgency. *They were all of them family tales,* she realized with a shivering gasp. The girl rushed out into the orchard, a huge glass bowl in her arms. Though the others wept and moaned and whimpered, the little one's heart was thrumming with a jubilant song, an ancient melody that burst from her heart and was joined by the voices of leaf and trunk and root. The stars seemed to dance in time to its waltzing, sparkling tune as she skipped to the river's edge, certain of what had to be done.

Back in the Big House, the great-grandchildren had gathered round her silent form, memories blurring their sight as her stories echoed in their souls. Suddenly a sweet forest scent compelled them all to turn their heads to see a smiling girl with white magnolias in a bowl. Ignoring grown-ups' cries, Rosamaría rushed to the bed and with a laugh showered petals on the storyteller's eyes.

With a wondrous sound like the coming of spring, the woman burst into a swarm of golden butterflies.

They lifted in a cloud to the high ceiling, and then streamed merrily down at Rosamaría, enveloping her as she laughed and laughed. Soon the startled adults and weeping children began to laugh as well.

The butterflies swirled about Rosamaría for a time, singing for only her. And their song burrowed deep. And when they finally drifted into the night, the storyteller's gift had settled within the girl to wait in soft, quiescent sleep.

Till the following year, on the anniversary of the Miracle, when her cousins gathered round the magnolia tree, as if to hear the storyteller weave once more her tale.

They all stared as Rosamaría walked to the rocking chair and settled in it with a smile. She paused for a moment, readying the spell, plucking softly at the weft that bound the tales together, bound their *souls* together. Then she closed her eyes and whispered:

"Would you like to hear a story?"

— SUMMER SKIN —
by Zin E. Rocklyn

I saw her on the D train and she looked like an auntie so I sat down next to her and started asking her questions, but she moved away. You see, I've got this thing with my skin and it's been so long since I've been around family. I miss my family.

We had all these remedies, all these bush baths and teas and draws that would cure you or make you shit or both and either way, I'd never felt so loved in my life.

But this thing with my skin...

It molts.

But before that, it bubbles, inflames kind of. It doesn't itch, but it's rough, like the surface of a dried out clementine. It becomes extra sensitive, as if my nerves are sliced open and breathing, cresting the surface of my dermis and flirting with the air.

It hurts.

It wasn't always so bad, but it seems like I've always had it.

Started as a tiny, bumpy patch on the back of my knee when I was four. I'd fallen in the front yard and my mom swooped down and carried me into the house while I screamed myself breathless. Nothing was wrong with me; no broken bones, no deep cuts, just a little scrape on the hand that prevented my forehead from smacking into the pavement.

And that little patch.

My mom noticed when she bathed me that night in the normal concoctions that I'd hissed the moment I touched the hot water. The temperature didn't bother me, it never bothered me, but my skin, it stung. It felt like it was being peeled away from me, from my body, and I hissed, then screamed and mom smacked my mouth, shutting me up, so she could turn me over.

She cut it off, that patch of skin. Right there, in the bath.

She took the small paring knife to it and slipped the layer right off, so quick, her wrist, that I barely felt it.

The odd thing? There was no blood.

There never is. There's this viscous clear liquid instead. Plasma, it's called, I think. I know I'm not supposed to, but I pick at it. I can't help it. When I'm not staring, I'm picking. It's fascinating. And repulsive. And it's me.

She gets up, but we're between stops so there's nowhere to go. The train is packed and the route all fucked up because there's forever construction so there's a lot of white people asking questions to the kindest, yet brownest people they can make eye contact with.

People tell me I have a nice smile, but it doesn't outshine my skin. Still, it would be nice to be asked. Not just about the trains, about anything, really. It would be nice to be noticed.

She's stuck in the midst of a Swedish family, all blond and milky, and the father looks like he wants to ask her where the fuck we're going, but she's got that look on her face, the look that says "leave me the fuck alone."

I stare at her until she worms her way through the bodies towards the middle of the car. I stand, just to keep an eye on her, and a young pregnant woman slides into the empty seat, next to the one that her man had taken when my auntie had gotten up.

Don't think me presumptuous; I know she's pregnant, I can smell it. It's strong, like a pretty perfume amped by sweat. Her and her man, they smell alike, but he's not hers. Not really.

Anyway, my auntie, she's made it to the doors on the other side, so when we pull into West 4th she doesn't have time to look up and see me step off with her.

She's following most of the rerouted crowd for the F train and I'm following her. I'm kind of short and with the exception of my skin, I blend into the other black and brown faces, though we seem fewer and fewer these days at stops like this. No one notices my skin while rushing to another train or place or meeting, there's never enough time, so I always find a little peace in the frantic rush. Stopping makes me nervous.

It's hot, but the F is running on a higher line so we get some breeze. Still too hot for my jacket, though.

The sweat stings like hell.

I hide by the Swedish family until the little girl notices and starts staring and the mother, the smooth cream that is her face tinges with a delightful smack of strawberry jam, and she says something in her native tongue because she's so nervous she forgets the perfect English with which she'd asked questions and it sounds somewhat apologetic, so I smile at her and nod, accepting her daughter's rudeness. It's not the smile I get compliments on, it's the kind that's tight, kind of mean, expected of a Black girl with an attitude problem.

I look down and see that I've begun oozing.

Before I can start to blot, the train arrives.

Me and Auntie step on through separate doors.

Summer was the catalyst.

Once the humidity set in, there was no controlling it. My skin would explode, hives turning into sores on top of blisters until every piece of clothing hurt.

Before the buds of my breasts came in, my mother used to let me run around the house naked. Those were the summers mom would dress me in a smock on weekends and I'd lay down in the back seat of daddy's car under a blanket until we pulled up in front of my aunties' house in Canarsie.

Usually at night. *Always* at night.

I had seven aunties. They all lived together. No uncles. Mom's family didn't have any men until my dad. I supposedly had a brother, a twin, but he died before we were born. I had cousins, but I haven't seen them since I started to bleed. I overheard my aunties and mom talking about sending them "home" the morning I woke up with a pain my belly and the sheets stuck to my bum when I was fourteen.

They'd given me a special bath that day, a blue one, one that didn't sting. They told me it was nothing to be ashamed of, that I was a woman now.

And there'd be changes.

I hardly felt any of them, these changes. Except my belly hurt a lot of the time and I was hungry. Constantly hungry.

But my aunties kept me well-fed. With my cousins gone, I could eat their plates, plus some. So my mom left me there that summer.

I never saw my mom or my dad again.

There's more room on the fake F train so hiding is a bit difficult, but my auntie doesn't notice me anyway. I can't lie; it hurts a little, but it won't matter soon enough.

The F follows the E until we get to Jay Street/Metrotech. There's a mass exodus as the connections and corrections are mumbled through the PA, but it doesn't include my auntie so I drift further down the car and sit next to the homeless man everyone is avoiding.

He stinks, but I don't mind. I have this thing where I can filter smells if I want to. It's useful when traversing the tunnels.

My auntie pulls out a book and my heart leaps with joy. I love books, always have. I love reading. My dad taught me when I was really young. I was the smartest kid in pre-K, so they say. I skipped a few grades, but then my condition spread and kids are mean and I started having this temper problem...

The F is skipping a lot of stops, but Auntie doesn't seem to mind. She's casually paying attention as we roll past the elevated stations and I try to keep an eye on her and where we are. I know these boroughs fairly well, well enough to get back to where I need to be, but I don't like feeling unmoored either.

As we pull away from Neptune Avenue, she puts her book away—some crime novel, dog-eared and shitty—and stares out the plexiglass windows.

She has beautiful, clear skin...

Winter is the kindest to me. At that point, my skin is no longer oozing or blistering. Instead it becomes hardened, dry, flaky. Feels like a callus in some spots, horny bedsores in others.

But the relief is palpable.

It's then I try to take oat baths, like my aunts taught me. It helps keep the new skin underneath healed so when my summer skin slips, it's just a matter of peeling it away. Sometimes I get too eager and make new scars but—

Oh, yeah, there are scars.

They're not so bad. It's better than the condition.

Anyway, Spring and Fall are my transitions, from relief to pain, pain to relief. But I've learned to live with it. There's no cure so there's no point to yearn for one.

But there is a way to find respite, if only for a season.

We get off at West 8th street and this butterfly lets loose in my belly because we're close to the boardwalk and the aquarium and I haven't been there in years. My dad used to take me—never mind. I keep lamenting the past when my present is gaining distance.

So Auntie, she's not going to the aquarium or the boardwalk. She lives here, in the Luna Park Projects. She's in the building right on West 8th, closest to that concrete park. There's a lot of people outside, but none pay much attention to either one of us. The security door is broken so walking in a moment or two behind her is no big deal. The elevators are working and she steps on but no one else does so I put on my jacket and lift the light hood and step on and stick myself in the far corner away from her.

She doesn't seem to notice me or at the very least recognize me. I'm short and plump and I look like everyone else when my jacket is on so she has no reason to. She gets off on the 15th floor and I wait a few seconds before following her out. Her apartment is closer than I think and she's almost got the door closed before I realize which one it is.

I take a breath, raise a fist. Knock.

I hear her suck her teeth—steups is what we call it—I hear her steups as she approaches the door, but then she opens it and I try on one of those smiles for size, the good smile, the smile that people like so much, but it doesn't relax her.

It does the opposite.

Her eyebrows knit hard and she's looking me up and down like she's trying to figure me out and she sees my hands, my stupid fucking hands give me away because they're bubbling up really bad and they're oozing, too, so there's no hiding it and my auntie, she sucks in a breath, a tiny little panicked breath and moves to close the door, but I stop it with my foot and everything goes black.

My aunties taught me everything I know.

I thought they knew everything.

But they couldn't control me.

Turns out I had plenty to be ashamed of once I started to bleed. And my aunties, they tried. When the past failed them, they tried to learn me, but it was too late.

Turns out they knew nothing at all.

I come to in her small living room on a cracked leather couch set.

Auntie's laying on the love seat while I'm in the arm chair. She's got a shiner that's swelling before my eyes and her beautiful square jaw line is lumpy. Blood fights melanin as both discolour the surface.

Her skin is still beautiful.

Not a mark on it. No scarring, no acne.

She's got a high forehead like my first auntie, the oldest, but she favours the youngest the most, the last auntie, the one after my mom. Same burnt umber skin, same beady black eyes, same pillowy lips. Even the slight arch in her thin, short eyebrows mocks the memory of my prettiest auntie. The nose is different though; hers is thinner, straighter, almost violent in its slope. I don't like her nose.

But I like everything else about her face and her skin so I sit up and smile at her until her eyelids flutter open and those beady eyes are staring back at me.

I smile harder. Show all my teeth.

Of all the other things my body has failed me with, my teeth remain pretty and white and big. Not sure why. Genetics, I suppose.

Auntie sits up and by the look on her face, perhaps a little too fast. She touches her eye, then her jaw, then whimpers, tears brimming those bug eyes.

"You okay?" I ask. My voice is rough, croaky. Before today on the train, it'd been a long time since I'd spoken.

No need to when you're ignored.

I clear my throat. "Are you okay, Auntie?" Old habits kick in, remembering the licks received for addressing elders as if they were friends. The question is intrusive enough to catch a hard side-eye, but this is a new auntie. She wouldn't do that.

She blinks at me, five tears running down the slopes of her face, then says, "Yes, I'm fine."

"Good! You have any squash?"

Squash is my favourite. My dad made it best, but I've learned to live with substitutes.

She frowns for a moment. "Y-yes. Yes, I do."

I knew it! I knew she was an auntie! There's no accent but I know my aunties anywhere!

"May I have a glass, please?" I ask patiently, though my excitement for the sweet, tangy drink is making my heart pound.

Auntie stares at me for a long time, then nods slowly. She stands with some trouble, then shuffles her way towards the tiny kitchenette. I watch her giddily, practically climbing over the top of the chair to keep an eye on her movements. She pauses by the sink and pats her pockets, then looks around patiently. There's a cell phone charger but its empty. Right next to it, she finds what she's looking for, smashed to pieces.

"Sorry about your phone," I say. "I can get you a new one." This is a lie and we both know it but she smiles softly anyway and turns to the fridge. She takes out an old-school, probably early '70s, plastic pitcher and dumps the remains of the squash in a plastic dollar-store cup. Bright red. Red is one of my favourite colours. She looks around the kitchenette again, tugging drawers open, and sighs with disappointment. I know those sighs all too well.

Her shoulders fall a bit and she trudges back into the living room and hands me the squash, of which I greedily gulp down. Still not as good as Dad's, but better than any of my aunties' attempts. She needs more Angostura.

She sits back down on the loveseat and her body begins to shake. "Are you going to kill me?" she asks.

I frown, tears prickling my eyes. "No, Auntie, no!" I cry out. "I just—I need a bath. One of those baths. I can never get the ratio right, you know? The Florida water versus the Rose. It doesn't make sense and I can never get it right and my skin—," I tug the sleeves up with care, but it still catches on the plasma and sticks until I have to tug harder, "—it's really bad this summer and I need help."

Her apartment has grown warm so I roll the sleeves back down and take off the jacket. The acidity of my sweat has made things worse, some areas of my arms and chest cracked so bad, I can see fat. The skirt and tank top I'm wearing is sealed to my skin and this stupid fake leather chair isn't making things any better but this is the only place to sit. She doesn't even have a table set with dinner chairs.

I shift in the arm chair and a small flap of flesh from the back of my knee comes away. It doesn't hurt compared to the area that was stuck in the jacket so I don't howl, but I do pick the piece off the chair and study it.

"Oh, Father God," Auntie says in a breath.

"See?" I say, showing her the piece. "I *need* a bath!"

"O-okay," she sputters.

"Do you have the stuff? All the different waters?" I ask. I'm being rude, but I'm desperate, Auntie has to understand.

She nods slowly.

"Do you have air conditioning?"

She nods again.

"Can you put it on? It's hot in here. And I'll have to nap afterwards, you know that, right? So put on the air in the bedroom, if you have it."

"I do," she says.

"Good," I say.

She stands and runs her hands on her thin thighs. She's small, my new auntie. Not at all like my other ones. They were all big women with broad shoulders and huge guts and far-reaching breasts. I loved cuddling with them. This auntie is bony and I realize she looks a lot younger than I'd originally thought. Almost too young to be an auntie.

"Where... where did you put my knives?" she asks, her voice shaking.

I shrug. "I don't know what I do when I'm in the black," I say and it's the truth and we both know it, so she nods and walks towards to the large window and turns on the air. It takes a minute, but the stale air turns cool, then cold and I'm sighing in relief. She returns to the loveseat and I stand up so quickly she flinches but I ignore her to stand directly in front of the unit.

I don't know if it's real or a psychosomatic relief, but I swear I hear my skin crinkle and sigh.

Once the pain subsides, I walk back over to the arm chair but I don't sit. Instead, I say, "May I have more squash, please?" I'm being greedy, I know, especially since it's before dinner, but I love squash and it's been a couple years since I've had some.

"I don't have any more limes," she whispers, her eyes widening with something like hope. "I can get some though."

I grit my teeth. "No store."

"No, just down the hall. Miss Toddy always has limes," she says desperately.

"No. No neighbours." I blow out a breath and try not to let the disappointment turn into tears. "No squash then." I sigh again. This really hurts. "What's for dinner?" I flinch, remembering the last time I'd asked something like that so casually.

Whatever in de fuck I cook, das what!

I whimper, then shake my head. "I can cook," I say, trying to pep up. "It's been a while, but I never forget."

"I don't have anything thawing," she says. "But I can order Chinese."

Again, I'm fighting anger through my jaw. "No. Stop trying to leave before giving me my bath. I need to eat before you do, though, so what do you have that I can cook?"

Finally, she's had enough. Her whole face sets hard and she shoots up from the couch. "Go look in the fucking fridge, crazy-ass bitch." Almost immediately, she stops herself, sobers as if someone popped her on the mouth after a bad word flew from it, but I'm too sad to do anything but deflate and drag my feet towards the kitchenette.

I open the fridge first, then freezer, then cabinets and see that she's right, she doesn't have much, barely anything at all, just some chicken quarters in the freezer that will take forever to defrost.

I have to eat and I have to do it soon.

She's a terrible auntie.

My skin ripples and my belly growls for the first time in a very long time. I try not to let it growl ever because when it does, it's almost like being in the black—I have no idea what will happen.

But when I look at her, I don't feel sad or scared, I feel angry. I feel like she deserves whatever is coming to her for being so horrible to me. I've been nothing but nice and respectful and she can't even feed me before my bath.

My belly growls again.

And I change.

I come to naked in a bathtub full of cool water, my ruined clothes on the floor beside me, and a little bit of blood on the tiles. I shift and various perfumes tickle my nose, meaning I attempted the concoction again.

This one smells a little closer to home.

Florida, Kananga, Rose, *Aqua Divin*, and Holy. No one would be able to tell, considering how murky and thick the water has become, but I can smell it. All of them.

I smile. Then sit up and pass my hands along my arms, watching in fascination as the old Summer Skin sloughs away, revealing new, soft, gorgeous mahogany flesh. It's perfect, my new skin. Perfect and beautiful and condition free.

My smile grows wider as I continue the shed. From my breasts to my feet, my legs to my belly.

I am brand new.

When I think I'm done, I stand in the water and let the few chunks plop back down. I step out and dry my feet on my old clothes stiff with plasma and reach for a decorative towel drying the rest of my skin. I do something rude to the embroidered flower in between my legs for a little mischief, then turn to drain the tub. I'll have one shitty clean up to do, but it won't matter. The task won't be halted by cracking, tight, swollen skin.

I use the same towel to wipe down the droplets on the tiles, then hang it back. I search through her lotions and pick the least scented one, slathering it almost erotically slow over the smooth expanse of my skin. Once done, I look at myself in the mirror and for the first time in years, I like what I see.

I need a plan, but for the next few days I'll have to lay low here. My new skin will be sensitive and highly reactive to the outside. The sun is my enemy. Summer makes it worse. I want to enjoy the gift my auntie has given me. As long as the air is still kicking, I'll be fine. No food, but I'm satiated beyond normal means.

I'll have to work on a story though, like one of those mysteries I used to love reading. Because there's a knock at the door and a body in the hallway and I don't want to hurt my new skin.

— COLT'S TOOTH —
by Linda Robertson

My pa always said I was ornery 'cause I liked playing in the creek, watching cattle being driven by, and climbing trees with my goats. But back in the early months of 1867, I was six and I was sick. When a boy so full of piss-and-vinegar spends the winter stuck in a drafty Texas cabin because he's feeling lower than a snake in snowshoes, you can bet your boots he's spent too many hours thinkin' of ways to make up for lost time.

As the days got longer, Ma decided that I needed some sunshine and figured some wagon rides into town would do me good.

Today was my third trip in two weeks. Now, I'd never paid much attention to the townsfolk, more concerned with whether or not I was gonna get a piece of candy, but having been cooped up for so long, I found these strangers more interesting than usual.

On my first trip, I saw a fellow walking out of a certain brown and blue door holding a bloody rag at his mouth. Stunned me, it did. So much so that on my second trip, I kept my peepers trained on that same door. I wasn't disappointed.

After the newest bleeding man hurried off to the saloon, I pulled my ma's sleeve and asked, "What kind of place is that, behind that brown and blue door?"

"That's the barber's shop, Colt."

I didn't know about hair cutters then, as ma trimmed my and my pa's hair. But I did know about the barbs on a wire fence, and my young mind imagined some mighty scary possibilities about why people were a-leaving there with bloody mouths. Of course I probably wouldn't have envisioned such wild ideas if Ma had enlightened me as to what a barber does, or bothered to add the fact that the local barber also dabbled in dentistry... but then she would've had to explain about teeth as well, I suppose. And at that time, I felt mighty sensitive about my teeth.

You see, I had a loose one. My first. She'd told me the tooth fairy would give me a penny if I yanked it out and left it under my pillow. But I couldn't stand the thought of losing part of myself, much less selling it to some tiny winged woman whom my parents didn't mind breaking into our home at night.

But things being as they were, by that third trip, Ma had noticed the attention I paid to that particular establishment. Worse, she'd decided that maybe I ought'n to visit that there barber...

"Don't wanna," I grumbled. My tongue pushed at the loose tooth.

"Colt Tanner, you want me to tell your pa you made a fuss?"

Chin dropping down, I kicked at a little stone. "No."

I stepped onto the boardwalk and held her skirt tight as I followed her through that dreaded brown and blue door, eyes wide as a barn owl's. The first thing I noticed was the pale and stooped man behind the counter. The second thing I noticed was the dark drops staining the floor. I reckoned I knew a bloodstain when I saw one, so while ma spoke with the man, my single thought was: escape.

Ma had properly shut the brown and blue door. She grabbed me before I could get it open and out. She pulled me around to face the narrow room with its big ol' chair in front of a large square mirror. Beyond that seat was another room, and at the back of it, an open door and freedom beyond its window. I was ready to run—

"Jump up in the seat, son." The barber's voice was a husky rasp. He patted a plank he'd slid across the arms of the chair. "It's up so high; won't that be fun?"

My toes dug into my worn shoes like the roots of an oak.

"Go on, boy," Ma said. She leaned down and whispered, "You didn't pull your tooth so the fairy couldn't leave you a penny, but be good and I'll get you a candy when you're done."

That sweet word loosened my "roots," and I walked stiffly toward the big seat. Halfway into the chair, I gandered up at the barber and went stock-still. The man was sleight with gangly arms as long and thin as willow branches. His dark eyes sat too close, and his nose protruded from his face like a sharp beak, but he had the smoothest shaven chin I had ever seen on any grown man. And on the subject of hair, this barber had none on his head, but there were bushes poking out of his ears that sparrows could have nested in.

"Well come on." The man patted the plank. "You're a-burnin' daylight." Then he grinned.

From my low angle I could see what others couldn't. This man's mouth had more teeth than any person I'd ever seen—as in a whole second row behind the first. With a gasp I backed out of the chair.

Ma scooped me up and plopped me on the board. "Stop acting the fool." Her tone conveyed all the fury of a mule chewin' up bumble-bees, so I stayed put.

There was a blur of white and the snap of fabric as the barber threw a cloth around me and tied it behind my neck. When he turned away to reach for his scissors, I was gobsmacked by the size and shape of the hunch on his back and the knobby shape of the man's head. I glanced at the mirror and saw him notice how I was looking him over. He spun back, holding the shiny scissors open like two silver knives. Menace gleamed in his eyes.

I ain't ashamed to admit it. I started to shake.

"Sit still." The barber gave the scissors two quick snips, and they sounded real sharp.

Unable to help it, I shook even more. I cast a look at ma, but she was studying the trinkets on the front counter. I was about to cry out for her, but the barber leaned closer, gagging me with a stink like rotten eggs, and whispered, "I learned to cut hair in prison, son. You know what that means?"

I shook my head side-to-side.

"It means if you *don't* sit still, you'll be taking one your ears home in your *pocket.*"

I blinked once, twice, and decided this wasn't worth the candy. I dived off the seat, got hung up in the white cloth, twisted, and rolled across the floor. Ma squealed. The barber stomped on one frayed end of the cloth, and it ripped even as I threw a hand between my neck and the cloth, forcing the tied end to let loose. I rolled twice more and clambered to my feet.

Evading the barber's long, spindly arm, I raced through the back room and, heedless of Ma hollerin' for me to get my ornery ass back in there, I sprinted through the open back door.

I ran like the homestead was on fire, faster than I thought I could after having been sick so long. But it felt good to run, and since my only thought was keeping away from that barber, I made a straight line across the prairie. When I came upon a creek, I leapt over the embankment. My feet splashed in the shallow water and slid forward off a slimy stone. Arms flapping, I threw myself backward trusting the embankment to catch me.

But it didn't.

Though my hands slapped against dirt, the rest of me kept going into a giant hole. It started about even to my knees, widened outward and rose up past my head. My fingers dug in, but I couldn't hold myself up.

I fell, screaming, then lost my breath as I hit rock two feet down. I bounced and began sliding, headfirst, down a steep slope. My chest hurt, and I hadn't the air to shout anymore or I would've. Twisting onto my belly, I threw my arms and legs around, trying to stop or slow down, but this wet and muddy surface had soaked my clothes, and I was as slick as the greased pig at the county fair. Then, finally, I plopped into a thick mud puddle and stopped.

I clawed into a sitting position and wiped the crud from my face. It was all dark around me. Darker than night.

When I'd recovered my breath and my heartbeat stopped roaring in my ears, I could hear Ma yelling from far above.

"I'm here! I'm sorry! I'm so sorry."

"Are you hurt?"

"No." I tasted something funny in my mouth, pushed my tongue at the spot. "My tooth's gone!"

"That's okay, boy."

Realizing that I was tasting blood, blood like that on the rags of everyone leaving that brown and blue door, panic tried to set in. Then Ma shouted, "Can you climb up?" It gave me purpose that fought off my fright.

I tried and tried but couldn't climb. "I can't! It's too slippery."

"Stay right there. I'll get your pa."

For the first few minutes I listened to water dripping somewhere far away and remained perfectly still. Except for my tongue, that is, which kept flicking over the spot where my tooth had been. *It's gone. Gone!*

I felt my chest, then all around me. Mud, more mud, and even more mud. My eyes adjusted so I could detect my hand in front of my face now, but I couldn't find the tooth. Without it, there'd be no penny from the little winged woman, and now that it was out, I reckoned I ought to have given her a try.

I shed a few tears, but it was cold as a frog's butt sitting in wet and mucky clothes, and soon I was thinking how this wasn't so different from how I started getting sick before the winter came. I'd played in the creek near the cabin, found a baby bear and followed it until its momma found *me*. I'd run across the creek, fell in the water, and come up with a mouthful of moss and a crawdad pinching my nose. After yanking it off, I ran and ran... going farther up the creek than I'd ever been. When I'd lost the momma bear, I'd stopped. The creek bank was high and slick, and I couldn't climb out, so I'd rested on a rock until I was ready to head back.

Ma said that spending most of that afternoon and evening with my feet wet and cold, with maybe a belly full of crawdad water, was what made me get so sick.

The last thing I wanted was to spend another season in bed, missin' out on all the fun I could've been havin', so I kept feeling around, determined to find some way of getting out of this cold mud. I discovered a ramp of smooth stone angling upward a few feet away from the thick mud puddle. Crawling onto the edge of that slope, I sat and scraped the mud off as best I could, then wiped my hands on the walls around me, thereby realizing this tunnel was smooth and round.

Every other cave I'd been in—and I'd been in several—was jagged and irregular. Only people made things like this. And if someone had made it smooth and round, there had to be a reason.

That was when I realized, I wasn't in a hole in the ground. I had discovered a secret *place*.

The distant dripping sound seemed louder and caught my attention. In moments, it became clear that it was not dripping but small splashes, like steps.

Someone's comin'!

Facing the sound, hopeful and frightened, I spied a dim glow. Despite having just cleaned myself off, I crawled across the mud pit I'd landed in and learned that I sat in a hole high up on the wall of a great stone room. A few inches down from the hole sat a fancy platter. Beyond, it was a long way down to the floor.

As the light grew brighter, I drew back from the edge so I wouldn't be seen. But I couldn't see who had come in with the light. Just as I dared to peer out, the platter was jerked away, and the barber hurried to the table, examining it.

Spinning around he shouted, "Come out of there, you little rat!" He dragged a chair closer to the hole. The barber's lanky arm lunged into the hole and flopped around like a fish out of water. "Come out! You've ruined everything!"

I didn't dare say a word. I scarcely breathed.

"I know you're there, boy."

Throwing myself out of his reach and across the mud puddle, my fingers scrubbed along the shaft I'd fallen down, hoping to hear Ma and Pa above. "Hurry," I whispered.

"I know you're bleeding. I can smell it. Reckon I'll have to come get you."

Unable to reach me, the barber's arm slithered from the hole, and he began to moan and groan and mumble to himself. Little by little, I eased toward that edge again, curious but wary of being tricked. I noticed three flat-topped pegs in the wall just under the opening. The platter had been resting on these. Below, the barber wandered about the stone room like a blind horse in a pumpkin patch, struggling to remove his jacket over the hump on his back.

On the table sat the platter. With the barber's candle beside it I could tell it was like the offering plate at church. It had little puddles of dark blood on it, and a handful of small white stones.

With a gasp, I realized why I'd seen men holding bloody rags at their mouth. The barber had pulled their teeth!

Why bring them down here?

A pain-filled cry drew my attention back to the barber. The man had fallen but managed to remove his jacket. He tore a padded shirt over his head, revealing an inhumanly thin torso underneath, and a wad of bandages upon his back. "Got to fit in that hole," he grumbled.

His talon-like fingers plucked away the bandages, revealing two stumps sticking up from his back like another pair of arms cut off above the elbow. The skin was a mess of scabs, bruises, and dark blotches. I didn't much want to have sympathy for the barber, but it looked like it hurt a lot.

"What are you, and happened to you?" I asked, horrified. "What do you want people's teeth for?"

The barber sneered up at me. "Why does anyone want teeth?"

"To chew food."

The barber growled in frustration. "Why does anyone want teeth that aren't in your head?"

"To get candy money from the tooth fairy?"

The barber's eyes locked on my mouth. With a sudden shout, he put one flat foot on the floor and clambered onto the table. "You've lost a tooth."

He looked mean enough to hunt bears with a hickory switch. I scurried backward, fast.

"Where is it? Give it to me!"

Clinging to the edge, the barber used the pegs to pull himself up. "I need it!" One hand punched into the hole, then the other. "Give it to me now!" The barber pulled himself forward until those two stumps stopped him. He grunted and gnashed his many, many teeth and tried to flatten himself so as to fit into the hole.

"She imprisoned me, boy. I broke out and she took my wings to punish me." His voice had gone all whiny and sad. "Now she comes for the teeth, comes down this tunnel to collect them... but all I get are the teeth of old men." He looked pathetic. "Take me a hundred years to pay my debt with those rotting teeth... but if you'll just give me your tooth, maybe a few more, it'll be over." His eyes begged me.

But he wasn't gonna euchre me; I was no ninnyhammer. "No!" I shouted.

At that, his wicked expression returned, and I swear that peck o' trouble would've fought a rattler and given it the first bite! He strained his twiggish arms so hard something snapped loud—one of his stumps. The barber screamed. I covered my ears.

"Your teeth," he growled, "are young and new." Another snap. Another scream. "So white." Panting loudly and filling the space with a horrible smell, he wriggled forward. "I must have them. Just three or four. You're young enough others will grow in!"

"Can't have 'em."

"I'll give you a bag full of candies..."

"I said no!" I grabbed a wad of mud and threw it into the barber's face.

"You wretched guttersnipe!" He growled and tried to wipe it away, but his gangly arms were too long to bend in this cramped space. He had to move his head against his upper arm to wipe the muck from his eyes.

I threw clump after clump into the barber's face until I heard, "Colt! You there, son?"

"Pa! Help me!" I squirmed up into the shaft as far as I could.

"Ropes a-coming down. Put the loop under your arms, and I'll pull you up!"

I clawed desperately around the shaft. "Hurry Pa!" I felt the edge of the coarse rope.

The barber's fingers snatched around my shoe. "You're not going anywhere 'til I get those teeth!"

I jerked the rope down and around me with one hand and dug another handful of mud to throw with the other—but I felt something small scrape between my fingers. Searching the thick stuff, I found my lost tooth.

The barber's one clean eye widened. "Mine!"

Then Pa pulled.

I was hauled a few feet up into the shaft, but the barber held tight to my shoe.

"You're heavier than I thought, boy," Pa shouted down into the tunnel.

I kicked at the barber with my other foot, keeping him from moving his grip higher.

"Hold on, boy," Pa shouted. "Need a break. Good Lord. Shoulda hooked the rope on the saddle. Ma, bring ol' Nellie over here."

"Don't stop, Pa!" I pushed the tooth into my shirt pocket and twisted onto my stomach, trying to climb up the rope. The weight of the barber kept me from it.

"Give me that tooth!" The barber pulled himself up and wrapped the tail of my shirt in his fist.

In that moment, I got so angry. Far angrier than I was scared. I was determined to fight like Kilkenny cats and keep this skeersome snapperhead from getting my first tooth.

I rolled to my back again and shouted, "You can't have it! If she wants teeth, you've got plenty to spare!" and thrust my heel against the barber's mouth. I felt teeth break.

The hole filled with the barber's shout as he slid backwards, but his grip on my shoe stopped him.

I pushed the toe of my free foot at the heel of the clasped shoe.

"No! NO!" the barber cried.

My shoe slipped off and the barber raged as he fell away.

I was quickly hauled up and into Ma and Pa's arms.

I clutched them so hard. "Sorry I ran. I promise to do my chores every day, just say you'll never take me to a barber again."

— THE EDITORS —

Alana Joli Abbott is the author of interactive multiple choice novel apps including *Choice of the Pirate*, the "Redemption Trilogy," and comics including *Cowboys and Aliens II* and *Ithaca*. Her game design has been featured in *Tiny Dungeon 2e: The Hatchling Edition* and *Serenity Adventures*. She is Editor in Chief at Outland Entertainment where she co-edits anthologies like *Kaiju Rising 2* and *Knaves*. Alana has visited ancient ruins around the world; sung madrigals semi-professionally; and earned her black belt in Shaolin Kempo Karate. She lives near New Haven, CT.

National bestselling and award-winning author **Cerece Rennie Murphy** fell in love with writing and science fiction at an early age. It's a love affair that has grown ever since. In 2012, Mrs. Murphy published the first book in what would become the "Order of the Seers" sci-fi trilogy. Mrs. Murphy has since published seven books.

In addition to recently publishing her first time-bending romance titled, *To Find You*, Mrs. Murphy released the 2nd book in the "Ellis and The Magic Mirror" children's book series with her son. Mrs. Murphy is currently developing a fantasy adventure, titled *The Wolf Queen* and a 2-part space opera. Mrs. Murphy lives and writes in her hometown of Washington, DC with her husband, two children and the family dog, Yoda. To learn more about the author and her upcoming projects, please visit her website at www.cerecerennie-murphy.com.

— THE AUTHORS —

C.S.E. Cooney lives and writes in the borough of Queens, whose borders are water. She is an audiobook narrator, the singer/songwriter Brimstone Rhine, and author of World Fantasy Award-winning Bone Swans: Stories (Mythic Delirium 2015).

Her work includes the novella *Desdemona and the Deep* (Tor.com 2019), three albums: *Alecto! Alecto!*, *The Headless Bride*, and *Corbeau Blanc, Corbeau Noir*, and a poetry collection: *How to Flirt in Faerieland and Other Wild Rhymes*. The latter features her 2011 Rhysling Award-winning "The Sea King's Second Bride."

Her short fiction can be found in Ellen Datlow's *Mad Hatters and March Hares: All-New Stories from the World of Lewis Carroll's Alice in Wonderland*, the *Sword and Sonnet* anthology, edited by Aidan Doyle, Rachael K Jones, E. Catherine Tobler, Mike Allen's *Clockwork Phoenix 3* and 5, Rich Horton's *Year's Best Science Fiction and Fantasy* (2011, 2012, 2014, 2015, 2016, 2018), Jonathan Strahan's *The Best Science Fiction and Fantasy of the Year Volume 12*, *Lightspeed Magazine*, *Fireside Magazine*, *Strange Horizons*, *Apex*, *Uncanny Magazine*, *Black Gate*, *Papaveria Press*, *GigaNotoSaurus*, *The Mammoth Book of Steampunk*, and elsewhere.

David Bowles is a Mexican-American author from south Texas, where he teaches at the University of Texas Río Grande Valley. He has written several titles, most notably *The Smoking Mirror* (Pura Belpré Honor Book) and *They Call Me Güero* (Tomás Rivera Mexican American Children's Book Award, Claudia Lewis Award for Excellence in Poetry, Pura Belpré Honor Book, Walter Dean Myers Honor Book).

His work has also been published in multiple anthologies, plus venues such as *Asymptote*, *Strange Horizons*, *Apex Magazine*, *Metamorphoses*, *Rattle*, *Translation Review*, and the *Journal of Children's Literature*.

Carlos Hernandez is the author of more than thirty works of prose, drama, poetry, and fiction. He is also a game designer and served as the lead writer for *Meriwether*, a computer role playing game that explores the Lewis and Clark Expedition. He is an associate professor at CUNY and a member of the doctoral faculty at CUNY Graduate Center. In addition to his adult short story collection, *The Assimilated Cuban's Guide to Quantum Santeria*, he is also the author of the "Sal and Gabi" middle grade science fiction series. His short stories have appeared in *Uncanny* and anthologies including *The Year's Best Science Fiction & Fantasy, 2017*.

Jim C. Hines is the author of the "Magic ex Libris" series, the "Princess" series of fairy tale retellings, the humorous "Goblin Quest" trilogy, and the *Fable Legends* tie-in *Blood of Heroes*. His latest novel is *Terminal Uprising*, book two in the humorous science fiction "Janitors of the Post-Apocalypse" trilogy. He's an active blogger, and won the 2012 Hugo Award for Best Fan Writer. His short fiction has appeared in more than 50 magazines and anthologies. Jim lives in Michigan with his two children. Online, he can be found at http://www.jimchines.com.

Minsoo Kang is a historian specializing in the intellectual and cultural history of Western Europe in the eighteenth and nineteenth centuries, and a fiction writer. Due to his father's occupation as a diplomat for South Korea, Kang has lived in Korea, Austria, New Zealand, Iran, Brunei, Germany, United States, and other places for shorter periods. He served in the army of the Republic of Korea and earned his Ph.D. in European History at UCLA. He is an associate professor at the history department of University of Missouri - St. Louis. He is the author of the history book *Sublime Dreams of Living Machines: The Automaton in the European Imagination* (2011: Harvard University Press) and the short story collection *Of Tales and Enigmas* (2006: Prime Books), and the translator of the Penguin Classics edition of the Korean novel *The Story of Hong Gildong* (2016). His short story "A Fearful Symmetry" was included in the 2007 *Year's Best Fantasy and Horror* collection, and "The Sacrifice of the Hanged Monkey" in the 2018 *The Year's Best Science Fiction & Fantasy*.

New York Times bestselling author **Alethea Kontis** is a princess, storm chaser, and geek. Author of over 20 books and 40 short stories, Alethea is the recipient of the Scribe Award, the Garden Sate Teen Book Award, and two-time winner of the Gelett Burgess Children's Book Award. She has been twice nominated for both the Andre

Norton Nebula and the Dragon Award. When not writing or storm chasing, Alethea narrates stories for multiple award-winning online magazines, contributes regular YA book reviews to NPR, and hosts Princess Alethea's Traveling Sideshow every year at Dragon Con. She currently resides on the Space Coast of Florida with her teddy bear, Charlie. Find out more about Princess Alethea and her wonderful world at aletheakontis.com.

Seanan McGuire is a native Californian, which has resulted in her being exceedingly laid-back about venomous wildlife, and terrified of weather. When not writing urban fantasy (as herself) and science fiction thrillers (as Mira Grant), she likes to watch too many horror movies, wander around in swamps, record albums of original music, and harass her cats.

Seanan is the author of the "October Daye", "InCryptid", and "Indexing" series of urban fantasies; the "Newsflesh" trilogy; the "Parasitology" duology; and the "Velveteen vs." superhero shorts. Her cats, Alice and Thomas, are plotting world domination even as we speak, but are easily distracted by feathers on sticks, so mankind is probably safe. For now.

Seanan's favorite things include the X-Men, folklore, and the Black Death. No, seriously. She writes all biographies in third person, because it's easier that way.

Raised in the wilds of countless library stacks, **Gwendolyn N. Nix** has forged her skills in writing and science in the shark-infested waters of Belize, by researching neural proteins, inducing evolutionary pressures in green algae, and through the limitless horizons of her own imagination. A born seeker of adventure, she saw her first beached humpback whale on a windy day in New York, met a ghost angel in a Paris train station, and had Odin answer her prayers on a mountain in Scotland. Her short fiction has appeared in *StarShip Sofa* and *The Sisterhood of the Blade* anthology. *The Falling Dawn* is her first novel. She lives in Missoula, MT.

Physician **Glenn Parris** is a Fordham University, SUNY Buffalo School of Medicine graduate, and Native New Yorker, but this Emory Medicine alum and Georgian forevermore, writes science fiction, medical fiction, historical fiction and fantasy. He's lived in suburban Atlanta with his wife Carla for over 28 years.

He joined the Atlanta Writers Club in 2011 and credits much of his growth as a writer to that organization's support and activities. The opportunities to belong to a local community of writers has proven invaluable.

He is a regular guest at the DragonCon diversity track Labor Day weekends. Author of the "Jack Wheaton Mystery Doc" novel series, *The Renaissance of Aspirin*, and the dark fantasy short story, *Unbitten: A Vampire Dream*, and the speculative science fiction novel, *Dragon's Heir: The Archeologist's Tale*.

A fan of Michael Crichton, Stephen King and Frank Herbert, Glenn's vison is to develop his writing skills in several genres of fiction.

L. Penelope has been writing since she could hold a pen and loves getting lost in the worlds in her head. She is an award-winning author of fantasy and paranormal romance. Equally left and right-brained, she studied filmmaking and computer science in college and sometimes dreams in HTML. After living on both coasts, she settled in Maryland with her husband and their furry dependents. Sign up for new release information and giveaways on her website: http://www.lpenelope.com.

Linda Robertson is the internationally published author of the Persephone Alcmedi series set in Cleveland, Ohio. She's also published a handful of short stories, is a graphic artist, and an unrepentant former lead guitarist who presently writes musical scores for her books. In 2006 she won the Florence B. Allen writing competition. Linda's website is: www.authorlindarobertson.com

Zin E. Rocklyn's stories are older than her years, much like the name she's chosen to pen them under. Of Trinidadian descent and hailing from Jersey City, NJ, Zin is influenced by the everyday curiosities of the terrifying unknown and the fascinating weird. Her work is currently featured in the anthologies *Forever Vacancy*, *Sycorax's Daughters*, and *Kaiju Rising: Age of Monsters II*. She also has a non-fiction essay "My Genre Made a Monster of Me" in Uncanny Magazine's Disabled People Destroy issue. Her personal website, terizin.com, is currently under construction, so stay tuned for all of her weirdness in HTML form. In the interim, you can follow her on Twitter @intelligentwat.

Shanna Swendson earned a journalism degree from the University of Texas but decided it was more fun to make up the people she wrote about and became a novelist. She's written a number of fantasy novels for teens and adults, including the "Enchanted, Inc." series and the "Rebel Mechanics" series. She devotes her spare time to reading, knitting, and music. Visit her website at shannaswendson.com.

Grey Yuen is a writer based in Singapore. He was raised on a mixed diet of eastern Wuxia, western Fantasy, and Southeast Asian folklore. This has resulted in a terrible allergy to badly-translated old Shaw Brothers movies, as well as a fascination with stories that break new ground with old cultures. He writes locally, but has published in anthologies such as *Sword & Mythos* (2014). A high caffeine-to-haemoglobin level in the system helps, as always, a habit left over from his Dark Days as a mild-mannered IT Engineer.